SMALL TOWN
MONSTERS

SMALL TOWN
MONSTERS

DIANA RODRIGUEZ WALLACH

Underlined

Text copyright © 2021 by Diana Rodriguez Wallach
Cover art copyright © 2021 by Nicholas Moegly

Visit us on the Web! GetUnderlined.com

Educators and librarians, for a variety of teaching tools, visit us at RHTeachersLibrarians.com

Library of Congress Cataloging-in-Publication Data
Names: Wallach, Diana Rodriguez, author.
Title: Small town monsters / Diana Rodriguez Wallach.
Description: First edition. | New York : Underlined, [2021] | Audience: Ages 12 and up. | Summary: "Outcast Vera and popular jock Max are up against dark forces that stretch much further than their small, coastal town—and into the very heart of evil."— Provided by publisher.
Identifiers: LCCN 2020056816 (print) | LCCN 2020056817 (ebook) | ISBN 978-0-593-42751-4 (trade paperback) | ISBN 978-0-593-42752-1 (ebook)
Subjects: CYAC: Demonology—Fiction. | Demoniac possession—Fiction. | Cults—Fiction. | Dating (Social customs)—Fiction. | Popularity—Fiction.
Classification: LCC PZ7.W15885 Sm 2021 (print) | LCC PZ7.W15885 (ebook) | DDC [Fic]—dc23

The text of this book is set in 11-point Berling LT Std.
Interior design by Andrea Lau

Printed in the United States of America
10 9 8 7 6 5 4 3 2 1
First Edition

To everyone who stands up to monsters

And to Jordan, who believed I could write about them

For the Angel of Death spread his wings on the blast,
And breathed in the face of the foe as he passed;
And the eyes of the sleepers waxed deadly and chill,
And their hearts but once heaved, and for ever grew still!

Lord Byron, "The Destruction of Sennacherib" (1815)

SMALL TOWN
MONSTERS

CHAPTER ONE

Vera

A darkness surged through Roaring Creek, casting a shadow upon its modest homes and oozing onto Vera Martinez's hands—and it all began, at least for her, the day that Maxwell Oliver's pale brown eyes turned her way.

He was staring.

Vera flipped a fistful of curls in front of her face and pretended not to notice. This was an unfamiliar situation. Boys never looked at Vera, and certainly not like this.

She opened an eight-hundred-page novel, reduced to the five-inch screen on her phone, and pretended to read. Discreetly, she scratched her scalp with a nail chipped of black polish and let her gaze slip between her wavy strands. Yup, he was still looking.

"All right, class!" Ms. Spuhler cleared her throat to begin their last day of eleventh-grade English. "Settle down." The teacher grabbed the TV remote, the only tool necessary on the final day of classes.

Roaring Creek High School had the feel of an iPhone powering down one app at a time. Science teachers cleaned lab equipment, jocks threw out ratty sneakers, and theater kids sobbed over the end of another magical season. Vera, however, was the app that no one clicked. She was "Keynotes" or "Numbers," an icon you couldn't delete due to manufacturer settings but was rarely engaged.

So why was Maxwell Oliver suddenly taking notice?

"We'll be picking up *Jane Eyre* right where we left off," said Ms. Spuhler. So far today, Vera had watched *Saving Private Ryan* in AP History; *Hidden Figures* in precalculus; and now *Jane Eyre* in Advanced English.

He's not looking at me, she reasoned. Then, because she had to prove herself right, Vera glanced at the window behind her, expecting to see a flying squirrel or mating robins drawing Maxwell's attention. But there was nothing. Not even a breeze.

Her brow furrowed. Vera and Maxwell had never spoken, not directly, or at least if they had, she couldn't remember it. They'd never been partners on a project or run into each other at the beach. To say they moved in different social circles would imply that Vera had a circle, which she didn't. Unless you counted her family, and that was just sad. Vera preferred to be thought of as sans-circle. The loner. The outcast. The . . . well, all the other names that people called her.

Her parents had *unconventional* careers, the kinds that caused dog walkers to cross the street when they passed the Martinez home and mothers to refuse to let their children go over for playdates. Vera had long since accepted this, because what other choice did she have? Hating her reality would mean hating her mom and dad, and she refused to go there.

Maxwell Oliver, on the other hand, was an athlete, an honest-to-goodness *I competed in the Junior Olympics* sprinter. He was beloved. Janitors high-fived him in the hallway, and girls, if given the option, would line up in formal wear for a chance to accept his thornless rose.

Vera was different, for a slew of reasons that added up to her not being the type who'd catch Maxwell Oliver's eye. Yet he was *staring*, almost like he had something to say. It made no sense. Every cell in her brain screamed *Don't fall for it, it's a trick!* But still her stomach twisted with the toxic taste of hope. A shoved-down piece of her soul longed for someone to look at her and see something other than the five-year-old everyone avoided on the playground.

Vera tucked a thick lock of hair behind her ear and gnawed on her lip. She was under no obligation to pretend she didn't notice. *He* was staring at *her.* So technically *he* should be embarrassed.

She steadied herself, preparing to meet his gaze head-on. What was the worst that could happen? After today, she wouldn't see Maxwell again until the start of senior year.

Vera inhaled, summoning all her courage from down deep, when Jackson Johnson stumbled into the classroom. He tripped in a walloping belly flop onto the linoleum floor, and the room erupted into laughter. Jackson immediately bounced up, milking the crowd with his arms spread in a victorious V. "We're almost out of heeeere!" he shouted.

Applause broke out, everyone whooping and giggling as he danced about as if in a training montage. Even Vera chuckled as she stole another peek at Maxwell. His gaze still lingered, lips parted, and he was prepared to mouth something. Then both his friends abruptly turned her way. They whispered, chuckled, clearly talking about her. Vera's cheeks flushed, and she let her eyes flit about the room until the heat in her face subsided. When she glanced back, Maxwell's focus hadn't shifted. Only, before he could speak, Jackson snatched a notebook and smacked Maxwell on the top of his head. Ms. Spuhler dimmed the classroom lights.

And the moment was shattered.

But it *had been* a moment. Vera was certain of it.

She just didn't know what it meant.

She would soon.

The darkness hanging over Roaring Creek was inching closer to Vera Martinez.

And it all began with a single look.

CHAPTER TWO

Max

"Oh my God! You are so dumb!" yelled Leo Rambutan, thrusting his hands in frustration.

"Why the hell would I know where Indonesia is?" Jackson scrunched his eyes. "It's an island. I thought it was in the Caribbean."

"It's *thousands* of islands, and because I've been your friend since preschool!" Leo slammed the door to his empty locker.

Max Oliver watched as his best friends bickered, shoving one another, but didn't intercede, because (1) Jackson was that clueless, and (2) Max hadn't slept more than a couple hours a night for the past two weeks and he didn't have the energy to referee. His brain throbbed behind his eyes, and it took all his effort to fake some end-of-year enthusiasm.

"Max, please tell me you know my dad's Indonesian." Leo slapped his back as they trudged toward English. Only two hours left before the final bell.

Max debated staying home. It was a blow-off day, movie after movie after movie. He tried to get some sleep when the teachers dimmed the lights, but his classmates kept interrupting with invites to parties and flyers for bonfires. *Man, I sound pathetic.* It was the last day of eleventh grade, which meant it was almost the first day of senior year. He and his friends had been looking forward to this moment since they first stepped into the building, and now he was whining about going to parties? Nothing felt right anymore.

"Yeah, your father was born in Indonesia," Max said. "Which is somewhere in Southeast Asia. And your mom is, like, Polish?" It sounded like a question.

"Czech, but close enough." Leo nodded.

"Max got *that* wrong," Jackson huffed.

"Poland and the Czech Republic are right next to each other."

"Why would I know that?"

"Because one day, believe it or not"—Max wrapped an arm around his friend's broad shoulders—"you might actually leave Connecticut."

"Says the guy who's taking over his dad's business," Jackson quipped.

Max shut his mouth. *Touché.*

His family owned Oliver Seafood, one of the town's only restaurants on the waterfront. Max grew up waddling around picnic tables full of lobsters in plastic tubs, while his dad worked the kitchen and his mom kept the books.

Then, just like it had for many people in Roaring Creek on that same hideous, unforgettable day, his world changed.

"Sorry, man, didn't mean to bring it up." Jackson caught the change in Max's face, or the laser stare from Leo; either way, he shifted to pity mode. It always came back to the dead dad.

"Bring what up?" Max tried to brush it off. He didn't want to talk about his father, and thankfully, the moment shifted.

Jackson's gaze pointed across the hall. "Hey, Bridget! You comin' today? Devil's Pool!" Jackson strutted over to the redheaded volleyball captain, his arms spread like Bridget might actually hug him.

"That's never gonna happen." Max snorted.

"I know, right?" Leo smiled. "He's got about as much of a shot at hooking up with Bridget Levandowski as I do of getting into Harvard."

"What, Harvard doesn't take C students?" Max quipped.

"I'll have you know I ended with a C-plus." Leo pumped his brow.

They strode into English, and Max's eyes caught on a swish of wavy dark hair across the room—black locks to match her black outfit and black nail polish, as though there were a funeral about to commence.

Vera Martinez.

He'd never thought much about her. He'd heard the rumors—about what her parents did for work. And he'd laughed along with everyone else in grade school when they pretended that touching Vera would give you "the death disease." But lately, after tucking his sister into bed and trying to ignore the chill on his skin, he couldn't help but think of *all* the possible explanations for what was happening at home. Dark ideas sprang to mind, ones he was too afraid to say aloud but he knew existed, because of the whispers that followed one of the most infamous families in Roaring Creek.

Vera glanced up, and Max kept staring as he took his seat. He'd spent a lifetime avoiding the creepy girl with the bizarre parents, yet now he found himself parting his lips and searching for the nerve to say hi. Only, Jackson stumbled in behind them. His friend tripped over his feet and landed face-first in front of the teacher's desk, popping up to a standing ovation, arms spread overhead.

"Always classy," Leo joked when Jackson finally stopped milking the applause and plopped beside them. "You convince Bridget to come?"

"Of course," he gloated, then cocked his head. "And she's bringing Delilah."

"Great." Max grunted. They'd hardly spoken lately, which was fine with him. He had too much going on to worry about some girl screenshotting his text messages and sending them to all her friends for analysis. *What do you think he means by the word* the?

"Poor Max, the hot girl just won't leave him alone." Jackson pretended to pout, and when Max didn't react, his friend followed his gaze. "Dude, are you staring at the Wicked Witch of the Creek?"

"No," Max lied, shaking his head, though it was obvious he was looking at Vera.

"Seriously, that girl creeps me out," Leo added. "She's like a walking haunted house."

"No, she *lives* in a haunted house," said Jackson. "That's legit."

"Have you ever walked by there at night? I swear I saw lightning coming out of it once."

"Shut up," said Max, rolling his eyes.

"Ooh! You defending her now? *Maxwell loves the frea-eak!*" Jackson singsonged, stealing Max's notebook and swatting him on the head. Max shoved him off.

"Hey, I'm just sayin', be careful, man." Jackson raised his palms. "She might be undercover hot, but she'll make a voodoo doll of you."

"I'm not defending the freak," Max said. "I just . . . Could you imagine growing up like that?"

"Nope." Jackson shrugged. "And I can't say I've thought about it much."

Max peered at her again, his eyes hovering until she caught him staring. He didn't look away, because the truth was, he *had* thought about her a lot.

He just couldn't tell his friends why.

———

"Wanna beer?" Leo reached into the cooler and pulled out a dripping can.

Max shook his head. "Nah, I'm good." He knew it went

against the rules of teenage coolness, but Max thought beer tasted like gym socks. Sometimes he pretended; sometimes it wasn't worth it.

He stretched his legs as he lay in the back of his pickup truck, his bare heels kicking at dried leaves. All he wanted to do was sleep, curl in a ball, close his eyes, and forget everything.

"You cool?" Leo asked, reading his face.

"Yeah. Fine." Max cleared his throat.

As soon as the last bell rang, they'd headed to Devil's Pool for the first real day of bathing suits and beers. All the tourists in Roaring Creek clogged the beaches—at least, they used to back when it was a more popular vacation destination. The locals (or the local teens) took ownership of the creek. Devil's Pool was the nickname for a stone bridge that crossed over the deepest section, which was only about twelve feet, but that was enough for kids to cliff-dive like they were in an ad for the Bahamas. Max had taken the plunge only once—early last September, on a dare. His toes torpedoed all the way to the murky weeds on the creek bed, slamming onto a rock. He thought he broke a toe; his entire track season dimmed behind his eyelids. But it was only jammed. Still, it was enough for him to never do it again.

The next week, the accident happened. Five of their classmates died in a car crash while driving home from Devil's Pool. Max had been at the creek that day. He'd watched them drive away. This was his first time back.

Max swiped at the sweat from the blazing evening sun.

He should get home, make sure everything was okay. Maybe he could pick up dinner?

He sat up, reaching for his tattered backpack.

"You're leaving? What about the bonfire?" Leo swigged his beer.

"I can't. Too much crap going on. But maybe I'll come back later."

Leo narrowed his gaze like he didn't believe him. "Your mom still sick?"

Max's mom hadn't been to the restaurant in nearly two weeks, but his claims that she had the flu, in June, were getting harder to sell. Still, if he told them the truth about the way she'd been acting lately, they'd ask if *he* was feeling all right.

"Yeah, but she's getting better," Max lied.

Leo and Jackson had known him since preschool playdates. They were around for the dark days after his father's funeral. They knew about the periods when his mom didn't leave her room, or worse, when she parked her car on the lawn. But they also saw her cheering in the stands at every track meet.

Only six months ago, his family celebrated his sister Chloe's seventh birthday, and everything was normal. His mom made breakfast for dinner and gave Max an "unbirthday" present—ever since his dad died, birthdays were a celebration for everyone. Max opened the box to find a new Mets cap, just like his father's, the original lost in the flames, charred and gone.

Touching the hat was like getting a piece of him back, a physical reminder that they were still linked, father and son.

Where had *that* woman gone?

Max shoved his feet into his dirty flip-flops, then hopped out of his truck and slid on the cap, ignoring the stench of sweat. He refused to wash it. Dad said cleaning a baseball hat would curse the team, like getting up to pee during an inning with two runners on base. Dad's superstitions were to be respected.

Leo hopped down beside him. "See you later, bro. Want me to tell Delilah anything? She's gonna notice you leavin'."

Max looked toward the tall blond in the turquoise bikini, her toes in the chilly creek and her hand clutching a can. He pursed his lips. He and Delilah had an on-again, off-again thing all year, if you even wanted to call it that. She wasn't his girlfriend, but she had made it pretty clear that was what she wanted to be. Last month, she decorated his locker for his birthday, covering it with white and aqua streamers and all this gold glitter. You could see it from halfway down the hall (if not from space), and it was obvious it took her a lot of time. Max thought it was cool she remembered, but he also thought it was a bit much. When he said "Thanks, that's . . . nice," you would have thought he'd run over her poodle. She stomped away moaning, "You can be a real jerk sometimes." They hadn't spoken much since.

"Don't tell her my mom's sick." Max shook his head. "She'll show up with chicken soup or something."

"Dude, that girl *wants* you. I don't know what you're waiting for." Leo shook his head like Max was an idiot.

Maybe he was. Delilah was easy to look at, and he definitely thought about her that way (a lot), but his life was so messed up right now, he couldn't handle bringing a girl into it.

At least, not *this* girl.

"I'm not waiting for anything. I'm just weighing my options." Max smirked as he trekked to the driver's side.

"You hanging tomorrow?" Leo called after him.

"I'm working the dinner shift."

"I will make you have fun this summer!" his friend called.

Max plopped into his seat and slid the cap backward. "I'm all about fun!"

And he was, when he wasn't making sure his sister was safe—from his mother.

CHAPTER THREE

Vera

Vera scratched her back on the bark of a tree as lime-green strings of pollen showered her book. At school, she was reading *The Stand* on her phone. At home, she was reading a signed copy of *The Outsiders*, a prized possession.

Books, solitude, and work—that was her summer break in three words.

A metal screen door clattered in the distance, and she turned to spy white-haired Mr. Zanger following his little puff of a dog, nearly as arthritic as he was.

Seven years ago, during the worst hurricane their town had ever seen, Vera saved both their lives. She wasn't being dramatic. She was ten years old, and she ran out into gale-force winds to help the old man when he slipped while taking the dog out to relieve nature's call. Mr. Zanger hit his head, hard, and was motionless, faceup in the wind and rain. Vera jostled him back to consciousness, and when he opened his eyes, he clambered away as though she were scarier than the Category Two storm.

Sadly, that wasn't the worst thing to happen that day. Or the most dangerous.

Vera raised her hand in a neighborly salute. Mr. Zanger turned his back. The dog, however, locked its black eyes on her and released a series of piercing yelps. Then its gray mustache twitched, shifting into a throaty growl.

I should've left you both in the rain, she thought, though she'd save them both again tomorrow. *First, do no harm.* Med school was in her future.

"Vera! Dinner's ready!" Aunt Tilda called from the kitchen.

Vera set her bookmark and strode toward the back door, inhaling the savory scent of rosemary. Tilda McMahon prided herself on being "the best Irish cook in the family," though her only competition, Vera's mother, considered microwave popcorn a reasonable dinner. Vera's father could cook, mostly Spanish rice and plantains, but he only donned his *Kiss Me I'm Puerto Rican* apron on major holidays. Other than that, Vera boiled pasta and Aunt Tilda cooked potatoes with some form of meat that was hardly ever chicken.

"Smells good." Vera tiptoed in.

The oven was open, flooding the room with warmth, but Vera didn't fear *that* door. Instead, she nudged around the entrance to the basement, her whole body reacting to *its* heat. Behind those rustic barnwood planks rested a collection of artifacts from her parents' work, which Vera had never examined for herself, but which routinely haunted her dreams. *Never touch the door, never open the door*—those rules were uttered so much, her family should have had them cross-stitched on a pillow.

It was as if the basement held not objects, but energy. Vera swore she could feel the artifacts humming, a buzz crawling against her skin even from the other side of the house. But whenever she told her mom, the response was always the same.

There's nothing to be afraid of. Would Daddy and I do anything to hurt you?

Vera was certain they wouldn't, so she tried to ignore the internal pull she felt, and she convinced herself that it wasn't the call of evil, and that the call wasn't coming from inside her house.

"What did you make?" Vera asked as she sat down at their fifties-style dinette, the vinyl cushion sighing beneath her.

"Shepherd's pie, with lamb." Aunt Tilda kissed the top of Vera's head. "I saw your report card. I'm so proud of you."

Vera smiled as the gray-haired woman who practically raised her served up an overflowing plate of food. Then the table rattled, her cell phone vibrating. "It's them." Vera unlocked her screen, putting it on speaker. "Hola."

"Honey, you there?" She could hear the smile in her mom's voice.

"Yeah. Aunt Tilda's here too."

"Great! We just wanted to check in."

"How's Spain?" Vera asked.

"I made shepherd's pie," her aunt blurted, as if proving she kept their daughter well fed.

"Todo bien," said Vera's dad, also on speaker.

"We haven't seen much of Barcelona outside of the home where we're working. It's . . . a sad case." Her mom sounded tired. It was midnight there.

"Is the girl *afflicted*?" Aunt Tilda asked. *Afflicted* was their family's polite way of saying "possessed by evil demons." Her parents were demonologists. Exorcists. Or a few other words most people didn't understand.

"Sí, unfortunately. We've spoken with the church, and we're just waiting to hear back." Dad sighed deeply. "How's school?"

"Over." Vera shrugged.

"Oh, that's right!" Her mom's voice rose—she'd clearly forgotten. "Are you celebrating?"

Yeah, I sprouted friends and joined the Glee Club in the two weeks you've been gone.

"Aunt Tilda and I are living it up," Vera quipped.

"Great. Til, I *have* to tell you about dinner. We had this amazing paella. Did you know they leave the heads on shrimp here?"

Vera's face crinkled. *Seriously?* Did her life matter so little that they'd rather talk about entrées and appetizers? *Please, tell me more about the salad. . . .*

"And you should see the cathedral here. It's stunning, and Gothic, and unfinished," Mom droned.

"Espera. Don't forget about Father Chuck," Dad interrupted. "He's stopping by tomorrow because he has a wedding on Sunday. Someone needs to be there to open the basement."

Vera's eyes shifted toward the sub-level gateway to Hell, only steps away, like it was a charming breakfast nook.

"I'll be here," Aunt Tilda replied. "And that prayer candle he brought last time . . ."

"I got my grades," Vera cut in, since her parents didn't bother to ask. "Straight As."

"Oh, mija, wonderful," said Dad.

"Really, that's great. We're so proud of you," Mom cooed.

Vera's lips turned up. It was hard to feel special in a family of people who could do things few others in the world could, like in all of human history. Her parents saved people's souls. A talent that skipped a generation, which didn't go unnoticed. Vera wasn't like them. Sometimes at night when she was in bed trying to ward off impending nightmares, she let a dark thought slip in—if Vera didn't fit with the parents who made her and she didn't fit with kids at school, then it was possible she would never belong anywhere. Ever.

"God's certainly blessed us," Mom added.

Vera set her jaw. *God didn't take my finals.* It was *her* accomplishment, though it was sacrilegious to even think that.

"Thanks, Mom," Vera muttered, all sense of pride squeezed out. "So, tell me about *you.*"

She slumped in her chair. Only one school year left before Vera could put Roaring Creek, and everything that went with it, behind her.

CHAPTER FOUR

Max

Max returned home, creek sand still gritted between his toes. He kicked off his flip-flops and found Chloe perched in front of a flickering television.

"Where's Mom?" he asked, patting his sister's curly black hair, which looked somewhat brushed. He should be grateful for that, but instead it made his stomach turn.

Chloe had begun playing hide-and-seek with the comb, refusing to let Max brush her ringlets. Then last night, Max awoke to the sound of footsteps in the hallway. He crept out, upright hairs on his neck making him wish he slept with a baseball bat, and he spied his mother gliding into Chloe's bedroom. He watched Mom sit on the edge of his sister's mattress, wearing that tacky yellow T-shirt from her latest self-help group. She lifted a wide-tooth comb and brushed her daughter's tangled locks.

It was two in the morning.

When Max called her name, Mom didn't turn. When he strode to her side, she didn't react. Finally, he nudged his mom's shoulder, and she lifted her chin to display fluttering lashes and eyes rolled into the back of her skull. There were no pupils, only white pools marked with bloodshot veins.

His hands quivering, he said nothing more as he helped his mother back to her room. She sleepwalked the whole way. Then he spent the night on the floor of his sister's bedroom.

"Mom's door is closed. She's not answering," Chloe told him.

It was five o'clock. His sister must've gotten off the bus over an hour ago, and she'd been by herself the entire time. He never should have gone to the creek.

"How 'bout mac 'n' cheese for dinner?" he asked.

"Nope. Peanut butter and jelly."

"I think we're out."

Chloe turned his way, eyes tight. "I *want* peanut butter and jelly."

Max ground his teeth.

"Fine, I'll check the cabinet." He knew it was empty. He hadn't bought any groceries recently, and his mother definitely hadn't. She barely left her room.

He marched to the kitchen, past a bookshelf overflowing with self-help tomes. Mom bobbed from lifestyle blogs about organic eating, to yoga, to meditation, to mindfulness, to podcasts on living your "optimal life" and finding "happiness within," to large-scale arena events with high-priced gurus, to powering crystals in the moonlight, to her latest—the Sunshine Crew, TSC for short. It was a local group that not only advertised with cheesy yellow hats and T-shirts, but it was started by the family at the center of the town's worst tragedy, at the center of *his* family's tragedy. Creating this group seemed to be their way of atoning. Max didn't agree, nor could he understand how his mom swallowed any of it, but it was better than downing a bottle of booze or a handful of pills, so Max let it go.

That was, until lately.

He yanked open the cabinet door: crackers, Cheetos, a can of coffee. No peanut butter.

He dropped his head.

The store was a mile away. He could run there and be back before Chloe's movie ended. His legs needed it anyway. So did his brain.

He peered down the hallway, a pendulum clock ticking behind him. His mother's door was at the far end, closed, dark, and silent.

He grabbed his sneakers.

———

Max cradled the plastic jar of peanut butter in his arm like a football as he jogged down Main Street, dodging potholes. A streetlight flicked red, and he kept pace at the curb, maintaining his heart rate while he waited at the light. He swiped sweat from his brow as a horn blared. His head jerked in time to see a woman backpedal to the opposite curb, having stepped into oncoming traffic, her eyes blinking with shock, as though she hadn't expected cars to be driving on a busy boulevard. Max rolled his eyes. The woman kept blinking, adjusting her canary-yellow baseball hat—the same one his mother owned, featuring a cheesy eclipsed sun. Man, that group was everywhere.

The sign shifted to *Walk* and Max dashed across the street, the hospital looming ahead of him.

Vera worked there. His classmates whispered about the irony all the time: Vera Martinez, the girl with the "death disease," worked part-time at Roaring Creek General. Max actually found it relatable. Not a lot of his friends had part-time jobs, but with a family restaurant, Max began working when he was old enough to fold paper menus.

He eyed the hospital's sliding doors. If he wanted to talk to her, if he really wanted to continue what he'd tried to start in school, he could. It wouldn't be too hard to find her schedule.

He leapt over the flattened carcass of a dead squirrel and, as if on autopilot, his body led the way.

———

The hospital detour was brief and Max sprinted home to overcompensate, stagnant humidity filling his lungs, not a hint of a breeze. He reached the front steps and flung open the door. Instantly the smell of bacon coated his tongue.

Breakfast for dinner?

"Ma, you up?" Max sniffed. It was smoky.

"No, *I'm* cooking!"

That was Chloe.

"*What?*" Max yelped, sprinting through the house and rattling the good dishes in the china cabinet.

He entered the kitchen and saw his sister at the stove, standing on top of a plastic stool with all four burners blasting, only two of them covered with pans, and blue flames so high they nearly kissed her elbows.

"What are you doing?" he shouted, dropping the peanut butter as he dove for the gas knobs with such force, he knocked his sister off her stool.

Chloe landed on the linoleum with a thump. "Stop it!" Her voice was piercing. "Mom said I could!"

"Where is she?" He switched off the flames, cringing at the pan of burned, unseparated bacon slices. Another nonstick skillet held the charred remnants of what used to be pancakes. Chloe didn't know how to make batter. His mother had to have been involved in this.

"Mom woke up! She said I could!" Tears sprang to Chloe's eyes, her lower lip wobbly, and Max crouched by her side.

It didn't take much to make his sister cry, but still, he shouldn't have pushed her.

"You okay?" He helped her up.

She could have burned down the house, and he'd only left her with their mother for a short time.

Max glanced around the room. A gallon of milk was warming on the counter, bowls of gooey slop filled the sink, the faucet dripped a trickling stream of water as sticky serving spoons covered the Formica counter. Swiftly, he shifted into old habits, flinging open cabinet doors and digging for an open bottle. He couldn't go through this again. If his grandparents found out . . . No. He shook his head, refusing to accept that his mother would bring alcohol into this home. But then, why would she leave Chloe standing near an open flame?

The deck groaned, and Max shifted toward the storm door. Footsteps creaked on the wooden boards, the sound distinct, like the swirl of his mom's teaspoon in a mug or her cough echoing at night. It was her.

Sure enough, Mom appeared on the deck outside in a white nightgown that was almost see-through. *Ugh*. Max cringed.

"What are you *doing*?" he snapped, a breeze brushing through the screen carrying the sickly sweet scent of cheap perfume or maybe day-old flowers. "Chloe was in here, *alone*, playing on the stove."

Mom's mouth lifted in an unnerving grin, cheek cocked to the side. Max knew what she looked like drunk. Staggering, crying, and puking were involved. But his mom stood steady, and her eyes weren't glassy. Instead, her gaze was stretched wide and was oddly bewitching.

Who was she? He gulped. "You need a robe. Come in."

"Why? Don't like the way I look?" She slithered her lithe body, wind lifting her hair. There hadn't been a breeze during his entire sticky run. Now every leaf in his yard stirred and his mom's curls bounced.

"Did you know Chloe was cooking?"

"She said I could!" Chloe whined.

"Oh, I just love the smell of burned meat. Don't you?" Mom tilted her head, nostrils flaring above exposed teeth.

"Are you okay?" Max asked, carefully choosing his words. "You're acting . . . strange."

"Am I, little pet?" She never called him that. "Tell me, how should I act?" She snapped her teeth together in three quick chomps.

"For the love of God, Ma, what is *up* with you?"

"Love?" She laughed, only it wasn't her laugh. This was deep and rough. "Love is pathetic. It's weak. *I* bring you strength. I ease your suffering. I will resurrect your mind. Join me!"

She was making no sense. She'd been babbling nonsense like this for almost two weeks. At first, he thought it was self-help lingo; then she started spouting it in her sleep.

Behind her, the wind picked up, sending a plastic bag dancing about their yard with spinning emerald leaves. Next door, a German shepherd barreled at their wooden fence, rattling it with his heavy paws. His black muzzle growled, his dark eyes pointed at his mother like he'd never seen her before. She pet him almost every day. It hopped on hind legs, his bark growing vicious.

Mom laughed, cackles rising with a sound that wasn't hers. Instinctively, Max nudged Chloe behind him.

"Why don't you go watch TV. I'll make you a sandwich," he whispered, trying to sound normal, but his voice was shaking. "You want bananas with your peanut butter? Or jelly?"

"Jelly," she croaked, seeming unable to move. Max placed a clammy palm on her shoulder and pried himself from the spot where he'd been rooted. He guided Chloe toward the living room. "What's wrong with Mommy?" Chloe mumbled in a nearly inaudible whisper.

Max had no answer. Still, he parted his lips to respond, but—

"Oh, my little pets, Mommy's never been better."

That voice. What was wrong with her voice?

Woodenly, Max turned to see Mom hovering in the screen door, silhouetted by the sunset, ochre light emanating around her frame, gleaming through the sheer white fabric of her fluttering gown. "The pain is gone, little pets. I have been rewarded. And soon, I will take away your pain too, take away everyone's pain."

Max dug his fingers into Chloe's collarbone. "Go to your room," he ordered through clenched teeth.

"But—"

"Go." Max pushed her toward the narrow hall, and Chloe ran, bare feet squeaking on the floorboards.

As soon as she was out of view, Max swiveled back to the figure glowing in the doorway.

Her cheeks were pushed too high and her eyes offered a challenge. *Come, boy, come to Mommy. You're not afraid, are you?*

He was, but still he stepped toward her.

CHAPTER FIVE

Vera

Vera wriggled into her black scrubs and double knotted the dangling white string at her waist. Her shift started in an hour. She was a part-time "food service assistant," an overly official title for someone who delivered meals to hospital patients. Last year, during her first week on the job, her boss suggested she wear scrubs in "a cheery color!" like lavender or salmon; Vera chose black. She realized this was leaning in to her Cruella de Vil reputation in town, but she didn't think it was her responsibility to skip about in sunny yellow just so strangers would stop prejudging her. She wore what she wanted.

Vera bounded down the creaky stairs, her hand skimming the banister. Morning light glinted through the stained-glass windows that were the primary reason her parents had bought the house. Right in the center of the staircase, where the landing pivoted toward the living room, were three slender windows featuring artful glass patterns in ruby, sapphire, emerald, and amber. It was like living in a church, which was where her parents spent most of their time anyway, so why not bring their work home with them?

"Aunt Tilda, I'm leaving!" she called on her way to the door.

"Breakfast!" her aunt hollered, emerging from the kitchen with a spatula coated in egg. "I don't want you touching hospital food."

"That's literally my job." Vera cocked her head.

Her aunt rejected all forms of hospitals, doctors, pharmaceuticals, Western medicine, *Eastern* medicine. She believed in God. God will cure all. God's will be done.

Vera once told her that God created chemo; her aunt left the room.

Obviously, Vera believed in a higher power. She couldn't grow up in a family like hers, seeing the things she'd seen, and not believe there were other forces at work. She had faith, but that faith also extended to science. Whenever Vera wheeled her squeaky cart into a hospital room and saw a family collapsed in a puddle of helplessness, Vera dreamt of med school and one day being able to help sop up the mess.

"I'm gonna be late." Vera dashed into the kitchen and grabbed a piece of toast and a sausage link. "I'll eat a good lunch," she promised as she raced from the house, ignoring her aunt's pleas.

The front door yawned as she thudded across the porch toward her beat-up sedan. It was a guilt gift from her parents on her sixteenth birthday. The door was dented, and it slumped every time she opened it. The car also took two turns of her key to get it started, and the gas gauge didn't really work, but it had four wheels and drove. Vera loved it.

She navigated herself to work on autopilot and methodically moved through her day—fill the tray, serve the food, collect the dishes. Repeat. The smiles got her through the monotony, and the proximity to the medical world kept her coming back. Plus, every paycheck took her a little further out of Roaring Creek.

"Here you go, Mr. Gonzalez." Vera lifted the hospital-grade pasta off her cart and set it on the swivel table attached to the patient's bed. She made sure the steamed carrots were closest to him, because he liked those best. Then she peeled off the foil top to the apple juice, knowing his arthritis made it hard for him to pinch.

"Gracias." The old man nodded, wisps of gray hair dotting his sun-spotted head. He smiled with the glint of a young man. "I used to be a cook, you know. In the army. I peeled potatoes!"

"Hmm." Vera hummed, already knowing this story.

She headed back to her cart, and a woman wheeled past the open door, *Get Well Soon* silver balloons trailing behind her.

"My Maria loved my cooking," Mr. Gonzalez went on. "Especially my croquettes! Chicken, and sometimes a little jalapeño . . ." He winked.

Vera half listened, her eyes busy avoiding a makeshift altar resting on a small table near the window. Every time she passed it, the hairs rose on her arms. Vera supported religious expression. Of course she did. First Amendment and all that. But she swore the air in the room grew colder the closer she got to it.

Plus, it had grown. Atop a disposable tablecloth now sat fresh lemony carnations in a glass bubble vase. There were black and white candles—not burning, of course—along with a chocolate bar with frayed gold foil, a crumpled dollar bill, a small jar of what Vera hoped was dirt, and a gold-trimmed chalice seemingly filled with water. But it was the object in the center that caused icy fingers to slither down her neck—a twelve-inch statue of an ivory skeleton in a white robe with matching feathery wings. Its bony hands held an ivory torch, a skull carved into the handle, and it was upside down, the flame at its feet extinguished. It was weeping, black streaks marking its face.

"The Angel of Tears," said Mr. Gonzalez, noticing her gaze.

"Yes, I know." Vera nodded stiffly.

Just get out of here.

She tossed a polite see-you-later grin his way. Then she paused at the sight of his face. His smile looked off. His lips were turned up, the corners straining toward his ears as they had been earlier, but now his mouth looked too wide and his lips too moist. A sudden smell wafted through the room. Her eyes searched for a bedpan, but it wasn't human waste. The air was full of rotting sweetness, as if the carnations were dying, only the petals looked fresh. The stench hadn't been there earlier. She was sure of it.

"El Ángel was there for my Maria," he said, his voice suddenly scratchy.

Mr. Gonzalez suffered from dementia, had just had hip surgery, and was on a grand cocktail of new medications. Sometimes he thought he was back in high school and Vera was his date to the dance. Other times, he spoke at length about his days in Mexico. And almost every time she saw him, he mentioned his wife.

"El Ángel brings me good fortune. The spirit answers my prayers. It listens." His voice was deep, croaking almost, and there was thick drool dribbling down his chin. He made the sign of the cross with a shriveled hand, joints swollen and stiff like a claw. When he kissed his fingers, gums bared, she saw his teeth—tawny and crisscrossing as if threatening to collapse onto the floor. A moment ago, his grin was gleaming.

"I prayed to El Ángel, and my Maria was spared. Do you know my Maria?"

A patient moaned in the room next door. An alarm buzzed. At a quick clip, a police officer jogged down the hall.

Then a frosty wind blew on Vera's neck.

Go. Now, her brain ordered.

"Of course," Vera lied, hugging her chest. Her job was to deliver food pleasantly and with as little interaction as possible.

She turned back to the door and lengthened her stride.

"El Ángel is here for you too."

Three more steps. Just grab the cart and go.

A baby wailed nearby, rhythmic shrieks in bursts of three, and a heaviness fell in the room, the dust motes gaining density, growing more visible. What was that sweet stench? Like rotting lilies.

"My Maria is waiting for me," he babbled. "And soon my soul will be rewarded. El Ángel makes it so. You just have to believe."

Vera understood the intensity of belief. Catholicism flowed with the blood in her veins. Her aunt prayed to saints when she had so much as a flat tire. *"St. Eligius, please assist me in my hour of need,"* her aunt beseeched when their car broke down outside of IKEA. The woman was right: there was literally a patron saint of mechanics. But you know what else there was? Triple A. Vera called. Guess which one arrived first?

Now, if you asked her aunt, she'd tell you that St. Eligius sent the tow truck. Vera disagreed when it came to flat tires, and *definitely* when it came to medicine. Whether you prayed to saints or believed in nothing at all, a tumor was a tumor and the treatment was the same. For Vera, spirituality gave her a moral compass; it taught her right from wrong; it made her believe in a world bigger than herself; and it created a hopeful outlook more conducive to healing. But praying to what looked like the Angel of Death? When you're trying to heal? That seemed counterproductive.

Vera clutched the handle of her cart, the cool metallic feel conjuring an image of her basement doorknob. Why would she think of that?

Her grip tightened.

"Are you ready, Vera?" Mr. Gonzalez's words clawed their way to her ears.

That couldn't be him speaking. She turned, eyeing the face that matched the too-deep voice. His pupils were swollen, gobbling every speck of warm honey that normally spilled from his eyes, and his skin was ash gray with inky blue veins spreading like vines.

"It's glorious!" His tongue lolled. *"I've seen it. The end! You must not fear death. It's like fearing peace or harmony. Open your arms and let the warmth of the next life embrace you!"* Creamy spit splashed, his lips making the wet smack of a raft hitting a pool. *"Be ready, Vera. El Ángel welcomes you. Can you feel it?"*

He never used her name. The man had dementia.

And where had she heard those words before?

He cranked his mouth wide, glaring at the ceiling. The lights crackled, then flickered.

"Let go and your mind will be resurrected. For it is through suffering that we reach a pure state of being! Join me!" he called to the heavens.

What the h—

"Death is beautiful. It's just sleep. And it wants you, Vera. Oh, how it wants you. . . ."

A hollow laugh broke out, his bald head tossed back

with a film of sweat, black eyes crazed. *"It wants you. It wants you. It wants you . . . ,"* he sang like a child keeping time with a jump rope on a playground in Hell.

Vera didn't reach for a call button. She didn't check if he was okay. She sprinted, an animal fleeing with a pulse faster than her feet. She wheeled her cart down the hall, nearly colliding with a nurse. She didn't stop. She didn't apologize. Vera panted, clambering away from the room, from the shrine, from . . . whatever that was, *whoever* that was . . . until she couldn't hear his murderous laugh anymore.

CHAPTER SIX

The Gift

In a sterile hospital room, an old man begs for peace. His wife is dying, of that he is certain. The years have been good to them. Their children are healthy. Their days are quiet. But their minds, oh, their minds.

Age is a cruel beast.

The wife slipped first—years ago, maybe even a decade, if he were being truly honest. And at a time like this, why not be honest?

The first time he noticed, she forgot her father's name. Then she forgot what day it was. Then she forgot she had grandkids.

Their children decided on a "home." Though there was nothing homey about it. The room stank of Lysol, and the bed was lined with buttons. The walls were white. There were few pictures.

She slept. The light rise and fall of her frail chest the only way he knew she still existed. Through it all, the husband rubbed the loose skin on her hand. She was still her.

Then their son visited, dispensing questions with a familiar look in his eyes. Did he know what day it was? Who was president? The old man had watched this happen before. They'd stripped his wife of her humanity, her dignity. He'd let her become something they promised each other they would never, ever be.

Now he was next.

So he placed the statue of the Angel of Tears by her bedside, its ivory wings soaring toward the heavens, the extinguished torch pointed her way.

"Please show her mercy. Please give her peace."

There was no answered prayer.

Next, he brought an offering, a bottle of sweet red wine. "Please let her leave this earth with grace."

The following morning, a flush appeared on her cheeks.

He brought bread.

Then flowers.

With each gift, he felt a fresh vibration tingle within him, nothing dramatic, just a little hum. Slowly, she stopped moaning in her sleep. Her bedsores looked better. Her hair gleamed, more silver than ashen.

He was helping.

So on this day, he brings a candle, white for purity. He places it by her bedside and holds her hand. "Please, Ángel, show her kindness. Let her leave this world as herself. I will do anything. Anything . . ."

For the first time in days, her eyelids flutter. They peel open, blue as the day he met her, and clear, oh so clear.

"Héctor," she says, her breath sweet as candy. He can taste her kiss.

"I'm here, mi amor. I'm here." Tears drip from his eyes as

he touches her cheek, adrenaline coursing through him like a young man. He feels powerful.

"Te amo," she says.

His smile stretches so wide, it strains his cheeks.

"I see it, Héctor." Her eyes glow with the intelligence of youth. "I will see you there. I'll be waiting for you."

When the last breath puffs from her chest, it's as if it puffs straight into his own. He grows dizzy. Storm clouds swirl before him. Blue flames erupt in his temples. He reaches for the bed rail to steady himself, leaning his head on her chest, which no longer moves.

Fever rushes through him as he inhales her scent, sickeningly sweet, like August flowers.

She is gone.

And something else has arrived. It's inside him.

He lifts his head, his chest puffing for the both of them. His vision ripens. He removes his glasses and sees dust drifting in the air. He turns toward the closed window and hears a bee buzzing against the glass. Then the smells come—the pungent cleansers, stale air, and oh, yes, there's Maria, the perfume lingering in her hair.

Something is changing within him.

Something he can't control.

Something he doesn't want to stop.

"Mr. Gonzalez?" says a nurse rushing into the room. "Oh, Mr. Gonzalez! Oh, I'm so sorry for your loss!"

She fiddles with the machines, her hands busy and her eyes glassy. She is filling with grief.

Only he is not sad. He knows the truth.

His wife is not gone. She is waiting for him.

Soon he will join her, but not until he spreads the word.

His prayers have been answered, and others must know.

He must tell them.

CHAPTER SEVEN

Vera

Vera swirled her strawberry-banana yogurt, her eyes in a dead stare as she pictured Mr. Gonzalez's face morphing before her, his deep voice, and his thick drool. *What happened to him?*

"I once had a guy tell me I smelled like lasagna. I had actually eaten lasagna the day *before*, but I had showered since and brushed my teeth *twice*. Explain that," remarked Chelsea, a fellow food service employee, as she bit into a ham-and-cheese sandwich with glowing neon mustard. She was a sophomore at community college and managed to get her girlfriend hired two months ago. Technically, Vera was a third wheel on their lunch dates, but considering she sat alone in her high school cafeteria, this was better.

"I had a lady once ask me to pick food from her teeth. Like, she thought I was going to stick my fingers in her mouth and dig around." Samantha pretended to gag as she snagged a baby carrot from her girlfriend's tray.

"You know, I've seen that Grim Reaper thing in other

rooms," Chelsea said. "It's so creepy. The hospital should ban it."

"I don't know." Vera shook her head, the ends of her hair brushing her shoulders. "But the shrine is technically religious expression, so the hospital can't suppress that."

"It's the Angel of Death in a freakin' hospital. How is that okay?" Chelsea raked her blond hair, pulling long strands loose in her fingers.

"He also, kinda, threatened you," Samantha added, stealing another carrot as Chelsea swatted her hand.

"Technically, he said it *wants* me. I'm not sure if that's a threat," Vera corrected.

"Well, what's *it*? Is it his *it*? Like, his wrinkled old *it*? Because that's sexual harassment," said Chelsea.

Samantha scrunched her nose, disgusted. "And what about the other stuff he said?"

"Some of it I swear I've heard before." Vera chewed her cheek.

"Yeah, in your nightmares." Chelsea huffed. "Don't worry—if you complain, we got your back."

She and Samantha didn't live in Roaring Creek. This made them the two people in Vera's life who didn't know about her parents' work, so they treated her like a human being.

"He could have been hallucinating. Maybe it was the drugs from surgery? Or an allergic reaction?" Vera suggested. Typically, Mr. Gonzalez was a smiling old man telling tales of Mexico. He seemed young for his age, strong even.

But she couldn't conceive of a medical reason for his voice dropping, his mouth decaying, and his pupils swelling right in front of her. She could, however, think of another explanation, a darker one.

I've spent way too much time in my parents' world. Mr. Gonzalez is just sick and the doctors will figure it out.

"All I know is the hospital better take this seriously, because I feel like too many patients are coming in here high out of their minds or completely *possessed*," Chelsea griped.

Vera's eyes shot her way. Hearing the word *possessed* beyond the confines of her home was like hearing a trying-too-hard politician use eighth-grade Spanish: it might be technically correct, but it didn't sound right.

"I think he just misses his wife. They were married for over fifty years. Now he's sick, alone, and grieving," said Vera.

"We're *all* grieving something," said Samantha. "Speaking of which." She pulled a hardback book from her backpack with a bright yellow cover featuring an amateur design Vera was pretty sure she could duplicate in Word Art. The large typeface read *The Sunshine Crew*. "Look what my mom dragged home."

"Ugh." Chelsea rolled her eyes.

"I know they're *odd*." Samantha wiggled. "But she's been looking for the right support group ever since Brian, and this is helping."

Samantha's older brother died of an overdose last year. He was twenty-six. During the funeral, people kept muttering how he was "too young," and Vera watched as Samantha ground her teeth. Working in a hospital meant they were constant witnesses to the lack of sand in the hourglass. Life was always too short. If you miscarry a baby, you wish you could have at least held him. If you rock your daughter to sleep before she passes, you wish you could have seen her first day of school. If you lose your son after graduation, you wish you could have gotten to dance at his wedding. If your daughter dies as a young woman, you wish you could have gotten to meet your grandkids. And on and on and on it goes. They were always too young.

Now, nearly 365 days had passed since Brian's death, but it might as well have been three or three thousand; the wound would always be fresh.

"You know how much I care about you and your mom. What you're going through is awful." Chelsea lightly touched Samantha's hand. "But those people are the walking dead."

"No, they're not." Samantha scoffed.

"I don't even know what you're talking about," said Vera. Given her bookshelves practically needed a rolling ladder, she was surprised she didn't recognize the cover.

"Yes, you do!" Chelsea said. "It's that self-help crap *all* over town. You know the posters, with the eclipsed sun? They're all black and yellow, and way too dramatic. It was started by the *Durands.*" Chelsea whispered the name like *cancer.*

"Oh, *that* group!" Vera's eyes lit with recognition.

Seven years ago, a gas explosion at the community center

killed eighteen people. It was the worst tragedy to ever strike Roaring Creek. It was accidental; at least, that's what most people believed. But there was one gas works employee whose remains were found *inside* the building—Seth Durand. An investigation determined his "human error" *may have* caused the explosion, but there was no definitive proof either way. Still, saying *Seth Durand* three times in a mirror while spinning in a circle was a popular activity at Roaring Creek sleepovers. (Not that Vera had ever been to one.)

Despite that, his son, Anatole, had an immense following. He started a group whose members were identified by matching yellow hats; Vera was fuzzy on the details. From what she remembered, Anatole had been twelve years old and on the brink of death from some terminal disease the day his dad died in the explosion. Then, against all odds, the boy lived.

"That family is twisted," said Chelsea, unknowingly echoing exactly what was said about Vera her whole life. "I don't know why anyone would take advice from *him*."

"Because he *survived*. Amid all that tragedy, he lived, and now he's dedicated his life to helping the people his father hurt." Samantha sounded impressed.

"Oh, don't tell me you're getting into this!" Her girlfriend yanked away her hand.

"No." Samantha shifted awkwardly. "I'm not buying a yellow hat or anything, but my mom spent five hundred dollars on a seminar about grief and 'self-actualization,' which I thought was nuts, but she said it really helped."

"Self-actualization? What does that even mean?" Chelsea's face twisted.

"Finding your potential," Vera explained. She'd read a few self-help books in her day. But five hundred dollars?

"No, it means joining the Manson Family," Chelsea mocked.

"Shut up!" Samantha nudged her shoulder. She was smiling, but still, she shoved the book into her bag.

"Okay, back to Old Spooky McSpookerson." Chelsea crumpled her trash. "When does he get discharged? Because I don't wanna serve him any time soon."

"I think it was supposed to be in two days, but who knows now." Vera shrugged.

"Well, if he goes Grim Reaper–crazy on me, I'm busting out the garlic."

"Isn't that for vampires?" Samantha mocked.

"Good enough." Chelsea giggled, her hazel eyes shifting to something behind Vera. Then her face morphed into a smile—not the happy kind, but the this-is-gonna-be-good kind. Samantha's gaze immediately took on the same expression.

Vera craned her neck. *If there is an old man in a hospital gown standing behind me . . .*

Only, the person she found was even more shocking.

Hovering inches from Vera's face was Maxwell Oliver. He was staring. *Again.*

"Um, hey, could we talk?" he asked.

CHAPTER EIGHT

Max

She looked shocked, which made sense. While their last names were pretty close in the alphabet—Oliver and Martinez—and over the years they'd sat relatively near each other in a few classes, they'd never spoken. She caught him staring yesterday, and he'd wanted to talk to her; only not in school.

Then the bacon incident happened, and Max had to do something. He saw two choices. Option 1: He could take his mom to the hospital and get her looked over, but every instinct inside him shouted "No!" His mother loathed doctors, and Max feared what would happen to him and Chloe if the hospital admitted her, especially if it were for something (he hated to even think it) addiction-related. Besides, he'd searched the house for pills and liquor last night and found nothing. That left him with Option 2: Vera Martinez, the girl whose parents were so often whispered about they almost didn't seem real. He'd never given much thought to the rumors before; in fact, he figured most of it was elaborate bullying. But now his mom was morphing into a different person, with a disturbing voice, face, and smell. If he lived in a different town, somewhere far, far away, he probably wouldn't even consider this possibility. But he lived in this town, with this family, and this girl.

"I know we haven't spoken much." Max searched Vera's face. Her friends across the table gawked at him but wore smiles. Vera didn't. "I hope you don't mind. The front desk staff said you were working today and usually take lunch at this time. I was hoping we could, maybe . . ."

"You came to see *me*?" Her brows crumpled above big brown eyes.

"Well, yeah." He rubbed his neck, now heating to what was likely a blotchy shade of red. Her friends smiled wider, nudging each other as they watched him squirm. *Great.* "Do you think, like, maybe we could talk, you know . . . somewhere?"

"About what?"

Max swallowed (his pride as much as his nerves). Vera wasn't making this easy, but not too many people were ever easy on her. He cracked his knuckles, and her friend, the blonde, stifled a laugh. He did not want to have this conversation in front of two older girls he didn't know, who were kind of pretty. In fact, if he were being honest, so was Vera. *What did Jackson call her before? "Undercover hot"?* Max hadn't noticed until now. But her eyes had this cool way of turning up at the corners like a cat's, and they were flecked like warm apple pie.

His face flushed more. "Um, I think I need your help, or

maybe your parents' help. It's about my mom, and I know that your parents . . ."

Vera stood up so fast that her blue plastic chair nearly toppled to the tiles. "Um, yeah, sure, we can go somewhere." She snatched her purse from the back of her chair, bright roses blooming on her cheeks. "Follow me."

———

They sat on a splintered wooden bench in the shade of trees speckled with bright white blossoms. Tiny round petals snowed into their laps with the breeze, and his throat itched at the sight of them.

"Thanks for talking to me." Max coughed slightly.

"You didn't give me much of a choice. You showed up at my work." Vera's lips were tight.

"I wasn't sure where else to find you."

"So the one hundred and eighty days of school we had together this year weren't enough?" Vera tilted her head, dark waves falling over her shoulder. "Because I don't exactly remember you chatting my ear off, you know, since kindergarten."

Touché. "I couldn't say this at school. It's about my mom. She's been acting strange, and, well, your parents—"

"Look, I don't know what you think you know about my family," she cut him off, "but we're not a 7-Eleven. We're not open twenty-four hours to serve you whatever you need whenever you need it."

His chest clenched. He may not have hung out with Vera much (or at all), but he knew what a girl's face looked like when she was pissed, and this was it. When they didn't get a chance to speak in English class, or, more accurately, when he couldn't work up the nerve to talk to her in front of his friends, he thought he'd uncovered the perfect opportunity. He diverted from his jog to learn her schedule and even waited until her lunch break, thinking it was the polite thing to do. Besides, her friends didn't look annoyed by the interruption. *Wait, her friends . . .*

"Sorry, maybe I shouldn't have come to your work." He thought of all the school lunches where Vera ate alone. "I didn't mean to involve your friends, but I really need to talk to you."

"Of course." Her tone was flat. "That's why I'm here, in case *you* really need me."

Max squinted, his head throbbing. What was he supposed to do? He spent the last couple nights sleeping on the floor of his sister's room, not to fend off the nightmares, but to fend off their only surviving parent, who was now acting like a stranger. Like a threat.

No. He was blowing this out of proportion. He had to be.

He shook his head, throat squeezing tight.

A hand touched his arm, fingers light on his skin. "I was rude," Vera said, her voice softer. "I just like to keep my co-workers separate."

Max opened his eyes. Roaring Creek wasn't exactly kind to this girl. Neither was he. If the roles were reversed, how would he react if she showed up at his work one day, in front of everyone?

"Something's obviously wrong," she went on. "You came all the way here, so what's up? You said it's your mom?"

Max nodded.

How should he put it? It felt like a betrayal even saying it.

He took a deep breath and collected his thoughts.

"The past couple weeks, she hasn't been herself. It started small. She forgot to pick up Chloe from school—that's my sister." He looked at Vera, and she nodded like she already knew, which of course she did. Chloe's birth had been a bright spot after the explosion. She was headline news. "Then she started showing up to work late, then forgetting to place orders with our vendors, then she stopped coming in at all. I've taken over her job completely. At first, I thought she was sick. She's been sleeping a lot—"

"During the day?" Vera interjected.

"All day." He watched Vera check off a mental note. "But now her behavior is . . . bizarre." He didn't know how to put it. "It's gotten to the point where I'm afraid to leave Chloe alone with her. Then yesterday . . ."

He steadied himself and described the incident with his sister at the stove.

"Her voice was different?" Vera asked.

Max nodded.

"And she was laughing?"

"At the end, yeah." Max confirmed. "But it wasn't a

happy laugh. It didn't sound like her at all. I don't know how to describe it."

Vera's cheeks twitched like she was considering something, or maybe remembering something.

"And you're sure there was no alcohol? Pills?"

Max clenched his jaw. "She's been sober for four years. . . ." She has, right? Max knew the signs. "There was no alcohol on her breath, no slurring, no puking. And the stuff she was saying, it wasn't like she was drunk. . . . It was like it wasn't *her.*"

"When was the last time she saw a doctor?" Vera tried to sound official.

"She had her annual checkup on her birthday last month, blood work and stuff. Everything was fine."

"A psychiatrist?"

His gaze narrowed. What was this? Just because she was wearing scrubs (in black, no less, which was a little odd) didn't make her Vera the Teenage Doctor. Besides, he'd Googled every medical possibility, and nothing fit. That was why he came to Vera.

"She's seen a therapist, on and off, since . . . the explosion." He hated talking about his dad. Just brushing up against the memories of that day caused his body to tense.

"Depression can manifest in many ways, and it can be compounded with other illnesses. After everything your family's been through . . ."

"This is not about my *dad*!" Max slammed the wooden bench, regretting it the moment Vera flinched.

He hung his head, panting. He hadn't slept well in so long, and he was perpetually tired of the world pinning everything wrong in his life back on that one day. It had been seven years! It wasn't always about that.

He pinched the bridge of his nose.

Or maybe it was, at least in this town.

Half the residents had been flooded after the hurricane, and the basketball game was intended to raise funds for recovery efforts. Max's dad was captain of one of the teams. He and his mom were on their way to cheer him on, driving back from a "stress test" at the obstetrician's office. Mom was in her third trimester carrying Chloe.

When they arrived, the community center had already exploded. A mountain of tangerine flames roared so high Max could hardly see sky. Police were everywhere, screaming into walkie-talkies. Sirens blasted, firehoses spewed water, and crowds shoved and sobbed. Loved ones desperately clung to one another, to strangers, to anyone, pleading for help. Max stood on the sidewalk holding his mother's hand, helplessly watching the deadly inferno as it seared itself into the core of who Max would become. Then his mom went into labor, right there outside the blazing building. Chloe was on the front page of the paper. MIRACLE BABY! But what came next wasn't a miracle.

His mom healed, physically, from the emergency C-section, but the pills kept flowing. Max was too young to understand, but he noticed the alcohol. He raised Chloe during those early months, a ten-year-old warming bottles, changing diapers, and popping a pinkie finger into a shrieking mouth. Eventually, his grandparents came. Then the threats. Then the accident. And all of this because of a freak gas leak.

"Maxwell, I'm so sorry about your dad," Vera's voice cracked as she placed a palm on his shoulder—a classic move. It often came with thoughts and prayers. "I can't imagine what you and your family have been through. I don't know if you realize this"—she paused as if unsure whether to continue her train of thought—"but I met your mom once, in a way."

Max's eyes flung toward her.

"I started volunteering as a candy striper when I was thirteen." She wore the oddly embarrassed look of an overachiever downplaying her accomplishments. Meanwhile, if anyone understood working at a young age, it was Max. "I was in the lobby the night your mom was brought in. . . ."

Oh. Max grew rigid, his hands knotting in his lap. He should've realized.

Four years ago, on a sunny afternoon, his mother crashed her car on Main Street—it folded like an accordion against a telephone pole. Her blood-alcohol level mixed with the pills in her system was enough to render her a corpse, but somehow she survived. Her injuries were remarkably minor. But his grandparents hired lawyers. His mom left the hospital swearing she'd never touch another pill or another drop. She'd been sober for four years.

"You're blaming her addiction? You don't know anything about it," Max spat through clenched teeth.

"You're right, I don't," Vera reached out a hand. "I'm sorry. But substance abuse lasts a lifetime. It's a disease, like cancer or diabetes—"

"She wasn't drunk last night." If he couldn't make this girl understand, with her family history, then what hope did he have of convincing anyone else? "I remember what she looked like drunk and the things she'd say. She used to cry about my dad and feel sorry for herself. *Now* she's speaking gibberish, *incoherent* gibberish. She's spitting out phrases like, 'Your mind will be resurrected' and 'Join me in the next life.'"

Vera jolted, eyes suddenly alert. "That's what she said?"

Max nodded. He'd struck a nerve.

"Is she religious?" Vera asked.

"No." Max shook his head. "I mean, we were all baptized, but that's it."

"Does she have any religious objects in your house?"

"Aside from a Christmas tree?"

Vera snorted, but still, it sounded like she was listening.

"This is gonna sound weird . . ." Vera twisted her hands. "But have you seen a statue of a skeleton in your house? Maybe a shrine? Something that looks like a Grim Reaper, only with wings and a torch?"

"What? No," he spat. "Why would you ask that?"

"No reason." She shrugged.

"It sounds like there's a reason. That's pretty specific."

She bit her lip, not explaining further.

"Something's wrong with my mom. If you know what it is, you have to tell me," Max insisted. "I could sit here and pretend I don't know the rumors about your family, but we both know that's a lie. It's why I came. So while I have no right to ask for your help, if half of what I've heard about your parents is true, then it's possible . . ."

His voice trailed off as he watched her stare at the lawn, mowed in perfect rows, her sneaker kicking the freshly trimmed blades. The air smelled of baseball fields and summer. God, it was the start of *summer.* He should be with his friends. He should be at the creek.

"Even if my parents wanted to help, they're out of the country," Vera said, not looking him in the eyes.

Max's shoulders fell. "Where? For how long?"

"They're in Barcelona. On a case. I'm not sure when they'll be back."

"Are they helping someone who's possessed?"

Her eyes shot his way, surprised that he'd said it. He might have danced around it before, but it was time to put it out there—she knew about his dead dad and his mother's addiction, and he knew about her demon-hunting parents.

"I don't know what you think my parents do, but they work for the church. They don't just take on cases. The archdiocese fields calls, globally, from people who are troubled, possibly *afflicted,* and they can't send priests to investigate each one. My parents work as consultants. They check things out and report back. To the church. So even if they were here, what you're asking . . ."

"Is for help. I'm asking for *your* help. If your parents aren't around, maybe *you* can help me? Just see for yourself." Max was desperate. He sounded it and he felt it, but if she said no, what exactly was his next move?

If he brought his mother to the ER, if she was hospitalized for any reason, he knew his grandparents would win custody. And it wasn't that he didn't love his grandparents. He did. His grandma made the most amazing Jamaican food that reminded him of his dad's home cooking, and his grandpa played a harmonica and sang songs in Italian, but Max's mom was the only *parent* he and his sister had left. He couldn't risk them being separated from her; Chloe couldn't deal with that. She couldn't lose her mother too.

"I'm *not* my parents," Vera insisted. "They have skills, talents, that I don't have. Trust me. I'm useless when it comes to this stuff. The way I can help you is to tell you to bring your mom *here*. Let her be seen by a doctor. Let them run some tests."

"Oh, come on!" Max pushed to his feet. "They have a test to figure out why she smells like rotting flowers? Why her laugh isn't right? I can't believe you won't help me!"

"I *am* helping. If my parents were here, if you were speaking with them right now, they'd tell you the same thing— given your mom's history, she'd *have to* be seen by a doctor before they'd even consider talking to her. They'd have to rule out drugs, brain tumors, dissociative identity disorder, schizophrenia . . ."

"Oh my God! Are you kidding me?" He'd swallowed his pride and told this girl things he hadn't told *anyone*. Now she was blowing him off. It was *her* parents who fought demons. Shouldn't she be the one who believed in this stuff?

Forget her. He turned toward the parking lot.

"Maxwell, I want to help!" she called after him.

Sure you do. He spun back her way. "If that's true, then try *listening* to me. The doctors in there"—he pointed to the concrete building with gleaming blue glass—"they won't listen to the story of what I saw in my sister's room or on my back porch. Her raspy voice, her blank look, her strange grin, and her dark laugh—it wasn't *her*. She made my skin crawl. Through all the drinking and the grief, I was never *afraid* of my mother. But I have been these past couple weeks. I'm afraid to touch her or wake her up. I don't know how she'll react, because I don't know this person. And the worst part is, you *know* what I'm saying is possible. You might be the only person in this town who knows that, and you're sending me away."

Vera's mouth popped open, then closed. She blinked, shifting her weight, seemingly warring with what to say.

Okay, finally, I got through to her.

"When my parents get back, I'll tell them everything. I'll have them meet with you," she offered, chewing her lip.

His chest sank. Something told him he didn't have that kind of time. "You do that." He turned his back. "Thanks for the *help*."

CHAPTER NINE

Vera

After Maxwell stormed off, Vera headed back to work, grabbing her cart and pushing it to the next patient's room. Maxwell Oliver, who already lost his dad, was now begging for spiritual assistance for his *mother*.

Vera rolled her cart through the hospital halls, trays of food and silverware rattling while the back-left wheel squeaked with every rotation.

Step, step, squeal. Step, step, squeal.

Her shoulders pressed toward her ears as she turned a corner, the metallic squeak intensifying. Roaring Creek General was the perfect hospital diorama—pocked drop ceiling with too-bright greenish lights, upper walls crisp and ivory above a khaki bottom, with a mint-green chair rail cutting through it. Rectangular ceiling lights reflected on the shiny tan floor tiles, creating a band of white light.

Step, step, squeal. Step, step, squeal.

Vera knew Maxwell's mother had a history of substance abuse, but even if she was using, it wouldn't explain the odd changes to her voice, laugh, and smell. Plus, she sputtered

57

some of the exact same bizarre phrases as Mr. Gonzalez. Thankfully, she didn't have a shrine, or at least no Grim Reapers that Maxwell knew of, but still, Vera's gut sent up a flare.

She spun her cart around another corner. There were two vegetarian deliveries on this floor, one up ahead. Her eyes located the proper meal as she squealed past a bank of dusty gray office chairs bolted to the floor. Stagnant. Permanent.

Step, step, squeal. Step, step, squeal.

A janitorial cart rested ahead—Candace's. Vera could tell by the way she organized her bottles. A smile spread on Vera's lips as she prepared to say hello, then she spotted a canary book peeking from the cart's side pocket. The cover featured a sun engulfed by an eclipse. *Huh, that group really is popular.* How had Vera not noticed it before? A fog of Lysol enveloped her, chemicals slathering her tongue, and before Vera could glance in the room to find Candace, an alarm rang out.

A patient was coding.

Vera threw herself against the drywall, tugging her food cart closer to make room for a stampede of white-sneakered feet.

"She pulled out her IV and the oxygen tube," hollered a nurse as she raced by.

"Isn't she restrained, after last time?" asked the resident.

"Yes. *And* sedated."

"It must be delirium from the hypothermia."

"Maybe." Only, the nurse didn't sound convinced.

The staff charged into the room across the hall, its alarms blaring as they shouted commands.

Vera was supposed to keep moving. Privacy was paramount. Regardless, she stood still.

Feet pounded. Instruments clattered. A woman, maybe in her late twenties or early thirties, writhed on the bed. Her greasy hamburger-colored hair dripped into her mouth as her torso thrust up and down. The top of her checkered gown untied, tumbling to her waist, circular stickers adhered to her chest with no wires attached.

Vera couldn't look away.

"Hold her down!" the resident shouted.

"I'm trying."

"Try harder!"

The girl thrashed in the bed, her lower jaw jutting out in a fierce underbite, teeth gnashing together as sounds ripped from her chest. She snatched a bedpan and pitched it against the wall.

"The pain! You've brought it back!" Her voice was too deep for her frame.

Vera stopped breathing.

Flip-flops thwacked down the hall. "Camille! Camille!"

A middle-aged woman, maybe her mother, threw herself through the doorway only to be blocked by a nurse in lavender scrubs. "Mrs. Sheehan, we're doing everything we can. You can't be in here."

"Camille! Honey, I'm here!" The mom fought with the

same determination as her daughter, struggling to get inside. "What is happening?" The woman shoved, nearly knocking the nurse to the floor. "She's been so much better lately, best she's been in years. She said the pain was lessening."

The mom's back formed a comma as sobs tore out so forcefully, tears sprang to Vera's eyes. She was intruding; this raw, visceral, chest-cracking-open pain was not meant for her to witness, but still Vera stayed locked, bound by the undiluted agony that connected everyone.

There but for the grace of God go I. . . .

The mom hiccupped, wailing, "She was injured . . . in . . . the gas explosion."

Of course. Vera's jaw tightened. It always came back to that.

"You don't know what it's like, the constant aching, for years, never a moment of relief. Then she found this group. A mind-over-matter thing? I don't know . . . it's been helping." The heavyset mother clawed at the nurse, fingers pulling at her purple scrubs as if to force her words inside her. "Now this. Why was she in that water?"

"I don't know," the nurse replied, not releasing her grip. "The fisherman who found her is talking to the police. I can take you to them."

Then the daughter's shrieks quieted. Vera's eyes shot to the room in time with the mother, and they spied a syringe being pried from the patient's arm.

"*I've found the solution,*" the daughter mumbled. "*The*

pain doesn't matter. I can be reborn. Just let me go. . . ." Then she collapsed on the hospital bed, her eyelids shut.

The nurses got to work, placing an oxygen mask over her face as the machines beeped at a slower rhythm.

"What are you doing?" snapped a voice. It was aimed at Vera.

Her head wrenched toward the sound and spied the nurse in lavender scrubs snarling.

"This isn't a show! Move!" The nurse ordered, pointing. "You know better than this."

Vera's cheeks flamed as she awkwardly tucked her hair behind an ear. Then she swiftly spun her cart and marched away, not making eye contact with the mother.

The patient had been injured in the gas explosion, another life revolving around that single day. That and the hurricane. Tragedy after tragedy. Death after death. Pain upon pain.

Vera pushed her cart down the hall, machines still beeping, doctors still running.

Step, step, squeal.

Step, step, squeal.

CHAPTER TEN

The Swim

In a dusty one-room apartment, a clock strikes midnight. She rummages through a drawer, seeking—what's the word again?—yes, a swimsuit. She tugs it on, wincing as she lifts each leg. Then she limps to her car. She drives, the steering wheel guiding itself, her soul knowing where she needs to be.

She is returning to nature, arriving at the coast to complete darkness. There isn't even a moon.

Her bare feet sink into the cool sand, black waves roaring before her. She dips a toe, icy water slipping over her feet. It's June, a reminder of the days when the town still had tourists. That stopped the day her pain began.

Selling lemonade at the game, that was what she was supposed to be doing, if she hadn't been running late. She wished she'd run even later. If she had not sped through that yellow light, she still would have been behind the wheel rather than on the gymnasium's front steps at the fateful moment.

Blast-force trauma. That was what the doctors called it as they diagnosed her brain injury, back pain, hearing loss, PTSD, and constant, oh-that-constant, aching.

But not tonight.

She steps farther into an ocean not yet warmed by the sun's summer rays. It's too cold to be enjoyable, at least without a— What is it that surfers wear? A seal suit? No, a bodysuit. No, wait, a wet suit. Yes. She only wears a one-piece, solid crimson, legs cut high like a lifeguard's. She can barely swim.

Seven years of breathing techniques, meditation, compression, ice packs, supplements, and physical therapy, but nothing worked. Then she met him. Last year, on the anniversary of the explosion, his words echoed through the town square, rattling deep in her soul. Finally, someone saw her invisible pain, and rather than promise to take it away, he promised to make it not matter. Her agony was pointless. Her thinking shortsighted. She was experiencing a blip in a larger existence. There is more out there.

She wades deeper into the black water, a seagull cawing overhead as a white froth breaks on her knees. Freezing ocean water can wash away pain, he said. She must return to the elements, the greater universe. She must surrender.

"You have been trained by society to limit your thinking. There is so much more than this life. Open your mind, release your fear, and you'll see the vast sea of possibilities." Even now, in this moment, she feels his words. She swallows them whole, absorbs them into her very essence, and lets them take up all the space inside her.

He has the answers.

A wave crashes against her chest, the saltwater frigid, stealing the air from her lungs. The wave's force lifts her toes from the murkiness below. Her muscles tighten. Her teeth chatter. Seaweed wraps around her calves, holding on; she shakes it loose and, with it, the pain. It releases. She releases. The current shoves her faster than she's moved in years. Her eyes lose focus as she lies back, submitting, ice hugging her shoulders, pulling her deeper, past the breakers, toward that eternal horizon.

He has delivered the answer. Her pain is gone. It no longer matters.

Nothing matters.

CHAPTER ELEVEN

Vera

Vera's car wouldn't start. It wasn't the first time. Her senior citizen sedan suffered from a not-too-accurate gas gauge. She never knew when the tank was empty, so as a precaution, she put in twenty dollars' worth of gas every Friday. That typically got her through the week, but she drove her aunt to a church function on Tuesday. It was two towns over; maybe that pushed her to E?

Vera hoped so. Because broken parts meant money, and every dollar she earned went to her college fund. She slammed shut the dented white door of the car, which sighed heavier than she did, and tossed her leather bag over her shoulder. A two-mile stroll on a warm summer night wasn't so bad.

Her Converse scraped toward Main Street to the symphony of cicadas playing their violin wings. The fog was so dense individual droplets hovered in the strobes of antique-replica streetlamps. Salt air slid down her throat. Roaring Creek's proximity to the beach attracted the tourists, and its central location between Manhattan and Boston kept the locals. Either metropolis was a reasonable two-hour drive, even shorter if you took an express train. This meant townies got loads of educational and employment benefits while living in the backdrop of a Lifetime movie where a woman abandons the big city for the joy of running a fledgling ice cream shop.

Vera smiled as she eyed Igloo Ice Cream nestled next to Must Love Books, her typical Saturday-night suitors. It was Wednesday, which meant Janet was managing the bookshop and likely about to finish the new Nora Roberts. Last week, she was reading Betty Friedan. The week before, she'd recommended a tome on the ethnomusicology of heavy metal music. Vera waved at her through the plate glass, and Janet returned her greeting with a smile that crinkled her eyes. See? Vera had friends.

A seagull called in the distance—a high-pitched squawk that echoed in four staccato wails, bouncing off the concrete. Gulls usually pilfered French fries during the lunch rush and gave it a rest after the sun set. The bird called again, piercing her ears. It was high in a tree. A breeze rushed in, salty and cool. The temperature dropped. Vera crossed her bare arms, shivering as she shuffled past shops.

Then the seagull swooped down, a blur of white feathers nearly slicing her nose. Vera swatted her hands, sneakers skidding to a halt. A squawk ripped from its golden beak as a baby stroller was pushed from a shop. Vera jolted, avoiding a toddler collision.

"Omigod! Sorry!" Vera blurted.

The mom adjusted the brim of her bright yellow hat, shooting her a look.

A bird just dive-bombed my head! Vera thought as the gull perched on a telephone pole, black eyes trained on her. It let out another repetitious squeal; Vera's shoulders pushed to her ears as a car missed a stop sign.

Horns blared, and Vera spun toward the sound, catching a white SUV swerving into a crowded crosswalk. Pedestrians scattered, yelping. More drivers slammed on their brakes and laid on their horns.

"Watch where you're going!" a driver yelled.

The white SUV peeled off, not pausing, not apologizing.

"You're gonna get someone killed!" another screamed.

Vera's heart thumped at the scene.

Earlier this school year, five of Vera's classmates died in an unexplained car wreck. It wasn't an isolated incident. Local news consistently raised alarms about the increase in vehicular deaths over the past several years. The per capita rate for Roaring Creek far exceeded the national average. So did the town's drug problem and its rate of tragedy in general.

If you asked anyone, they'd likely say the problems in Roaring Creek began with the gas explosion. And that was probably true, just *not* for Vera. Aunt Tilda had been the executive director of the community center at the time, only, she wasn't working that day. Still, she stepped down immediately after the tragedy, not because of any wrongdoing, but because she didn't want to be near "so much darkness." A new director handled the rebuilding, and Aunt Tilda dedicated herself to the church (even more so than before). She also became Vera's primary caretaker when her parents were out of town, which was often.

It was Maxwell's family whose pain was exploited on national TV. A photo of young Maxwell holding his mother's hand while she went into labor, the baby's father burning in the flames behind them, instantly went viral. Chloe's birth was the miraculous moment the town, and the nation, desperately needed. But the reporters didn't follow the aftermath. They didn't cover the past seven years of walking depression from citizens who lost limbs, sleep, and loved ones. That wasn't sexy. That wasn't a "miracle." That was just real life.

You're sending me away. . . . Maxwell's words haunted Vera as she trudged past the florist filled with splashes of petal-infused sunshine and a clutter of antiques. It was owned by Seth Durand's widow, Mary. Despite whatever role her husband may have played in the explosion, no one blamed *her.* She was caring for a terminally ill child at the time. In fact, many believed that if society, if employers, had been kinder, then her husband would never have been working during such a difficult time. The human error was likely caused by his emotional distress.

If he'd only known his son would live.

Vera ran her hands up and down her icy arms, unable to get warm. She couldn't shake the image of Maxwell's pleading face. What would she want someone to do if she was as desperate as he looked today? What might have happened if someone intervened when Seth Durand was at his lowest, too distracted to make good choices?

But I can't do anything, Vera reasoned. *I'm not my mother—I'm not clairvoyant. And I'm not my father—I'm not an exorcist. Even if I feel bad for Maxwell, I can't help. Not in the way he wants.*

Over the years, Vera had watched her mother convulse in fits of uncontrollable "visions." Her mom could enter a home and tangibly feel spirits, the way others sense tension. She could *see* them, black shadows clinging to the possessed, or former residents roaming the halls. And her father had an otherworldly strength of body, mind, and spirit, with enough faith to actually drive out inhuman spirits. He and a priest routinely descended into the basement to bless the artifacts they kept locked away from the world. Vera had heard families thank her parents for saving their lives and their souls. Her parents' work was real.

But Vera wasn't like them.

She chewed her lip as she neared the end of Main Street, preparing to turn off onto Broadway with its double yellow lines and cars swerving too fast around curves. A man walking a rottweiler approached wearing yet another highlighter-yellow cap. The Sunshine Crew. The book, the hat, it seemed to be everywhere now. Or was Vera just noticing it more?

She met the man's eyes with a friendly, it's-dark-and-I-don't-want-you-to-assault-me smile, and he held her gaze, staring intently, his smile eerie. His gaze never shifted, and slowly her brain registered his face, same as the image printed on the back of Samantha's book. It was him, Anatole Durand, the creator of the Sunshine Crew.

"Hello," he said, his tone formal. Then he nodded his head and lifted the brim of his yellow hat in an almost Victorian gesture.

The look in his eyes, it was playful. Vera broke away, staring into the middle distance. "Hey," she muttered, ignoring the ice luge forming down her back.

This is the guy everyone's obsessed with? She smiled, friendly, as her arms wrapped tighter around her chest.

"Have a lovely evening," he added as he passed. His guard dog sniffed her leg, straining against its leash.

Vera kept moving, quickening her pace, eager to put distance between them.

She shook it off, feeling guilty for being rattled. Anatole Durand was not responsible for his father's mistakes; he was literally a child on his deathbed at the time. Now he was giving back to the community and making things right. She, of all people, knew not to judge others by their parents' actions. She should have been nicer.

Actually, she should have been nicer to Maxwell today too.

Her rubber soles halted at the *Don't Walk* signal, and she tugged her necklace from the V-neck of her scrubs, squeezing the golden cross between her thumb and forefinger. It was a gift from her parents. She closed her eyes, a warm breeze brushing over her, lifting her wavy locks from her shoulders.

Then a melodic pulse rang out, and she opened her eyes to see the signal changed—*Walk.*

I'll call my parents, she thought. There was no harm in telling them what was going on. She could ask for their advice. They could point Maxwell in the right direction, whether that be the hospital or *somewhere else.*

Vera turned onto Broadway, the cracks in the sidewalk disappearing into an even denser fog. She squinted into the mist and reached for the elastic around her wrist, tying back her damp hair. She checked her phone's battery; plenty of charge, no messages. A car rumbled past, its high beams blinding. She flinched, shielding her face with her palm, and caught a swish of movement in the powder-blue hydrangeas lining the grass. She gazed into the haze, expecting the yellow corneas of a deer or a raccoon.

Only, what she saw lacked life.

Hovering in the air a few feet ahead were the black-pitted holes of a skeleton, formed from a dewy cloud. The image was distinct—two hollow pits hung above the angular holes of its fleshless nose, black tears streaming toward the silent shriek of a gaping mouth. Behind the bony face, white wisps of fog formed long, feathery wings.

This wasn't her imagination.

It was the Angel of Tears, dancing so close she could extend an arm and touch it.

A vision of Mr. Gonzalez's shrine flashed in her mind, and every hair on her body spiked. Her pulse turned into the rattle of cymbals.

Then a seagull called in the distance, and her face shot up, unable to see the bird in the haze. When she lowered her head, the skeletal face was gone.

She dropped the necklace she was clutching and reached into her pocket.

This was a sign.

She pulled out her phone and found Maxwell's number.

CHAPTER TWELVE

Max

Max sat on the edge of his sister's bed, her black curly hair fanning across every speck of her pillow. Their Jamaican, Dominican, Swedish, and Italian roots left them both with hair so spiraled that Max buzzed his scalp rather than learn to care for it. Chloe's hair was his mother's responsibility, or it used to be. This week, Max was forced to tie an elastic at the base of Chloe's neck, opting not to comb it at all and instead grouping all the knots together. She was teased at school, Chloe told him at dinner, and a stiff jab to the kidney would have hurt less.

He thought of his mother sleepwalking into Chloe's room to comb it out. Part of him was grateful, and the other part was terrified.

"One more book," his sister pleaded.

"I've already read three." He cocked his head.

"Maybe Mom could read one?" Chloe's voice was soft like she knew the answer, but she was asking anyway.

His sister was young, but not that young. She knew something was up.

"She will soon."

"When?" She pouted.

"When she's better." Max reached for the Hello Kitty night-light on her bedside table and flicked on the rainbow strobes.

"What's wrong with her?" Chloe's eyes flexed the way kids' do when they know they're not being told the whole story. But the truth was, Max had no idea what was wrong with their mother.

"She's sick. You know how sometimes you get a stomachache, and you have to stay home from school?"

"Her stomach hurts?" Chloe wasn't buying it.

"No, more like her head."

"Well, she seems better to me."

Max jutted back. "Why would you say that?"

"The other night, when she came into my room, I told her what happened with Sophie, about her calling me a poufy poodle." Chloe scrunched her nose at the memory. "Mom said if I left a gift by her door, she'd make my troubles go away. So I put the chocolate bunny I had left over from my Easter basket by Mom's bedroom, and at recess, Sophie played with me. She didn't say anything about my hair."

Somewhere in Max's brain, a plug got pulled and all the blood drained to his toes.

When did his mother speak to her? He thought he caught her before she'd said anything. Had this happened more than once? And what was the deal with the gift?

"Maybe Mom *is* feeling better." This was a lie. "But be careful around Sophie. Bullies usually stay mean."

"How do you know?"

"I've met a few in my day."

"Yeah, well, maybe Mom can make Sophie stay nice. I have more Easter candy!" She smiled wide.

Moms didn't help their kids in exchange for gifts, but he wasn't about to rip that grin away from his sister. Besides, Chloe deserved a caring mother who helped solve her problems at school—the kind of mom that Max grew up with.

He said good night, and Chloe hugged her pink seal, rolling onto her belly.

He left her bedroom door cracked, then headed toward the kitchen. The dryer buzzed in the basement as Max stepped on a creaky floorboard, the wood buckling. He pulled at his tense neck, moving about three steps before the smell hit his nostrils, rolling him back onto his heels. That scent used to permeate the house—back when his family was happy and his father gave flowers to his mother.

Lilies.

Sometimes pale pink, sometimes goldenrod, sometimes as orange as the sunset through a windshield, but always so fragrant it would make Max's throat itch.

Robotically, he turned toward the source, expecting his father to be standing in the hall holding a bouquet. But the scent was coming from the master bedroom. They didn't grow lilies in their yard, and his mom hadn't had a car all day. Either someone sent her flowers, or they miraculously appeared. He padded to her door and reached for the long, curved handle.

He didn't push. Instead, he leaned closer, almost touching his ear to the wood. Pollen seeped in with his every breath, watering his eyes. A clock ticked at the end of the hall, keeping time with his heart. Sheets rustled inside.

"It is through suffering that we reach a pure state of being. . . ." The voice was so deep and flat that at any other point in his life, Max would have grabbed the fireplace poker and flung the door open, expecting to encounter a stranger. But he knew it was her.

"Death is just sleep, just sleep . . . ," she groaned, then broke into a throaty sound (maybe a chuckle?) that squeezed at the depths of Max's chest.

He let go of the handle, blinking rapidly as he fell back a step.

He should go inside. He should check on her. But he couldn't stop backing away. He clutched the sides of his head, trying to block out the laughter, knowing that his mother was not only aware of his presence, but that she was laughing at *him*.

Only, that wasn't her laugh.

He stumbled farther, still choking on lilies as he fumbled for his phone. He yanked it from his pocket, and it vibrated in his hand. He glanced at the screen.

The text read:

Hi, Maxwell. I hope this is your number. It's me, Vera.

CHAPTER THIRTEEN

Vera

Vera sat on an unpainted wooden picnic bench, peeling a thick splinter from the board. When she texted Maxwell last night, it was as if he'd been waiting by the phone. He called her back immediately. He didn't text; he *called*. She didn't have too many phone conversations with people who weren't her parents or who weren't offering her a free cruise, so the entire interaction should have been awkward, but it wasn't. It was almost prophetic.

"You'll help me?" Maxwell said as soon as she picked up, like he already knew.

"Yeah." She nodded, though he couldn't see her, and they arranged to meet at his family's restaurant the next day.

Vera had the day off, and thankfully, with a spare gallon of gasoline, she was able to get her aging hunk of metal started. Maybe there really was a patron saint of mechanics. Or maybe she was supposed to walk home and see that winged skeleton in the fog. Either way, it brought her to Oliver Seafood.

She glanced around the open-salt-air restaurant. Galvanized

metal buckets rested on tables holding laminated menus, paper napkins, and condiments in yellow and red plastic bottles. Live lobsters crawled in a tank near the register. Through a giant glassless window, Vera spied chefs bustling in white coats, steam rising into their faces. At the table with the best view sat an elderly couple with a fully unobstructed expanse of ocean spread before them. The afternoon sun was high in the sky, a breeze fluttered the woman's white hair, and seagulls called in the distance. The tables around them were empty.

It was June, in a beach town, during what should be the lunch rush, at one of the only oceanfront restaurants in town, and Vera made up fifty percent of their tables. She wasn't even eating.

Maxwell stepped out from a door marked *Employees Only*.

"Benny, thanks, man." Maxwell slapped a heavyset guy on the back. "I owe you one!"

"Don't worry about it," the middle-aged man replied, scratching his bushy black beard.

"Someday, and that day may never come," Maxwell lowered his voice into a husky gruff, "you may call upon me to do a service for you. . . ."

Benny let out a hearty laugh you wanted to hug. "You're quoting *The Godfather* to your godfather—I love it!"

"Always!" Maxwell extended his arms and Benny squeezed him so tight, he lifted Maxwell's six-foot frame from the ground.

"You tell your mutha to get well soon, capisce?" He placed Maxwell back on the floor.

"I'll send your love." Maxwell straightened the hem of his shirt, smiling all the way to his ears.

He watched Benny leave, and as soon as the man stepped into the parking lot, Maxwell turned to Vera and his face collapsed.

He plodded over and sank onto the wooden bench across from her, no longer pretending. "Sorry about that. He's a family friend, and our seafood vendor, and now sort of a manager. He's helping us out. Things have fallen . . . behind."

"I understand. You're busy." As she said it, her eyes flitted between empty tables, not intentionally, but she couldn't stop herself.

Maxwell caught her meaning. "Yeah, every summer there seem to be fewer tourists. Ever since the hurricane."

Vera bit her lip. While the gas explosion gripped the nightmares of most people in Roaring Creek, it was the hurricane that plagued Vera, with images of rain battering her house and sounds of glass breaking. The fear of that day lived inside of her.

Maxwell sighed. "We've had seven summers like this. It's so weird, 'cause it feels like yesterday and a million years ago all at the same time."

Vera nodded. It was hard to remember life pre-hurricane, or pre-explosion, as if her time before had been shot on grainy black-and-white footage that was starting to erode. "Do you go to the memorials?"

The first year after the explosion, the town carved the names of those lost into a fountain. The next year, they planted eighteen trees in the park. And every year, they held vigils and rallies. Society excelled at remembering the dead, but it didn't always do so well at supporting the living.

"I used to, but it made my mom so much worse afterward, and it didn't help me at all. And as Chloe got older, I mean, it's her birthday, so it feels twisted to make the day so dark for her. She didn't even know him, which is . . . just . . . sad. Half the people here still go—they all lost somebody or knew someone who was hurt. It wasn't just my dad." He waved his hands around at the restaurant staff who weren't at all busy, but who continued to show up knowing the tips weren't flowing in. Vera didn't lose anyone that day, and she felt guilty about that. They all grieved something so specific, yet her world was spared. "Those memorials, everyone's all smiling and singing, but their eyes, it's like they're *blank*." He shivered.

"It's called walking depression." Vera picked at another splinter on the table, not wanting to sound like a premed know-it-all, but she did work at a hospital. She wanted to specialize in psychiatry one day. "They go about their lives to 'do it for the team'—or the town, in this case—but inside, they're counting the seconds until they can go home and pull the covers over their heads."

"God, isn't that everybody?" Maxwell huffed. He smiled like he was kidding, but it didn't sound like he was.

No, Maxwell, it's not. Vera's chest ached for him. "It

sounds like your mom had gotten a little better. She's been sober a while?"

"Four years. The car accident was rock bottom. And counseling worked. Then she dove into self-help." He picked at a packet of sugar with a chewed nail, looking uncomfortable. "She was in TSC. You know them? She's got the yellow hat and everything."

"I've been seeing them everywhere lately. Some of my coworkers are into it." She thought about the books popping up in janitor carts and on reception desks. "I hear it's expensive."

"Yeah, I freaked. I mean, the restaurant's not exactly rolling in cash. But my mom was able to renegotiate our debt and practically saved the place. She said it was all because of the almighty Sunshine Crew. They taught her the 'communication and assertiveness skills' she needed to make it happen." He sounded like a phony sales pitch as he smirked condescendingly.

"What do you think really happened?"

"I think my dad was a lifelong customer of the bank, and he graduated from high school with the new manager. But whatever, if my mom wants to credit TSC, fine. Either way, the place got back in the black, and the group made her happy."

His lips pursed as his heavy gaze moved toward the ocean. Vera wrung her hands, wanting to touch him, comfort him. Kids their age shouldn't have lives this tragic or problems this massive.

"You wanna talk about last night?" she asked, almost hating to bring it up.

"I'm not sure where to begin." Maxwell flicked his gaze her way, his eyes intense and the color jarring—pale wet sand with rims dark and stormy. Vera's cheeks flushed.

Then he drew a long breath and told her about the unsettling smell of lilies and his sister leaving their mother chocolate. It wasn't until he recited the words *It is through suffering that we reach a pure state of being* and *Death is just sleep* that Vera's stomach sank. Those were Mr. Gonzalez's words. Again.

"Did you find flowers in her room? The source of the smell?" she asked.

"I checked this morning, and there were no flowers. At all. But I swear I could *still* smell lilies. I'm not making this up. I *hate* that scent. It reminds me so much of my dad, and the pollen makes me gag." He clucked his tongue. "That stench was *there*."

Vera smelled something similar in Mr. Gonzalez's room, only it didn't make sense.

"You wanna know what my parents would say?" she asked rhetorically as Maxwell nodded. "Demons do emit smells. I've heard them talk about it a lot. But those odors are horrid, sulfuric, the essence of evil mixed with rotten fish and baby diapers. Demons don't smell like fresh-baked cookies or wildflowers."

"But they could. Maybe you just haven't met *this* demon."

Actually, Vera hadn't met *any* demons. "If you think

what you went through seven years ago was bad, if you think your mom's addiction was bad, then you have no idea what my parents' work looks like. It's Hell—not metaphorical, not in the dramatic sense, but actual, literal Hell."

Maxwell grunted. "I'm already living in Hell." His gaze held the same broken cast as the crowd of mourners he described at the memorials. This was so different from the role of the big man on campus that he played at school; it was as if he were a weary method actor unable to keep up the ruse anymore.

"When my dad died, it wasn't just a hole in our house, it was a black hole that swallowed everything—the restaurant, our livelihood, our activities. I *hate* basketball now. I hate driving anywhere near that site. I hate when other people talk about the deaths in their families, because I find myself comparing our losses. How sick is that? And I know I sound ridiculous, but I also know what's happening in my house right now. I'm not asking you to be your parents. I'm just asking you to come to my house and see for yourself."

Vera nodded. It was a reasonable request, and honestly, she'd decided to get involved the moment she saw that skeleton in the fog. "When should I come?"

"Tonight. We can't wait any longer."

CHAPTER FOURTEEN

Max

Chloe stampeded toward Max's legs, hooking herself around him so hard he stumbled back.

"Did you miss me?" she screamed.

Her friend Alexis Tenn charged in behind her squealing "Cats rule! Dogs drool!" with her mom right on their hyperactive heels.

"Sorry," mouthed Mrs. Tenn.

Max shrugged. If he knew how to lower the volume of a seven-year-old, he'd have a yellow Lamborghini in his driveway.

"Did you have fun?" he asked.

"We went to a cat café!" Chloe cheered.

"And had ice cream!" cooed Alexis.

"I'm returning her high on sugar." The mom approached the table grinning, her dark eyes shifting to Vera.

Slowly, then all at once, her face changed.

Max watched it happen. First, Mrs. Tenn maintained the forced look of politeness that adults reserve for semi-strangers. *Well, hello, Bob. Your lawn is looking healthy. . . ."*

Then she must have placed Vera, because her eyes flexed, her head tilted, and her eyebrows pinched together.

"Oh," she said. Like, *Oh, you invited a serial killer to lunch.* Or, *Oh, my daughter is within striking distance of a Salem witch.*

To Vera's credit, she didn't react.

"Hi," Vera said. She even smiled.

Mrs. Tenn blinked, her body otherwise motionless so as not to make any sudden moves. There was actual fear in her eyes. Vera was the only person in this town helping Max right now, and she was doing it even though he had never been particularly nice to her. Apparently, no one was nice to her.

"Um, Alexis, we have to go." Mrs. Tenn grabbed her daughter's hand and tugged so hard, Alexis slipped from her flip-flop.

"Mom! You said we could stay for lunch!" she whined.

"We can't. I forgot." The mother bent down and snatched her daughter's shoe, then continued yanking her through the restaurant with one bare foot.

Max looked at Vera, her eyes focused on the sugar packets so as not to reveal what she was thinking (though he had a pretty good guess).

"Alexis!" Chloe yelled with the melodramatic flair of a lover in an old movie.

Max grabbed his sister's hand, stopping Chloe from darting after a mom convinced a tantrum-throwing seven-year-old was easier to deal with than Vera Martinez.

"It's okay, we'll have lunch together." He tried to make it sound like a treat when really, it was their normal routine.

Vera continued organizing the sugar container, lining pinks, yellows, and whites together as if the task were vital. What would he be teaching his sister if he let someone treat her like that?

"Chloe, this is my friend Vera," he said.

Vera's eyes sprang up.

"Hi." Chloe's voice held the choked tone of a kid who just lost her best friend—at least for the afternoon.

"I like your shirt." Vera pointed to Chloe's teal T-shirt featuring a cat in sunglasses. "You like cats?"

"Duh." Chloe cocked her hip. "My mom said I can get one when I turn ten. She and my dad had one before I was born."

Max nodded. "Yeah, Lupi. We called her The Hisser. She died when I was five."

"Sorry." Vera's face looked sympathetic, for a mean-as-shit cat.

Actually, the day the cat died was the only time Max had ever seen his father cry. Until then, he hadn't known parents could do that.

His dad had spent most of the day cracking jokes. As always.

Hey, Maxie-boy! What did one plate say to the otha? Lunch is on me!

He was full of the worst dad jokes in the world, but man, his laugh—it reverberated through the entire restaurant.

Sometimes Max swore he could still hear it. But then that day, his mom showed up with blotchy cheeks and glassy eyes, and Max stopped coloring on his paper menu. She whispered something and Dad removed his Mets cap, dropping his chin to his chest, tears streaking his plump, stubbly cheeks.

It was Max's first experience with death, the finality of it. He had no idea that just a few years later, grief would shape his entire world. And that seven years after that, he'd be running his father's restaurant.

It was a bait-and-tackle shop when his parents bought it, and they turned it into the number one restaurant in Roaring Creek. Busboys, drivers, and kitchen staff said it was the best job they'd ever had. It was why they still worked here, because they could feel the ghost of Tony Oliver coating every speck of dust in the place.

Max turned to Vera, about to ask her to stay for lunch, when the rumble of a busted muffler puttered in the parking lot. A country tune drifted inside. Then he heard the familiar laughs.

Crap. He groaned, spying his friends piling out of Leo's flatbed, including Delilah.

"Chloe, wait here." Max looked at Vera. "Is that okay?"

"Sure." Vera nodded, shifting down on the picnic bench to offer his sister a spot. Then Vera reached into the galvanized tub and pulled out a kids' menu, which featured an octopus in a sailor hat. She handed Chloe the complimentary crayons. "What color should we make him?"

Max grabbed his dirty Mets hat off the register and headed toward his friends in the gravel lot, who were joking at a volume that made his sister seem muted.

"Maxwell!" Jackson swung his arms wide and barreled in for a hug, but he tripped over his flip-flops, catching himself just shy of falling on his face. "My bad!" He bounced up smiling.

"What are you guys doing here?" Max asked, adjusting his brim in the noonday sun.

"We're here to rescue you," said Leo. "From boredom."

"*Shheriously*, the day's too nice for you to be stuck inside." Delilah batted her lashes, which looked twice as long as they had last week. "Come hang out with us."

She tugged at the string tying her bikini around her neck. Her suit was covered (somewhat) by a loose-fitting tank top with armholes cut for a professional wrestler. She shifted her frame, offering Max a glimpse of her curvy figure.

"I'm working." He looked at his feet.

"Please, is there even anyone in there?" Jackson plopped a sweaty palm on Max's shoulder, his beer breath smacking him across the face. "Just close up. Screw it!" He peered into the restaurant, and Max sidestepped, hoping to block Jackson's view of Vera.

"Dude, we feel bad you're here all day." Leo ran his hand through his spiky black hair. "When are you off?"

"Late. We're short-staffed."

"You have, like, one customer," Jackson mocked, not caring how rude he was.

"It's just . . ." Max fiddled with his hat, still trying to block Jackson's sight line. "I got a lot going on. Chloe's friend dropped her off early."

"*Sho? Where'sh* your mom?" Delilah asked, slurring slightly.

"Not feeling well."

He looked at Leo, clearly the only sober one in the group and the only friend who bothered to check up on him. Max tried to communicate telepathically: *Leave. Now. Please.* But Leo's eyes narrowed and his gaze flicked to the restaurant's interior. Then his face shifted. So did Jackson's and Delilah's.

"Dude!" Leo yelped, eyebrows pressed high above his sunglasses.

"Holy shit! Is that Demonic Barbie?" Jackson shouted, fist kissing his mouth. "I knew it! I knew it when you were looking at her in school! You've gotta thing for the ghoul!"

Jackson's voice couldn't have been louder if he were holding a megaphone and pom-poms.

Max's stomach formed a slipknot. "It's not like that. She just came in for lunch."

"Is she sitting with your *shister?*" Delilah slurred, sounding offended that Vera was with his family, like she thought Vera was his girlfriend. It wasn't like that. But he couldn't exactly tell them what it *was* like, either.

"I told you. Chloe just got back," Max explained, though he shouldn't have had to.

Jackson stumbled toward the entrance, angling for a

better look, and Max grabbed the back of his sweaty T-shirt (yuck) and yanked him to a halt.

"Oh, come on! I just wanna say hi," Jackson said, then his head whipped around in alarm. "Did she cast a spell on you? Is that why you're with her?"

"I'm not *with* her. I'm serving her lunch in the place where I work. She's nothing to me." An anchor of guilt instantly dragged his heart somewhere down into his belly, and he prayed Vera couldn't hear. But the real reason Vera was meeting with him was something he wouldn't share with these people if they stuck branding irons to his chest.

"All right, all right." Leo held up his tan hands. "We'll go. You're working. We get it."

"We do?" Delilah countered.

"Yes, we do. Max is busy. We'll check in with you later. I hear Marissa's parents are away." Leo tried to steer the conversation back to the typical, but Max knew the second they drove off, his friends would talk about him for the rest of the afternoon. He'd be lucky if he and Vera weren't trending on social media.

"Hey, if she turns you into a frog, hop to my house, okay?" Jackson teased. "We're turning on the hot tub."

Max squinted with annoyance—*Please, shut up*—and when he opened his eyes, Delilah was right in his face.

"I *guessh* I know why you don't text me back anymore." Her tone was curt. "Thank God I *shaw* this, because I will stop texting you now."

Seriously? That was a bit much. Max's brows knitted together. "You don't know what you're talking about."

"Then explain it."

"I don't have to."

They were barely together when school was in session, and now she, Leo, and Jackson were making him feel shitty when *they* were the ones being jerks—to him *and* to Vera. So far, Vera had shown no reason to deserve the crappy treatment she'd gotten from the student body over the years. If Max felt guilty about anything, it was how he was acting right now. To her.

His friends climbed back into Leo's pickup, and as soon as the engine started, Max swiveled toward Vera. She met his gaze head-on, and he saw it right away.

She'd heard everything.

CHAPTER FIFTEEN

Vera

Vera scribbled her best rendition of an anime cat on the back of the paper menu using a cheap blue crayon—not cobalt, sky, or sapphire . . . just "blue." Chloe leaned closer, studying her every waxy line.

"I love the eyes!" said Chloe.

"I saw them in a graphic novel."

"Oh, I love manga!"

"Me too." Vera handed her the crayon.

She could see Maxwell in the parking lot, lit by the blazing noon sun, talking to two of his friends, Leo and Jackson, and a girl from their grade, Delilah Pazinski. Delilah might be his girlfriend, or at least Vera remembered her decorating Maxwell's locker—and by "decorating," she meant decoupaging it with every trinket found at the dollar store.

She turned back to Chloe, who had impressively replicated Vera's cat eyes. "Awesome."

Chloe beamed.

Laughter floated from the parking lot and Vera shifted

her chin, straining to hear, though she needn't bother. Their voices were loud enough.

Demonic Barbie.

Ghoul.

The words wrapped themselves around Vera's chest and squeezed.

She closed her eyes. *Demonic Barbie. Okay, that was a new one. Maybe it's sort of a compliment. Barbies are pretty.* Her brain tried to convince herself of this, but it didn't stop her stomach from falling to the floorboards.

She opened her eyes and spied Maxwell grabbing the back of his friend's shirt. He seemed to be pulling him away. Was Maxwell Oliver defending her? The corners of her mouth almost twitched up, then she heard Maxwell's voice. "She's nothing to me."

The breath kicked out of her chest.

Her head hung.

Okay, he doesn't know you any better than they do, she reasoned. *You just started talking to him. Technically, you're not friends. He just wants help. This is a business arrangement.*

But, deep down, she didn't want this to be a business arrangement, and for a moment, idiotically, she let herself believe that Maxwell saw her as something more than a green-faced ghoul with striped socks on a broomstick.

"Do you like my picture?" Chloe pointed to her blue cat with gigantic sad kitten eyes.

"Hmm-hmm." Vera nodded, swallowing the insults.

She regained her composure as Maxwell sauntered up, his frayed surfer shoes stopping right beneath her line of sight. She didn't meet his eyes.

"Sorry about that," he said. "I didn't know they were coming."

Vera nodded, pressing her lips together.

"They have a history of jackassery."

At that, Vera lifted her eyes.

"I'm sorry," he muttered again, lips downturned.

You weren't sorry enough not to say it.

Maxwell peered at the drawings on the table, his sister happily scribbling, then he glanced at Vera with honeybrown eyes full of . . . what? Remorse? Good. He should feel bad.

"Will you still come tonight?" he asked, his voice croaking with fear that she'd change her mind, that she'd no longer be at his beck and call.

Demonic Barbie.

Ghoul.

Frog.

She owed him nothing. She owed no one in her school, in this town, a single thing.

But it wasn't just about Maxwell, it was about Vera. She wasn't the type of person who could ever say, "No, let your mother suffer!" It was also about his sister, a seven-year-old currently smiling with a gap where a front tooth should be.

And it was about his mom, a woman who had already experienced enough trauma for a lifetime.

Besides, it was just a business arrangement.

"What time?" Vera asked.

CHAPTER SIXTEEN

Max

Max didn't know if Vera would show. In fact, she had every reason not to. He scratched his buzzed head, regret coursing through him.

When he'd walked back to the table, her big eyes held the droopy gaze of a girl who heard too much. He'd called her nothing, and she was anything but. Only, he couldn't explain that to his friends—he just wanted them out of there. Not because he was embarrassed of Vera, but because he didn't have the energy to pretend to be the guy they wanted him to be, and he didn't have the words to make sense of this for them.

Vera understood—at least, as much as anyone could understand. His mother was infected. No, *afflicted*.

Max popped to his feet, pacing alongside a coffee table blotted with water stains, and glanced at the clock on the cable box. Vera said she'd come at midnight, which was when the late-night wanderings and ramblings with Mom seemed to occur. Vera was sneaking out. It was now three minutes after twelve.

What if she decided he wasn't worth it?

Christ, I am waiting in my house, in the middle of the night, for Vera Martinez to tell me if my mother is possessed by de- mons. FML . . .

He reached for the remote, thinking he'd put on music, the TV, anything to fill the too-silent hum of the house, but he dropped it before touching On. His sister still believed their mother was sick (and possibly a genie who could grant wishes). He didn't want to wake her and shatter her with visions of rolled-back eyes.

Max hung his head, smelling the dried sweat on his skin. He'd run three miles after he left the restaurant, needing to let his legs loose and feel the drum of his feet on the pave- ment. He thought it would clear his head. It didn't, but he should have showered.

Now I'm rude, smelly, and possibly delusional.

Headlights beamed from the street, and his gaze shot toward the bay window as decrepit brakes squeaked out- side. A white car pulled alongside the curb, its lights flick- ing off.

He exhaled all the way from his belly. *She's here.*

He watched as Vera climbed out of her car and slammed the door (which required some effort). As soon as she marched across the grass that he should have mowed last week, his heartbeat picked up. It was happening.

He opened the door before she could knock.

"Hey," he said. She might as well have been wearing a superhero cape (black, to match her outfit).

"Hey," she replied, tone flat and face annoyed.

Okay, fine, he deserved that.

"Come in." He held open the door.

She was wearing a black cotton tank dress, and her fair skin glowed almost lavender in the moonlight. She tucked her wavy hair behind her ear, and he felt an odd desire to hug hello.

What is wrong with me?

She stepped inside, looking everywhere at once—at family photos, trinkets, vases. Then she rested her bag on the ground.

"How is she?" Her voice was all business.

"Right now? Quiet." He gestured for Vera to sit, and she plopped onto the khaki sofa, which sank too low from years of overuse.

Max rested on the arm of a rosy wingback chair. "Thanks for coming. Really, I mean it. I wasn't sure you'd show."

"Why? I said I would." She tilted her head, lips pursed.

Oh, that's right. I'm the asshole here, not you.

"Well, I mean, today . . ." He bit his thumbnail. "My friends, they don't know what's going on . . . with my mom. I don't think they'd understand."

"People rarely do."

Damn. He'd watched two separate groups be rude to her in a single day, in a single hour. "What happened with Chloe's friend, her mom—"

"It's no big deal. Happens all the time."

Max frowned. *But it shouldn't. . . .*

Vera stared at her toes spread wide in her flip-flops. They were painted pink, which made Max pause. He didn't know the girl who chose pink nail polish, and for the first time he realized that maybe he wanted to, in a way that stretched beyond what was happening with his mother.

"Vera, I'm really sorry."

She shrugged, maintaining her tough facade. She opened her lips to say something, when a creak echoed from the hallway. Their eyes shot toward the noise. Max's ranch house featured three bedrooms down a hall right off of the living space. His mother's room was at the far end, the last one.

He knew the sound of her door opening as well as he knew his ringtone. Lately, it was what woke him up most nights.

He looked at Vera. "It's her."

She nodded and they both stood, then she waved for him to lead the way. This was what she came for.

Max stepped in front, right arm outstretched like a protective crossing guard as they inched silently into the long hallway, sidestepping the floorboards he knew always groaned. His grandmother's pendulum clock ticked on the wall behind them, the sound oddly deafening. A fly buzzed past, skimming his nose. Then his mother slid out of her room in the same alabaster nightgown, lace hem ruffling by her ankles. He couldn't remember the last time she'd bathed, yet her tight black curls flowed down her back in perfect ringlets and her tan skin gleamed like she'd spent the day at the beach. She looked healthy and beautiful, and Max feared Vera would think he exaggerated his stories. Then he noticed his mom's eyes. They were open too wide, not rolled back this time; instead, all the chocolatey warmth was replaced by charcoal bricks.

Max stopped, he and Vera hovering beside a pair of never-lit candle wall sconces so thick with dust he could smell it. He felt Vera's breath on his shoulder as they watched his mother glide dreamily, her gaze pointed in their direction, but she showed no signs of awareness. Instead, she peered with pupils dilated more than should be possible. She lifted a graceful arm toward her daughter's door and pushed down on the handle. It opened with the drag of wood against carpet.

Max turned to Vera, looking for instruction, but her cheeks were bleached and her mouth hung open. He inched to the doorway. Vera followed. His mother stood in the rainbow glow of a Hello Kitty night-light, swaying with limbs flowing, hair swishing, and her head awkwardly bent like a severed branch. She was watching Chloe sleep.

His sister rolled over, sighing in dreamland.

Max shifted to his toes, flexing his muscles all the way to his clenched fists. He craned his neck to whisper to Vera, but a sudden stench of lilies gripped him by the throat.

He gagged, reaching for the neckline of his T-shirt, but Vera grabbed his forearm.

"Lizards . . . Mankind is a cesspool of lizards. Humanity is an artifice." The voice scraped at Max's ears, his mother's arms spread wide, her chest wrenching with the words. *"I bring a revolution! Salvation! Shed your bodies!"*

Max's face twisted, and he shook his head. *No. This isn't her. No way* . . . He pressed his hands to his ears, trying to block out the guttural sounds gnawing the woman who raised him.

Slowly, a slender black shadow crept from her bare toes, skinny as a sapling tree, its branches stretching all the way to Max's feet. He stepped back in time with Vera, and the fear he saw in her face, from a girl who lived with *those* parents in *that* house, sent a rush of heat through him that dried the moisture in his mouth.

"Remove the bonds of suffering. Embrace the self beyond the mortal flesh," his mother moaned in a hollow voice, her neck bent toward Max. Her hair puffed wildly, all shiny curls now burned to brittle black coils. Her stiff fingers clenched the air near her shoulders as tendons painfully protruded from her taut neck.

"Maaaxweeelll, heeelp meeee!" it screeched.

No, *she* screeched. *That* was his mother, with the voice of a woman tied to the stake as the flames licked her calves.

Max blinked rapidly, his chest collapsing, the room blistering, and his feet locked. She needed his help. Why couldn't he move?

Her body contorted, spine arching violently as her murderous gaze shot at Vera.

"Show your claws! Bare your fangs! Unleash your true selves and finally awaken!" The baritone returned.

Bloody spots danced before him. What was happening?

A hand slinked down his arm. Fingers interlaced with his, the grip tight.

"Breathe," Vera whispered.

The stench of rotting flowers grew more intense as his mother's face began to morph. Her skin cracked like packed desert sand, lips peeling back from her gums to reveal green dumpster-tinted teeth. Wrinkles spread to her squinted eyes, and a snarling gaze aimed straight at Vera with such rage that Max stepped between them.

Then he heard the strike of a match. No, the strike of a match*book*, the multiple crackles of flint popping in quick succession.

Vera shifted first; she knew what it meant. Max didn't. He followed her line of sight and saw that the wall sconces were lit. The two ivory cylindrical candles in the hall flickered with golden flames, the heat emanating off them so hot it scorched Max's cheeks from twenty feet away. Or maybe the heat was coming from his mother, the woman who braided Chloe's hair, who taught him how to drive a car, and who sang lullabies in Spanish.

But that wasn't the person in front of him now.

Sweat dripped down his face. "Is she sleepwalking?" he asked Vera.

"She is definitely *not* asleep." She squeezed his hand.

"Drunk?" he asked, even though he already knew the answer.

"No."

"What do we do?"

"I'm gonna leave."

"What?" he yelped. *Is she freakin' serious? She's abandoning me!*

"I'm making her mad," Vera explained. "She doesn't want me here. Can't you feel it?"

Well, yes, he could. The rage in the room practically wiggled in the air around Vera, but that didn't mean he wanted her to leave.

"The past few nights, you've walked her back to her room, right?"

"It wasn't like this."

"I know, that's because *I'm* here," Vera said through her teeth, as if moving her lips too much might make the room explode. "You can't leave her here with Chloe."

No shit. But he couldn't do this alone.

He slumped forward, hands on his knees, a sudden urge to vomit rushing through him. Vera placed a hand on his back; there was a gentleness to her touch.

"I'll be right outside. *Trust me.* It'll work."

She better hope it would. That was his sister in that bed!

But before he could reply, Vera turned for the door and left.

Max was alone, with Chloe, and with whoever, *whatever*, that was.

CHAPTER SEVENTEEN

Vera

What. The. Literal. Hell!

That was not sleepwalking and definitely not a sloppy drunk. *Holy Mother of Hades. How long has this been happening?*

Vera collapsed against the side of her car with the breathlessness of the mental marathon she'd raced inside. The texture of the air in that house, she *felt it*. As soon as Maxwell's mother left her bedroom, Vera didn't hear it— she sensed it, with the force of a hand shoving her shoulder. *I'm here. I see you.*

And the woman did see her, though not the teenage girl who was supporting a classmate—she saw *inside* her. She saw her parents. She saw what they could do. That woman wanted Vera *out*. Vera didn't know how she knew that, but she did.

She looked toward the front door, a coil of energy surging beneath her skin. Vera could hear the crispy rustle of leaves swaying in the trees. She could smell the mossy stench of algae from the creek a mile away. She could feel every prickling speck of rust on the car beneath her fingertips.

The adrenaline made her feel electrified, bouncing on her toes with her skin tingling.

Come on, Maxwell, get out of there. . . .

Vera didn't know how to help him, but that creature *thought* she did, and that alone put them in danger. Those candles it lit, throughout the *entire house*, were not a warning but a demonstration. To Vera. Of what it could do. Somehow Vera's mind cleared of all clutter, and that truth was implanted in her very cells.

The demon believed Vera possessed her parents' gifts, and right now, she wished it were true. Vera reached for her phone, fumbling inside her purse with quavering fingers.

What time was it in Barcelona? Morning—early morning, but still morning. She could call them.

Where was Maxwell?

Breathe, just breathe. . . .

Gusts puffed out audibly as she peered at the modest ranch house, bopping on her toes, her phone gripped in prayer position at her lips. "Please, God, let him come out safe. . . ."

Moments passed. The trees stopped moving. Not a bird cawed.

Silence. It had a weight, and she felt it climb onto her back and hold on.

Finally, a shadow shifted. A curtain twitched. Her heart leapt to her throat.

The door creaked open, and a silhouette emerged.

Maxwell.

"Thank God! Thank you! Thank you!"

It took all of her mental focus not to sprint across the lawn and risk upsetting the beast more. She stayed put and he bounded toward her.

"She went back to her room. As soon as you left, she went back to her room," he explained before even reaching her.

He was panting, his fear so thick she could reach out and grab a fistful. He stepped within range, and she flung her arms around him until they crossed on the other side. Maxwell gripped her just as tight.

"We'll figure this out. I swear," she promised in his ear.

Their arms locked so fiercely that the heat of their bodies, the smell of their sweat, almost fused them together.

She heard him sniffle. *Oh God, he's crying.*

"It's gonna be okay," she whispered. "I'll call my parents. I promise. It'll be okay."

She knew she couldn't really promise that. She didn't know when her parents would be home, and that left Maxwell and his sister sleeping down the hall from whatever *that* was.

"She . . . she lit those candles. They were everywhere," he stuttered.

"I know."

"And the lilies. Did you smell the lilies?"

"Yes."

"It was like she was burning. It was *so* hot in there."

"I know. I felt it." Vera's lips practically touched his ear.

"How did her voice go normal? For a second, I heard *her*. Did you?"

Vera nodded.

"She was in so much *pain*." The crack in his voice nearly shriveled Vera's insides.

"I'm sorry. I know. But it's a good thing. It means she's fighting."

"Fighting what?"

"I don't know."

Maxwell sniffed and shuddered against her; a drop fell on Vera's bare shoulder. Then he took a big inhale, snorting back the last of his tears, and slowly loosened his grip. He shifted back a step, wiping his eye on his sleeve. Reluctantly, Vera let go.

"What . . . what do we do?" he stuttered.

She lifted her phone; it was one in the morning here, which meant seven a.m. there. "My parents should be awake, if not now, then soon. I'll tell them what happened and see what they say. I'll let you know as soon as I hear anything."

"Good. That's good." He shook his head stiffly.

"Maxwell, I don't think you and your sister are safe here. Do you have somewhere you can go? Maybe to your grand-parents?"

He shook his head, running his hand along his neck, so tense she could trace the tendons with her fingers. "My grandfather, my mom's dad, he died. And my grandma, she moved back to Sweden."

"You're Swedish?" Vera didn't mean to sound shocked, but she was.

"Yeah, I'm pretty much what you get when you mix everything in a pot and stir."

She smiled slightly, and he seemed to like the distraction. For a moment, the expression on his face lightened.

"What about your dad's parents?"

"That's . . . complicated."

"Well, you're in complicated territory now."

"So you believe me?" he asked, shoving his hands in the pockets of his tattered khaki shorts. "This isn't just some medical condition?"

"No." Her voice was definitive. "Something is wrong. Maxwell, I'm so sorry."

Oddly, he looked relieved, like he welcomed the confirmation that this wasn't all in his head. This only made Vera's chest ache more, because it proved what she'd already suspected—he truly had no idea how bad this was going to get.

———

Vera cracked open the back door to her house, millimeter by millimeter, and crept inside. But before she could carefully close the storm door, her neighbor's little white puff let out a yap. She swore that four-legged snitch was out to get her.

She narrowed her eyes, and the dog yapped on.

Vera shut the door, muffling its calls, then crept up the stairs and past her aunt's room—not a stir. She slipped into her bedroom and tiptoed into her private bathroom, tempted to take a shower and erase the smell of flowers that clung to her hair and the tears that had dried on her skin, but it would be hard to explain a post–one a.m. shower to her aunt.

She clutched her phone. She'd called her parents during the drive. They didn't answer. She left a message, not divulging everything but professing it was an emergency. She promised to stay up for their call. So she washed her face and waited for the ring.

Something happened back at that house. Not just with his mother, but with Vera. When she stood on the curb waiting for Maxwell, she wasn't just drowning in fear and sadness, there was something else, something more shameful coursing inside her. Exhilaration. Vera's world shifted into a primal battle of good and evil, right and wrong, black and white, and she could see how her parents would be seduced by this. There was a rush in knowing you were doing something life-altering, soul-transforming. All these years, her entire childhood, creeping past that basement door like a constant game of Operation where you couldn't graze the edges, now gained a fresh perspective. Her parents were protecting the world from darkness; she knew that before, but she didn't get it. Now she did.

Vera dried the water drops from her face, inhaling the scent of detergent on her terry cloth towel. It was *her* scent, *her* home. She padded across her bedroom floor, toes sinking into the soft fibers of her area rug, pink nails flashing back. She couldn't believe she'd painted her toenails for him, like she actually thought this somehow mattered. Everything seemed so trivial now, the entire world outside of this situation dimmed, no problem nearly as vibrant.

She peeled back the covers to her bed and slipped in, the sheets cool from the hum of the air conditioner lodged in the window. Her eyes fixed on her whirling ceiling fan.

First Maxwell lost his dad in what she thought was the most horrific way possible; now he was losing his mother. His sister was only seven years old.

Vera refused to let this town devour another family.

This town . . .

What was wrong with this town?

Her eyes felt heavy, and she struggled against her exhaustion, gripping her phone. She forced her lids open, but sleep soon swaddled her tight.

———

In her dream, he's wearing coveralls the color of dried noonday mud. A scratched white hard hat is firm on his head, shielding the feral look in his eyes. His pupils are too large, but his crew members don't notice. It's another day on the job. Vera can feel their complacency.

A man struggles with a jackhammer, Hulk-like muscles straining as sweat soaks his stained white T-shirt. Cars pull into the lot beside the workers, a line forming down the block.

He strides past. Vera knows his face. It's been in the news.

He says he needs to enter the building, check the pressure before they disconnect the sensors and replace old pipes. No one stops him. He belongs here.

He cuts through the crowd in the lobby forming two messy queues beneath a sign that reads Tickets. A concession stand displays clear plastic cups full of ice and pink lemonade. The air smells of chocolate chip cookies. How can she smell that?

A frenzy of basketball sneakers squeaks in the distance. Vera's heart encrusts in ice. She knows what's about to happen; so does the man, yet calm emanates from his pores.

He descends the gritty concrete steps to the basement, and his dilated pupils cut across the dank room. The pressure gauge, it calls to him.

He approaches the round device, a white clocklike dial with crimson tick marks attached to a thick copper pipe. Its needle is steady and accurate.

He knows what he must do.

No! Vera mentally screams. Stop! Please!

A phone rings.

He doesn't react.

Stop! Don't do this! These people, they're innocent!

The phone keeps trilling, quick melodic bursts. It sounds urgent. No, it feels urgent.

Where is it?

Who is it?

He lifts a bulky metal wrench high above his head, prepared to hammer down on the gas gauge, his muscles bulging.

No!

The phone screams.

Someone should answer.

No, she *should answer.*

The call is for her.

————

Vera blinked open her eyes and found herself standing in front of her rustic basement door, her arm outstretched, fingers reaching for the scratchy brass knob.

Her hand jerked back.

What just happened?

She swung in all directions. She stood in the kitchen, lit by silvery moonlight wedging through the horizontal blinds. The sun had yet to rise.

Did she sleepwalk?

She'd never done that. Ever.

And to the basement door?

Do not open that door, do not touch that door, and do not break the seal of the blessings. It was the family mantra.

Her heart stuttered as she fell back a step, disoriented. How close had she come to unleashing a den of evil onto the world?

A phone rang in the distance. She spun to the clock on the microwave: 2:32 a.m.

It all rushed back. Maxwell. Chloe. His mom. *Vera's* mom.

She was calling.

Her bare feet padded through the living room and up the stairs, two at a time. She had walked all this way in her sleep, her body moving beyond her control. Her mind was someplace else—the dream, it felt so real, so vibrant. Like the others.

She threw open her bedroom door and dove for her cell phone on its final ring.

"Hello," she panted into the receiver.

"Vera, honey, it's Mom. What's wrong?"

CHAPTER EIGHTEEN

Vera

The next morning, Vera crawled into work with bleary eyes. After the conversation with her mother, following her dreamy wandering, questions bubbled in her brain all night. There were no good answers.

Vera yanked the metal latch on her hospital locker, tossing in a fresh set of clothes. She was meeting Maxwell after work to recap the call, which included her mother insisting Vera go nowhere near the Oliver house again, not until they returned home. That left Vera to decide whether to defy her parents or abandon Maxwell.

"Hey, you!" Chelsea cheered as she barreled into the changing room, her scrubs as bright as a fresh-cut lime.

Vera wore blackish-red scrubs so dark a patient could spit blood on her chest and no one would notice. She didn't understand why the entire staff didn't wear the same. She didn't understand a lot of things lately.

"Hey." Vera yawned.

"You look awful." Chelsea grimaced.

So much for the under-eye concealer. Vera slammed her locker.

The doors pushed open and Samantha sauntered through, pecking her girlfriend's lips and smiling as if they hadn't just seen one another the night before. Vera's chest sagged more. She'd never had that with anyone, and maybe for the first time, she wanted it—not in a general sense, but with someone specific, someone she was pretty sure didn't feel the same way. How could he? His family was in a deadly, otherworldly situation, and there was no way he had space to consider anything more than that. Vera was the girl he thought could help. He didn't choose her, at least not in the way she wanted.

"What's up with you?" Samantha eyed Vera's wilted appearance.

"I was up half the night." Vera pulled at her knotted neck, remembering her mother's words.

You are in too deep. That was what she'd said when she learned of Vera's sleepwalking. Not "You're okay," or "It's happened to me too," or, what Vera secretly hoped, "I always knew." A tiny piece of Vera's soul longed for the sleepwalking to confirm a connection to her parents. Maybe she was like them after all. But her mother stomped that hope under her foot, even from across an ocean.

The darkness is moving in, Mom insisted. *Do not invite the demon any closer.*

As if Vera were consciously choosing to wake up in the

kitchen with her hand stretching for the basement door. As if she were tossing around Evites to every demon on the block. Was it really that impossible to believe that Vera could be inheriting a smidge of the power her family possessed? Apparently, to her mother, it was. Vera could hear it in her voice—she thought that her daughter was too weak to handle this situation and that the demon was taking advantage.

Cue the late-night hours staring at her ceiling fan, afraid that if she closed her eyes, a hand with knives for fingers might pop through her mattress and lead her down to the demonic basement.

"You know, someone at TSC recommended this herbal Sleepytime tea. It's really helped. I could bring you some," Samantha offered.

"The Sunshine group? I didn't realize you were going to meetings." Vera cut her a look.

Last night, when she'd walked to the basement, she'd been dreaming about Seth Durand, that he caused the explosion *on purpose*. She watched him slam a silver wrench into the gas meter. She didn't know if the dream was true, or if it was just her overactive mind inventing scenarios, or if her brush with Maxwell's mother left a mark on her subconscious, but the Sunshine Crew was started by Seth Durand's wife and son. And despite the glaring hypocrisy, Vera didn't feel comfortable with her friend cozying up to that family.

Besides, Maxwell's mother had been a member and look at her now.

"Mostly I just go in the chat rooms." Samantha's voice was nonchalant.

"Well, I wouldn't get too close," Vera hedged, trying not to sound judgey.

"Why?" Samantha shrugged. "It's been helping. I think everything bothering me about Brian's death stems from a rigid mindset. I've been stuck in a cycle of destructive thinking."

"Ugh." Chelsea rolled her eyes. "Those are nonsense words."

"No, they're helping me find peace," Samantha huffed, slipping on her hospital sneakers. "My mom is like a new person."

"Because she's brainwashed," Chelsea mocked.

"She is not! Stop it." Samantha swatted her arm.

"Whatever. Just don't buy me a yellow hat." Chelsea shook her blond hair, swinging toward Vera. "By the way, did you hear about Mr. Gonzalez?"

"No. What?" Vera's brow furrowed.

"He croaked. Late yesterday." She sounded like it was good news.

Vera's shoulders caved. She had completely forgotten to mention him to her mother; she was too consumed with sleepwalking and Maxwell's mom. Now the old man was dead. Before that one horrible experience, Mr. Gonzalez had been a gentle soul who loved, and dearly missed, his wife.

Vera closed her eyes, offering a silent prayer. *Mr. Gonzalez, I hope you find peace with your wife. . . .*

"What are you doing?" Chelsea asked.

Vera lifted her lashes. "Saying a prayer?" It came out like a question.

"Oh, great." Chelsea's face twisted. "First *her* with the TSC. Now you're finding Jesus."

"Well, (a) I was raised Catholic, and (b) the man died."

"After he *threatened* you."

"He was sick and confused and alone."

"Actually, he wasn't *that* alone. His son was here earlier." Chelsea shifted to one hip. "And he threw that shrine in the trash."

"Really?" Samantha sounded shocked.

"Yes, *really*." Chelsea's eyes narrowed. "Those shrines are popping up all over the hospital, and they're freaking people out. A whole group is planning to bring it up at the next staff meeting."

"Good." Vera nodded. She didn't want to reveal how much she knew about the dangers of demons and idol worship, but the less creepiness spreading through town, the better.

"I thought you said it was religious expression?" Samantha glared at Vera like she'd switched sides. "Everyone has their own way of grieving. Peace comes in many forms."

"I know, but this isn't healthy," said Vera.

"Says who? Why is the Angel of Tears different from a cross? Or the Star of David? Or a statue of Buddha?"

Samantha knew the idol's name. Why? Vera's gaze narrowed.

"Because the Angel of Tears has nothing to do with

spiritual fulfilment. It's about taking advantage of people who are already vulnerable and suffering. Just look at the name. Kinda ominous, don't you think?" Vera didn't want to tell them about her parents' work, Maxwell's mom, or the face of the Angel appearing in the fog (they'd think she was losing it), but she had to offer a little glimpse behind the demonic curtain. "Besides, worshipping idols, especially creepy ones that cry black tears and convince you to pray *for* death, is like playing with a Ouija board in a cemetery on Halloween."

"Well, maybe death isn't so bad."

Vera blinked at her, momentarily stunned. Then she snuck a peek at Chelsea, whose lips were also parted in shock.

"Are you okay?" Chelsea put her hand on her girlfriend's shoulder.

"Just forget it," Samantha huffed, shaking her off. "When you guys lose someone close to you, come back and tell me how *you* deal with it."

Then she marched out of the room.

———

At lunch, Vera waited outside the hospital's main entrance. She and Maxwell agreed to find a place away from the clattering cafeteria talk.

Vera ran her hands along her cotton scrubs, scanning the cars for the candy-apple-red truck she'd seen parked in his driveway. Eventually, he emerged in a Mets cap, his sunglasses glinting in the afternoon sun.

"I parked in the far lot," Maxwell called as a greeting. "I needed some air."

"Understandable."

Then he hugged her. There was no hello, he just wrapped his arms around her like they were meant to be there. After last night, maybe they were. A collective fear had bonded them. She squeezed her hands around his neck, fingering the cotton seam of his hat.

"You okay?" she asked, her lips close to his skin.

"As good as I can be." He pulled back, not far, only a few inches, and he kept a hand on her hip. She liked that more than she hoped she let on. "Chloe is staying at her friend's tonight."

"The girl from yesterday?" Vera remembered the mom.

"Yeah. Her mom's not as bad as she acted. Really."

Maxwell didn't need to apologize. In fact, if he tried to atone for all the people in Roaring Creek who treated Vera like a wart-nosed witch luring them into an oven, he'd need to block off some serious time.

"Does Chloe have any idea what happened last night?"

"No, nothing. She slept straight through it. But get this." He took his hand off her hip. "Before she left for Alexis's, she told me she left an apple outside our mom's door, so—and I quote—'Mom will get Sophie to invite me to her pool party on July Fourth.' What the hell is that? Why does she think Mom can do stuff like that?"

An edge of uneasiness pricked at Vera's gut. Interacting with whatever was inside his mother was terrifying, but leaving it offerings or asking it for favors felt like DMing a serial killer. "Kids are really susceptible. They trust more. They're fooled more. You've *got* to keep her away."

"I will. I'm trying."

"I know." Vera nodded once. "How about you? How are you doing?"

He fiddled with the curved brim of his hat, hiding his eyes, but she could see the muscles flex in his jaw. "How do you think?" He gestured to the footpath. "Let's walk."

Vera followed him past the splintered bench where they had sat the afternoon he came to meet her. It oddly felt like weeks ago, not days.

Maxwell followed her stare. "I guess you believe me now," he joked, remembering their interaction.

"I'm sorry I was so tough before. It's not that I didn't believe you . . ."

"No, I get it. Anything makes more sense than what's actually going on." He strolled so close his fingers brushed the back of her hand, and she wondered briefly if he'd take it.

They neared the footbridge arching over the creek and traipsed to the center. Maxwell put both hands on the railing, carved from twisted natural branches, resting his full weight like he needed the support to stand. She pressed beside him, gazing at the rushing water. The sounds of a soccer game rose from behind the tree line—a whistle blowing, a crowd cheering. Farther down the creek, classmates lounged on the banks of Devil's Pool, where a taller stone bridge soared across the widest and deepest part of the stream. A figure in a cherry-red bikini dropped from the apex, plummeting to the rippling surface as her squeal traveled on a breeze that smelled of fresh-cut grass.

"You know, I've never swum in the creek," Vera admitted, watching her classmates bathe in the blistering sun.

"Seriously?" He side-eyed her.

"It always felt like something you needed to be invited to. I mean, I know it's a public place, but . . ." She gestured to the group, small as insects from where they stood, but unified as a swarm. "Everyone knows each other."

"We know *you* too. You go to school with us."

"Did you ever consider talking to me before *this*?" They both knew the answer.

"Maybe I should have." His voice was low. "You spoke to your parents?"

"Yeah." Vera nodded.

She told him about the conversation, which unfortunately included very little advice about what they should do, other than get "the kids" out of there and wait.

"Well, when do they get back?"

"In a week. Maybe."

He sighed like that wasn't fast enough. She agreed.

"What about a priest?" he asked. "Don't they do *exorcisms*?" He said the word like it was ludicrous. It was, to most people.

"They said it's extremely hard to get approval from the

church. It's one of the reasons they have jobs. The church hopes they can debunk most of the claims."

"But couldn't a priest come to see what's going on, maybe start the process?" He slid off his sunglasses, rubbing his eyes. The purple circles under his lashes were so much worse than her own; they were practically bruises, as if he'd been punched by life.

"We'll do everything we can. But involving the church includes a lot of red tape. It's our last resort. My parents are still the best option."

"Yeah, if they were here." Maxwell grunted.

From behind the oak trees, a gaggle of voices climbed up. *Kick it! Get ready! Come on!* A whistle screeched.

"I heard my mom's voice last night *begging* for my help." Maxwell's tone sounded broken, as though he'd relived the moment a lot.

"We're going to help her. I promise." Could she promise that?

A burst of clapping rang out from the trees. *Go, Jack! Get there! Hustle!* The voices overlapped, echoing against the bubbling surface of the water. A music-box jingle from an ice cream truck joined the cacophony, eliciting the Pavlovian response of salivation from anyone under the age of eighteen. Vera's cheeks puckered as she pictured hands slipping into wallets—*Okay, just one. Here's five dollars.* Simple. Normal. Happy.

"You know what I can't get out of my head? The way my mom looked." Maxwell's burned-out gaze turned her way.

"It's weird, but since this all started happening, my mom has never looked better. It makes no sense, because she's not showering—like, at all—but still, she's *glowing*."

"Well, she's beautiful," Vera agreed.

"She is. But last night, when you were there, she looked . . ."

Grotesque, Vera thought, but she didn't say it. Neither did he. "How did she look this morning?"

"Like she could walk a red carpet." He flung up his hands. "Some friend stopped by to see her, and I claimed she was sick, but really she was sleeping. Actually, she was snoring like a bulldog, which she never did before. But even asleep, she looked perfect. It's like she's morphing."

"I know."

Mr. Gonzalez looked similar with his rotten teeth and swelling pupils. How had she forgotten to tell her mother about him?

A shriek rang out from downstream, and Maxwell's chest leaned toward the sound, toward his friends. He tugged on his hat as laughter cartwheeled along the water.

"We should have invited you to the creek," he blurted. "*I* should have invited you."

Vera didn't move, his words rounding out a jagged little piece of her heart. She'd spent her last day of school in solitude under a tree, like she had so many Saturdays and Sundays before. She often avoided going downtown, because it was lonely seeing classmates you've known your whole life hanging out in groups who never considered inviting you.

"Thank you for that." She bit back a surge of emotion.

"It's true. We're idiots. All of us. Some worse than others." His tone turned heavy. "And honestly, the creek's not so great. There are a lot of days I wish I hadn't been here. This freakin' town . . ." His gaze grew distant, and Vera suspected she knew where his thoughts had pulled him.

The crash. Their classmates.

"Were you there that day?"

Maxwell nodded, eyes on his friends downstream.

It happened on one of the last September days warm enough for a swimsuit, and still the police had no explanation other than "maybe the kids swerved to avoid an animal." Their parents were suing. In a town used to constant mourning, this loss hit especially hard—five healthy, popular, gorgeous teenagers dead on a beautiful day.

"Everyone was there." Then Maxwell cringed as if to apologize because, of course, Vera wasn't. "We weren't even drinking. When I think of all the times kids *should have* gotten into crashes and didn't . . ."

Vera couldn't imagine anyone getting into a car with a drunk driver, but she was also an outsider worthy of a Ponyboy nickname, so her experience with peer pressure was rather limited.

"It looked like this." Maxwell gestured to the teens in the distance. "We were hanging out, having fun, then Rocco started acting like a jerk, which wasn't like him." He turned to face her. "He pushed Brooke off the bridge."

"What?" Her eyes bulged. Vera hadn't heard that. The bridge at Devil's Pool was higher than any platform dive.

At the wrong angle, hitting the wrong rock, it could kill someone.

"I know, but Brooke had been standing up there a long time. She wanted to jump; she was just chickening out. So Rocco pushed her. It was a dick move, for sure, but we thought he was joking around and took it too far."

"Now what do you think?"

"I don't know." He shrugged. "Brooke hit the water *hard*, and when she came up, she was hysterical. Everyone started fighting. And Rocco, he looked, I mean, he looked like he could have killed someone." Max shook his head. "He was normally the life of the party."

Vera didn't know him, but she was at the memorial. Everyone called Rocco a class clown. They spoke of his humor, his carefree spirit.

"Did you know he lost his dad in the explosion, and his mom lost half her leg?" Maxwell asked.

Vera nodded. She saw Rocco's mom at the services, collapsed in sobs as she physically leaned on her relatives, burying another loved one.

"That family is so wrecked now." Maxwell dropped his head back, squinting at the sun beneath the brim of his hat. "I don't know what happened in that car, but the only thing that makes sense is they were fighting. They *must have* been fighting while he was driving, and he got distracted."

In the nine months since the crash, this was the first theory she'd heard that actually made sense.

"Did you tell the cops? Their parents?"

"Yeah, but it doesn't change the fact that no one saw the accident. How can you *prove* they were fighting? And even if they were, it's just what happens in this town. People die. All the time." When he peered at her, his expression, his words, mirrored her own. "It freakin' sucks here."

Vera nodded. "It's like the town is cursed."

A wind gushed, carrying the tinkling toy sound of the ice cream truck moving on to its next location. Downstream another girl dropped, her body kicking and flailing, her scream wild. Their classmates cheered as she fell.

"Are you going to stay away from us now, like your mom said?"

Vera looked into Maxwell's eyes, and her response was simple. "No."

CHAPTER NINETEEN

The Crash

Filling every seat in a cobalt-blue Honda Accord, five teenagers leave the banks of a muddy creek. The gathering is an annual tradition, marking the last swimmable day before the trees put on their colorful show and yank the town toward the winds of winter.

A sixteen-year-old boy sits behind the wheel, the radio blaring to drown out the din of his friends' shouts. They're arguing. All of them. He's been impolite. He caused a scene. They needed to leave. He ruined their fun.

Their wasted words batter against him.

Meaningless.

His girlfriend grabs his arm, stretching from the passenger seat and jerking his hand from the wheel. He likes how that feels, letting go, losing control. She squawks like the birds overhead. Yap, yap-yap-yap! Yap, yap-yap-yap! He imagines her with a yellow beak. He pictures her tiny, unevolved brain.

He didn't push her; he released her. He gave her a glimpse of what's to come.

Soon.

The end is already reaching for a hug.

He rolls down the windows to let it in, hot wind blasting his face. Tangy sea salt hits his tongue as he traces a bird's path in the air, its wings flapping with enviable chaos. In the back, a girl cries for silence. She reaches between the seats for the radio, and he swats her hand, stinging her wrist.

She is not in control. None of them are. Not even him. He knows this. He knows the truth.

He adjusts the brim of his canary hat, turning it backward as he pumps his shoulders to a thumping rhythm.

The guys in the back join in, howling at the music, the wind. They feel alive.

For now.

He smiles.

Life is fleeting. Death is forever.

He presses on the pedal, the double yellow line curving, bright in places, covered in tar in others. It blurs. Life blurs.

He feels resistance against his foot, the pedal pressed to its maximum.

The girlfriend shouts. Shriller this time. Slow down. Please. Slow down.

The boys in the back continue hooting, whooping, and cheering. The wind rushes at them, spinning and spiraling. A bird swoops at the windshield.

The car is powerful. It is unstoppable.

So is he. He is following the teachings.

The girlfriend reaches for his arm, pulling, crying. He drops both hands to his lap. Challenge accepted.

He smiles wide as his eyes focus on the item atop the dash. The Angel of Tears.

He thinks of his father. His mother's leg. Their pain is temporary.

He just needs to ascend.

The girlfriend lies across him, grabbing the wheel, her body spread on his lap. He likes how that feels. She strains, and his foot presses harder. Friends lean from the rear, grasping for the wheel, vying for control. It is pointless. Don't they see?

They must accept it. They must worship it.

Death is forever.

He laughs, roaring, enjoying his final moments with such fierceness tears prick at his eyes.

He shifts to his girlfriend and smiles with all his teeth as the car fails to bank the turn. He watches her eyes as they leave the road. Isn't it thrilling?

They veer straight. Together. All of them.

They soar off the rocky New England cliffside.

He laughs all the way down.

CHAPTER TWENTY

Max

Max tossed his clunky key ring onto the mail table, the front door slamming as he caught an odd shift in the air, the twinge that tells you something's different in your home.

"Chloe?"

She spent last night at her friend Alexis's house, and she was being dropped off in a half hour. No mother, especially Mrs. Tenn, would leave a seven-year-old in an empty house.

But his house wasn't empty.

"Mom?" His voice shook.

It had been two days since Vera had been there, a day since they'd walked to the footbridge, and that time had been blissfully uneventful, because his mother slept the *entire* duration. Thirty-six straight hours. If his mom got up for a drink of water or to use the bathroom, Max hadn't seen her. Every time he cracked her bedroom door, he spied her sprawled beneath a white sheet, not only breathing, but snoring like a potbellied pig in the mud, deep throaty grunts that ripped through her chapped lips. He wanted to check her for fever, place the back of his hand against her forehead the way she'd done so many times for him, but he was afraid to get too close. It had come to that.

A whisper echoed through the house.

No, *whispers*. More than one.

"Mom, is someone here?" His gut tightened, the way it does before a punch.

The murmurs continued, a low hum.

He checked his watch. Anyone who would visit his mother, in this state, was not someone he wanted to meet. And Chloe would be home soon.

He'd called his grandparents in New Hampshire this morning. He didn't tell them what was going on (*Hey, Pops, everything's fine, it's just Mom's possessed by this demon. . . .*). Still, they heard the concern in his voice. Only, they were a four-hour drive away, and they worked Monday through Friday. They couldn't pick up Chloe until the weekend.

It was Tuesday.

The voices intensified, their tones deep, almost rhythmic, like chanting. It was coming from his mother's bedroom.

His breath quickened as he began to pace. *There are people in my house, possibly possessed people with my possessed mother, and my sister is coming home any minute. Seriously, what the f—*

His foot slammed into the curved leg of the coffee table.

"Goddammit!" he shouted, grabbing his big toe as he hopped.

"Ah, ah, ah." The voice was crystal clear.

He whipped around, heart bouncing to his tonsils.

"Careful what you say." It was *her*, her voice traveling from down the hall, but she might as well have been standing in the room. "He can hear you."

Max hunched over, gripping his throbbing toe, leg bent in a figure four as the other leg half squatted to balance his weight. The sound of her voice was not only loud, it was three Darth Vaders mixed with a Maleficent.

Max released his toe and stood upright.

"Join us," a voice said. That wasn't his mother.

"We are ready." This one was male.

Horror movies catch a lot of flak for characters stupidly investigating "strange noises," but really, the reason is simple—in moments of terror, your mind and body stop speaking. Right now, Max's head shouted *RUN!* in all CAPS, but his legs moved toward the voices. She was his *mother*. He had to see.

He robotically marched to the windowless hallway. All the bedroom doors were closed and the lights were off, making the beige walls seem black even in daytime. The clock ticked its swinging pendulum behind him. A car honked from the street, a peppy double beep. *Hello*, it said.

His pulse hammered beneath his skin, and the voices whispered, "The time is near. You are so blessed." Yet Max heard, "Come here, little boy, come closer. We won't hurt you. . . ."

The taste hit him first. His tongue slapped the roof of his

mouth—smoke. Not fireplace smoke, not kitchen smoke, not even the stench of burning leaves, but the rank clouds of cigarette smoke from the dark beer-soaked bar downtown.

He'd never seen his parents hold a cigarette. Patrons couldn't even light up in the parking lot of the restaurant. Besides, there was no shop that sold a pack anywhere within walking distance. He had the car all day. But the smell was distinct.

Max's shaky hand reached into the pocket of his shorts, and he slid out his phone. Vera was at the top of his text conversations.

He pounded with his thumbs:

Something's happening. People are here. I need you.

He slipped the phone back into his pocket, trusting she'd come.

He halted in front of his parents' door and could feel eyes sizzling from the other side. He groped the handle with a clammy hand and took one last breath of conviction.

Then he pushed.

The door swung open.

His mother stood near the closet, a vision in a long white sundress. Kneeling before her were two strangers dressed in black—black jeans, black T-shirts. One had a blond ponytail, and the other a graying black ring of fuzz around a balding brown skull. Their heads were bowed, small votives were lit on the ground around them, and smoke was everywhere.

Clouds plumed from his mother's nose and puffed from her mouth, thick and white, but there was no cigarette in her hand, no ashtray nearby. The smell. Holy shit, the smell. It was overwhelming. Max coughed, searching for what had to be a burning carton, but he saw nothing.

"Welcome, Maxwell." The blond ponytail turned his way. She wasn't much older than he was, with thick dark liner around her eyes and lipstick that was too purple.

"You know my name?"

"Of course," replied the older man. He had a graying goatee to match his head and the shoulders of an athlete.

"What . . . what are you doing here?" Max coughed, fist at his mouth.

"They're here to see me," Mom replied. The smoke came from inside her, like the cigarettes burned in her gut. "Where's your friend?"

"She's . . . at home." Max choked, throat on fire.

"Do tell her to stop by," Mom croaked. "We'd love to see her. I'm feeling so much stronger now."

For two days, his mom grunted and writhed, tossed and turned. Max welcomed her absence, and Vera sounded relieved. The sleep gave them moments of peace, along with time before her parents got home. Only, now it seemed Mom wasn't resting at all. It was like she'd undergone a metamorphosis.

She. Was. Smoking.

"Who are you people?" Max gagged, eyes squinting from the gritty air.

"Friends," the girl replied, rising to her feet. She was maybe five feet tall if Max was being generous, and she looked like someone he could be friends with. Yet she'd just been kneeling for his mother.

"Get out of my house," he ordered.

"Oh, don't be rude," his mother scolded. No, that wasn't his mother.

"Don't tell me what to do. This is *my* house."

His mom puffed her chest, standing tall with an odd expression, a *familiar* expression. *"Actually, Maxie-boy, it's my house."*

That was the voice of his *father.*

Time stopped.

His body was prepared for a blow, but not this. It was like preparing for an atomic bomb—there was nothing you could do, total destruction was inevitable. He heaved over in pain.

"Hey, Max, did you hear the one about the restaurant on the moon? It has great food, but no atmosphere!" The body let out a deep belly laugh that Max knew could be heard through the entire house, because he'd heard it before. For ten years, he lived with that laugh.

How could she?

Tears pricked at his eyes. He clutched his stomach, his insides, his every fiber to keep from unraveling onto the hardwood floors.

"Whatsa matta, Maxie-boy? You don't like my jokes no more?" The accent was thick and the conversation real, like they'd had it before, many times.

"Stop. Just stop." The agony in his voice couldn't be helped.

"She's not trying to hurt you. She's trying to show you," the girl said in a let-me-put-a-Band-Aid-on-that tone.

No. She didn't get to talk to him right now. Max let go of his waist.

"Your soul is a manifestation of your existence that lives on in the universe. She sounds like your father, because it is your father. It's his eternal force. She's offering a gift," she continued.

Max stood upright.

"Listen to the chick. She's a smart one, that girl," the voice of his father said through his mother's lips. And she looked like she wanted to wink.

"Get out," Max commanded, his voice strong.

"If you saw what we saw, if you let us explain, you could break free from your pain. . . ." The stranger clasped his palms, pleading.

"Get out of my house!" Max exploded, charging toward them. He'd never punched anyone before, but if he was ever going to, it was now, in this moment, with his mother pluming smoke and stealing his father's jokes. These lunatics, whoever they were, were not going to stand here and explain pain to him.

"Leave! *Now!*" He pointed a straight arm toward the door, and his mother let out a murderous cackle. Her head was thrown back, black waves falling all around her, perfectly styled. Her skin was radiant, and her hair luscious. The faint lines that sprayed from her eyes and crossed her forehead were Photoshopped away, making her body look ten years younger while her voice was a gateway to Hell.

She turned toward her visitors. "You may leave." She sounded feminine again. Not his mother's pattern of speech, but at least it wasn't his father's.

"Of course." The girl nodded.

"Your enlightenment is an inspiration," said the man.

"You cannot achieve enlightenment. You must be enlightened. And your time is coming. Soon," Mom bestowed.

The peons took their orders and exited the room. Max listened as they marched down the hall, creaking on familiar floorboards and slamming the front door. Finally, a car drove off.

"This has gone too far," Max spat through clenched teeth.

"I thought you missed your father."

"Mom, how could you *do* this?" He appealed to the woman who raised him. She was in there, somewhere, and she was torturing him.

"I thought we were past pretending I was your mother." Smoke gusted from her lips. "Mommy's gone, but you can join her if you want, her and your father. Dying's the easiest thing you'll ever do."

"My mother's *not* dead!"

"You sure about that?" Her lips pulled at the corners.

He cradled the back of his head, pressing his bent elbows to his temples, chaos raging inside him. Then the sound of brakes in his driveway pulled his attention. He spun toward the window.

The peons were back.

Or it could be Vera.

Only, when the car door shut and he heard his sister squeal, all the blood left Max's brain.

"No!" he hollered, spinning toward the door.

Footsteps charged into the house, along with the sound of a bag plopping on the carpet.

"Chloe, stay away! Get back in the car!" he hollered.

"What? Is Mommy awake?" she cheered, stomping down the hall.

"I said *get out*!" His head swirled with panic, and he reached for the wall to steady himself, but before his vision could clear, his sister was standing beside him.

"I wanna see Mommy!"

She pushed past his legs, and as his dizziness broke, he caught his sister's face as she spied the smoke rising from the creature.

"Mommy?" Chloe's head jerked back, puckered lips falling open.

"Come to me, sweetheart," the voice hissed, arms extended.

"Don't." Max clamped his sister's arm, probably too hard, but he would break her bone if it meant keeping her away from *that*.

"Why are you smoking? My teacher says it can kill you." Her eyebrows rumpled.

"It was a gift, my dear. Like *your* gifts." Dark amusement flashed in her eyes and sent Chloe creeping behind Max's leg. "Tell me, how's Sophie?"

"Okay," she squeaked, hands wrapping tighter around his leg. She got it now. Finally.

I'm so sorry. . . .

"Well, Sophie's a little piece of shit," the beast spat, head cranked. "Are you a little piece of shit?"

"Stop it," Max snapped.

"Mommy?" Tears choked Chloe's voice.

He turned to his sister, crouching down. "Get out of here. Go!"

"Go where? What about you? What's wrong with her?" Questions spilled out.

"Oh, don't go yet. Don't you want to be with Mommy forever? I can make that happen. It's easier than you think."

"Shut! The hell! Up!" Heat lapped at Max's skin; the room was burning, sweltering. He shoved his sister toward the door. "Run!"

Then the sound of another car squealed in the distance.

CHAPTER TWENTY-ONE

Vera

As soon as Vera placed a sneaker on the curb, she felt the tension crackle through the sticky summer air. Standing on the sidewalk, the wrath from Maxwell's mother pulsated from the home, across the weedy lawn, and onto Vera.

She sprinted across the too-long grass, and when she reached the front stoop, the door flung open. Chloe cowered in the entry with blotchy cheeks and snot oozing from her nose, shaking in hysterics.

Vera didn't have siblings, not even little cousins, and no one in Roaring Creek dialed her number to babysit. A few days ago, she'd say she wasn't good with kids. But it turned out she didn't need prerequisite knowledge to know to throw her arms around a sobbing child and drag her to safety.

"It's okay. I got you." Vera cradled Chloe's head.

She pulled her to the car and flung open the back door.

"Where is your brother?" Vera asked, guiding her onto a crumby seat cushion as the child gulped for air.

Chloe pointed, her mouth opening and closing like she wanted to say something, but Vera couldn't wait for her to choke out the words.

"Stay *here*! Do not move! Do not open this door for anyone!" Vera locked the vehicle and raced across the lawn, heart thundering against her rib cage.

She tore through the front door, knowing where she'd find him. That smell . . . What was that smell? She spun into the hallway, a blanket of night cloaking the house in broad daylight. Even still, she caught Maxwell at the far end, a silhouette backlit by the dim light of the bedroom.

She thundered toward him, rattling the pictures on the walls, and the closer she got, the more she smelled it, the more she tasted it.

She skidded to a halt behind Maxwell.

"Are you okay?" Vera whispered, then looked around him to see his mother. Instantly, she wrenched backward.

Holy Mother of Hell.

Maxwell's mom, or what used to be his mom, stood in a long white sundress, the flowy kind you might wear to a fancy garden party, and she was smoking. Literally. Thick white plumes seeped from flared nostrils and a gaping mouth. The clouds coiled from within her, stunning all rational thought. The smoke traveled *up*. It didn't exhale down from her nose then rise with a gradual drift. It was the smog of a chimney, swirling overhead.

Given Vera's family business, she was familiar with fear. The winds of a hurricane, the chill of a creepy basement, the crash of a demonic artifact—those, she suddenly realized, were pulses on the outer veins of terror. Now Vera was staring at its heart.

"I am definitely not okay." Maxwell's words were clipped.

His mother locked eyes on Vera, burning bricks of coal searing deep within her until she felt the flames in her chest. Then, as Vera watched, the woman's cheeks began to hollow, skin sinking and charring.

"I was hoping you'd show." Her voice was venomous. No, *its* voice.

Vera clutched Maxwell's biceps as they watched its hair morph from ringlets into oily black twists and its teeth brown with stains of unseen nicotine.

"I have Chloe. Come on." Vera tugged his arm. This was beyond her ability. Vera was not special. She was not gifted. They needed her parents.

"Oh, don't go so soon." Its cracked lips formed a grisly grin.

Then it started barking—literally, like a tiny dog— yapping in short, high-pitched bursts that matched the ones Vera heard at least five times a day from her neighbor's house.

"How's the little dog?" it asked, smoke gusting with each bark.

Vera's mouth grew dry, her tongue heavy. It knew about her neighbor's dog? Maxwell couldn't have told it. He'd never been to Vera's house.

No, it knew *her.*

Mr. Gonzalez's words rang inside her. *It wants you. It wants you.*

"Too bad Mommy and Daddy aren't around. Tell them I said hi." Its brow formed an unsettling V on its forehead, and it began to pace, staying inside a ring of small black votives, arranged as if for a séance.

"My parents don't give a shit about you," Vera spat.

Its eyes flexed. "I doubt that." Then it cocked its head, neck tendons tight. "What about you? Are you ready for me? It would save us all a lot of time. My friends can't wait to meet you—"

Vera's mouth opened to speak, but then its body seized, arms flailing as its rotted face whipped from side to side. The smell of decomposing roadkill filled the room, and Vera gripped her nose, gagging reflexively.

"Maaaxweeelll, gggooooo!" That was his mother. His real mother. And dear God, Joan of Arc would have sounded less horrific in her final moments on the stake.

Vera squeezed Maxwell tighter, tugging with all her might. Only, he was a marble statue, anchored to the ground by rusted screws as he watched his mother's arms rise, lifting the hem of her sundress. Wings. It almost looked like wings. A tornado of smoke spiraled faster as its eyes rolled deep into its sockets. *"There is no peace to be found here. Only death will bring peace! Rest! Rest with me!"*

It rasped the words, and a twister of smoke broke open the closet door with a violent crash. Vera stumbled back. A shrine, the Angel—a skeletal angel weeping black tears holding a skull-engraved torch, extinguished—facing his mother's bed. It sat atop a swishing black tablecloth, and at its base were packs of crumpled cigarettes and a bottle of wine. Three burgundy glasses were filled to the brim, but they looked untouched. There were more candles, all onyx, some in jars and some not, some tall and some short, flames crackling too tall for their wicks, too hot for their size.

"Maxwell! Let's go!" Vera carved her nails into the flesh of his arm and yanked him with a force she didn't know she had. He shifted.

Then she barreled toward the doorway, pulling him, dragging him, tripping behind her, his head constantly swiveling back to see the person who used to be his mother, to see if it all might disappear.

No, Maxwell, I'm sorry. This is real. This is horribly real.

She heaved him through the house and to the front door, and as soon as he stepped outside, he gobbled the air as though it was the first breath he'd taken since plummeting beneath the surface of that malevolent fog.

Then the gargling sound of tears rang out and his head spun toward his sister in the back of Vera's car. Her thin arms were wrapped around bent legs that were pulled forcefully against her chest as she rocked, wild black curls swishing with every sob.

Now it was Vera's turn to follow after Maxwell as he sprinted to the car like the devil was on his tail.

CHAPTER TWENTY-TWO

Max

Max clutched his sister to his chest, her feet kicking Vera's seat as she convulsed in sobs. His head throbbed, the smell of smoke still clinging to his clothes.

"My mother is still in there!" he shouted, rolling down the window. "You heard her! And before that, I heard my dad. My *dad*! We have to help them!"

"You heard *Daddy*?" Chloe screeched.

Shit, he shouldn't have said that, but Vera wasn't listening. She was driving, farther and farther away.

He released a hand from Chloe to shake Vera's headrest. "Vera, we have to go back! I heard them! Vera, come on, can't you get them out?"

She was a superhero, right? A demon fighter? This was what her family did.

He watched her knuckles tighten on the wheel.

"No!" she snapped. "I can*not* get them out. That's what I've been trying to tell you. I'm *not* my parents! I did what I could. I put Chloe in a safe place, and I dragged you away."

"But my mom—"

"Needs more help than I can give you!" she blurted, smacking the wheel. Then she sucked in a breath louder than the breeze from the window. "I'm sorry. I'm not trying to make this worse. I'm really sorry for what you're going through. And I'm going to get you help."

From where? Barcelona? They didn't have time to wait for her parents' case to wrap up.

Their level of hell changed in that room. This was no longer some potential sleepwalking and a little creepy babbling. There was an inferno with seven rings in there. His mother was breathing smoke! She was speaking in his father's voice! She tried to lure Chloe!

They pulled in front of Vera's home—a big white Victorian—and her aunt stood on the front porch like she was expecting them, long gray hair whipping in the breeze. Max stepped out of the car to the sound of yapping in the distance. His head spun to the neighbor's house, a white puff in the window. The dog. His mother knew about that dog. She'd sounded just like it. His eyes blinked, shock coursing through him as he cradled Chloe's tall, lanky body in his arms like a newborn. Then he marched toward the house.

"Bring her upstairs," the aunt instructed.

He hoisted his sniveling sister up the staircase, her long legs dangling past his knees, as he followed Vera into a guest room with a four-poster frame and a lace doily bedspread.

"I'll take it from here," said the aunt as she entered the room.

He lowered Chloe onto the mattress. The aunt sat and

hugged his sister's sweaty head to her chest, singing a song that might have been Gaelic. Before Max got back to the first floor, his sister's sobs had lessened.

About a half hour later, Chloe was still upstairs. Max was in the kitchen clutching a steaming mug of spearmint tea that he in no way wanted to drink, but that Vera's aunt insisted he finish.

"Every drop. It will calm you," she said.

Max grimaced at the minty herbal taste. The only warm beverage he liked was hot cocoa with mini marshmallows, but that felt inappropriate under the circumstances. He slumped in the chrome-framed chair, the black vinyl cushion squeaking beneath him.

"Chloe seems calm. I washed her face and gave her one of Vera's old stuffed animals," said the aunt.

What was her name? Aunt Tilly? Tully?

"Greenie is in capable hands. He's my mint-green tiger." Vera grabbed a plastic teddy bear of honey from a cornflower-blue cabinet. The counters were butcher block, and they had one of those big white sinks that sank super deep. His mom would have loved it. *No, she* will *love it. She's not dead.*

"I should check on her." Max stood.

"Sit," Vera's aunt instructed.

He dropped back down. It had been a long time since he'd been parented. And now his remaining parent . . . he didn't know who she was. Or what she was.

"How are you?" Vera sat beside him.

"Freaking out."

"The spirit's demonic," the aunt began, tucking a gray hair behind her ear. "I don't have my sister's gift, but I can sense evil, and there's evil in this town."

"Aunt Tilda, I said go *slow*," Vera whined, as if Aunt Tilda (that was her name!) had broken some sort of agreement. But after what just happened in his mother's bedroom, they could skip the honey and go straight to the heavy ingredients.

"Just tell me."

Vera sighed, setting down her tea. "Okay. That shrine, the one we saw in your mom's closet?" She paused as if needing to jog his memory. No, he was good. The whole thing was hard to forget.

"It's called the Angel of Tears," she went on. "It's the same one I saw in my patient's room. Remember I asked you about it that first day?" He nodded. Vera continued. "It's popping up all over the hospital—a Grim Reaper with wings and a burned-out torch. People are praying to it."

"That's why those strangers were in my mom's room?"

"Probably. And by the way you described them, it sounds like they're—"

"One flew over the batshit nest?"

Vera almost chuckled. "More like brainwashed, or hypnotized—"

"Or possessed?"

She nodded. "And they likely left the offerings."

"What offerings?" His forehead tightened.

"The wine? The cigarettes? I'm pretty sure that's where the smoke was coming from." Vera sounded calm, the perfect tone for a future doctor. *It's stage four, metastatic and inoperable. Can I get you a tissue?*

"My mom wasn't smoking a cigarette, *she* was *smo-king*, like it was coming from inside her body." He couldn't believe he was actually saying this, but he was.

"I know. And I'm not sure how, exactly." Vera took a sip. "But I think the gifts are left for *it*, the demon, or the inhuman spirit, or whatever you want to call it. And when *it* accepts the gift, when it grants a favor, then the gift manifests inside her body—the smell of lilies, the presence of smoke . . ."

Granting favors . . . his sister . . . the candy, the apple . . .

"What about Chloe?" Max spat, his brain clicking. "She left it crap, she said it did something, to a friend of hers—"

"I know." Vera touched his hand. "We looked her over. We spoke to her. She seems okay."

"I didn't sense anything dark inside her." Aunt Tilda agreed.

Oh, great! Aunt Tilda didn't sense anything dark. I guess I don't need to worry, then!

"What about my dad? I *heard* him." Max's eyes stretched.

"It's a trick. Evil spirits have many voices," said her aunt.

"No. It was *him*. He even told a bad joke. That was his thing. How could it know that?" His voice cracked. He didn't even have it in him to be embarrassed.

"Your mom knew that." Vera placed a palm on his arm.

"My mom wouldn't do that to me." His voice was small. It was the first time he heard his father's voice, outside of an old video, in seven years. It was real. He heard his laugh. Max's throat grew tight.

"That wasn't your mother," Vera said.

"Then what was it? How did it get there? Why is this happening to us?" He knew he sounded like a child, but that's how he felt. This wasn't fair. His family had been through enough; they didn't need this too.

"To be possessed, a person needs to *invite* the demon in," Aunt Tilda said matter-of-factly.

Max's head turned her way. "What do you mean? You think my mom *asked* for this?"

"No, not exactly." Vera shook her head. "You know all those horror movies about tarot cards and séances? Well, there's some truth to that. To be possessed, you need to *invite* the demon, you need to open a door to the other side."

"The shrine," her aunt explained.

"You said lots of people have the shrine. Are *they* all smoking?"

"No. I don't know. I'm not sure, actually." Vera raised her palms. "And I doubt your mom knew what she was doing when she bought it. Kids who play with Ouija boards don't think they're *actually* summoning spirits, but sometimes . . . they are." She shrugged. "The fact that she's fighting it, that you can hear her, means that she's regretting it. This is good. *But* the fact that there are so many people worshipping it . . ."

"You think they're *all* possessed?" He pressed his fingers to his temples.

"Maybe." Vera looked as confused as he felt. "I told you when you first came to see me, I'm *not* my parents. But I called them. I left a message. And they'll know what to do. In the meantime, we need to keep you and your sister safe."

"You're going to stay here," ordered Aunt Tilda. That wasn't a question. "I'll make beef stew."

Then she opened the fridge and began rummaging around, like what they were having for dinner was somehow a major concern.

Max couldn't stay here, in *Vera Martinez's* home. This was the first time he'd stepped foot in the place. He just met her aunt. He had his sister to think about. And what about the rumors? Was this house any safer? His eyes flicked around, not landing on anything specific, but searching for something to confirm or deny what he'd heard for seventeen years.

"What are you thinking?" Vera watched his face. "Are you worried about where you'll sleep? We thought Chloe could have the guest room, and you could sleep on the couch. It's not great, but—"

She paused and read something in his eyes, then sank back in her chair. "You're scared to stay here."

Her eyes fell to the floor.

Now he felt like a jerk. Max didn't know what he would do without Vera right now, and her aunt was like a real-life Mary Poppins with a spoonful of religion. He needed them, but they just said he shouldn't *invite* any more trouble, and this place had a reputation.

"Okay, I'm just gonna ask, because I think we're past the pleasantries." Max exhaled. "Is your house haunted? Do you make witch's brew? I realize my mom is currently possessed by a demon, so my options are limited, but if you have a strange collection of satanic objects hidden around here, now is the time to tell me."

Vera's eyes widened, then flicked to a nearby door. So did her aunt's.

Max sat back. Wait, was it true?

His mouth fell open.

"Okay, it's not what you think. . . ." Vera's voice was wary as she glared at an old barnwood door.

Are you kidding me? His sister was upstairs! And Vera was eying that door like even *she* was afraid of it. What was he supposed to think?

"I can see your mind spinning. Sip your tea," Aunt Tilda instructed.

No, you sip your tea! he thought, but robotically, he took a drink.

"Obviously, you know my parents perform *exorcisms.*" Again, she sounded clinical. *Your mother had . . . a colonoscopy.* "Afterward, there are sometimes objects connected to these cases that aren't safe to leave behind. What if the object holds residual power? What if another demon tries to access it? What if the demon they just expelled is still attached to it?"

"You're serious about this? There's shit like that in your house!" He must've looked like a cartoon character with a bunch of symbols and exclamation points floating above his head.

"Bacon! I found bacon!" Aunt Tilda cheered.

His face flung toward her as she yanked a plastic package from the fridge.

"She stress-cooks. Just go with it," muttered Vera.

Max rubbed his temples again, then glared at the wooden door, boards crisscrossing like *X*s on the upper and lower panels. An *X* usually meant stay away. "If it were just me here, fine. But my sister is upstairs."

"She's perfectly safe," said Aunt Tilda, plopping carrots onto a cutting board. She grabbed a chef's knife.

"She is." Vera agreed. "I wouldn't let you stay here if she weren't."

"How can you say that? You just told me that you have to *invite* a demon in. Well, how many demons have you invited in here?"

"It's not the same thing."

"How?" He knew he was frustrating them, but he didn't exactly have a lifetime of demonic background information.

"The objects in our basement—it could be a toy from a house that was haunted by the ghost of a child, or a mirror that was once owned by a warlock—my parents take them so we can watch over them. We have them blessed *every* week. We make sure their evil never spreads."

"But what if you're wrong? What if it doesn't work that

way?" His eyes narrowed. He couldn't believe she'd grown up like this, with evil artifacts steps from the breakfast table. A rush of pity swept over him. How was she not *more* messed up?

"My parents know what they're doing," Vera replied.

"Why? Because they have, like, superpowers?"

Vera's aunt chuckled. But he wasn't joking. What else would you call it?

"Yeah, something like that." Vera reached for his hand. "You're safe here. I promise."

No one could promise that.

CHAPTER TWENTY-THREE

The Storm

In a small coastal community, a hurricane rages. The eye is cutting an unrelenting path up the jagged coast, from Washington, D.C., to Atlantic City, from Lower Manhattan to Roaring Creek. The storm surge is expected to crest beyond the Great Flood of 1955—a historic squall still tattooed on buildings with fading lines that mark the day canoes rowed down Main Street.

A ten-year-old girl is huddled in a dining room, the most interior space in the house. Her only protection is her aunt and the packing tape crisscrossing the whistling windows.

"Pray, Vera, just keep praying," her aunt tells her, squeezing the girl to her chest, her long salt-and-pepper hair forming a shield to cover them both.

Outside, the wind howls like a mother who's lost her child, branches flinging violently into the air as if every spot must be searched, all debris upended. The roof groans from the blasts.

"Our Father, who art in Heaven . . . ," her aunt chants, rocking the girl who is nearly taller than she is as they cuddle together on the hardwood floor. The girl's parents are stranded overseas, unable to return.

They are alone.

"Thy kingdom come, thy will be done . . ."

For days, the governor pleaded for evacuations, but they didn't pack. There are items in the basement that cannot be moved, cannot be left unattended, and cannot be taken in a fire. The girl knows this. She knows what her parents do.

"Forgive us our trespasses, as we forgive those . . ."

The girl turns to the swaying lace curtains and catches a blur of movement in the deluge outside. Slowly, the figure takes the shape of a man. A man in a hat.

His evergreen poncho flaps like the frantic wings of a bird under attack, while his matching wide-brim fisherman's hat forms a bloated gutter above his gray beard. The aluminum awning above him offers no protection as the rain gusts horizontally, vertically, and circularly, mixed with bits of earth. A white puff of a dog is clutched beneath his armpit. He places it down, the puny animal determined to answer nature's call.

"Oh my God. Mr. Zanger is outside," the ten-year-old says, pointing toward the yard.

"Don't use the Lord's name in vain," her aunt scolds, then she follows her gaze. "What is he thinking?"

The man clutches a pole, struggling to stay upright as sheets of water crash on his face. The dog is barely visible through the murky haze, his yaps inaudible over the freight train rumbling across their ceiling. The old man releases the pole, stretching for the animal, as the posts of his awning suddenly lift from the ground like pegs from their slots, and the green-and-white metal sheet soars with the wind. The man crashes to the mud back-first. His head hits.

"Oh my God!" The girl leaps to her feet.

The wind shoves the small canine against the siding of the colonial, and the man lies motionless, faceup in the downpour.

The girl runs through the house, her eyes on the shuddering back door. She's aware of the danger, but she doesn't stop. She and fear are old friends. Best friends. The storm is no match for what's inside her house.

"Vera! No! Get back!" her aunt yells.

The girl reaches the door, Category Two gales fighting her push, thrusting her inside like even the storm doesn't want her stepping into its wrath. She barrels through.

There are no shoes on her feet as she stumbles blindly, toes squelching on the sodden earth and a skinny elbow bent in front of her face for protection. Three steps forward, she slides back one, three steps forward, she wobbles back again. The dog yelps, guiding her way.

She trips over the man before she sees him, dropping to her knees into clumps of clotted leaves.

"Mr. Zanger! Are you okay? Can you get up?" She shakes his shoulders, and his head lifts briefly.

"Vera! Vera! Come back!" her aunt cries in the distance.

The girl tugs at the heavy body, his consciousness slowly returning.

"Mr. Zanger, can you hear me?" She wipes the rain from his eyes, using her back as an umbrella to shield his face. He attempts to roll onto an elbow, but the hurricane throws him back like a wrestler who's won his match: stay down! "Mr. Zanger!"

"You? You!" He groans, squinting.

Then his dark pupils swell, fear taking hold.

Only, he isn't afraid of the storm.

"Get away! Get away from me!" He pushes the girl, tossing her into a puddle so deep it covers her hips. He crawls back on the seat of his poncho, giant galoshes kicking muck onto her cheeks.

Black hair sticks to her face as the rain blurs the look of disdain in his eyes. The old man reaches for his dog, who is cowering in a barren shrub, then scrambles up the two concrete steps to his home, the door slamming behind him.

"Vera! Vera! Come inside!" her aunt shouts over the wind.

The girl turns toward the sound, embarrassment surging within her. He fears her. Even now. Even in this. She spies her aunt's panicked face peeking through the door, and for the first time, she notices the wind—its odd dance, its strange pattern. Severed branches, plastic bags, autumn leaves, and trash can lids swirl around her property, twisting in a spiral, curling away from her home. It's as if her white Victorian were the center of the storm, everything whipping around it, not at it.

Even Mother Nature won't get too close.

The girl crawls on scratched knees, heavy drops pelting her back and mulch fumes filling her nostrils. Finally, her fingers graze concrete, the steps. Her aunt yanks her inside by a single arm.

"You could have been killed!" she hollers, shaking the girl's shoulders, water spraying onto the pine boards of the country kitchen.

The girl doesn't respond, her head flopping limply, as her aunt continues to grip her body.

"What if something hit you? What if you were hurt? What would I do?"

The words form a dull buzz in the girl's head as she shivers.

The chill deepens, but the source is no longer her sopping clothes. Her body stiffens. The aunt stops speaking. They both feel it.

Their eyes turn in unison toward the basement door, an unseen force tugging their chests and swelling their pupils. The dust in the room grows hefty as the silence builds.

Then the crash sounds. A cascading clink of shattered glass rings in the girl's ears, in her soul.

Something has broken.

No, it's broken loose.

She doesn't blink until an audible gasp rips from her aunt. Hairs rise on the girl's arms as the aunt begins to pray. The names of saints, God, Mary, and Jesus tumble from her aunt's lips.

But the girl knows it is too late.

They both do.

The unthinkable has happened.

Evil has been set free.

And God can't help them now.

CHAPTER TWENTY-FOUR

Vera

Telling a guy that your basement holds five or six dozen objects that at one time were possessed by inhuman, murderous spirits is not exactly the way to endear him to you. Not that Vera wanted to endear him. Or maybe she did. It was complicated.

She needed her parents.

They texted that they were in the throes of an exorcism and would call her later. How exactly could Vera tell them to ditch the possessed girl in Barcelona and come back to help the possessed woman here? Surely that girl deserved saving, but it was hard to feel sorry for her across an ocean when someone down the street was literally smoking. Vera dug her hands into her hair and groaned into her no-longer-warm tea. Maxwell Oliver was upstairs with his sister watching *Brave*. (A poignant title given the circumstances.)

"You know what I'm going to say." Vera peered at her aunt, who busied herself with chopped vegetables and hunks of meat.

"I know no such thing." Aunt Tilda swept her long silver hair behind her ear and poured chicken stock into a Crock-Pot.

"The hurricane."

Vera let the words hang.

She and her aunt rarely talked about it, as if giving what happened that day mental energy was giving it power. But there was nothing to give power to, right? They'd stopped it.

When Vera was ten years old, when she heard that object shatter behind the old barnwood door, she thought her life shattered with it. She had been told repeatedly to never touch that door, enter that room, or brush against a single object. Vera and her aunt gave those same instructions to Maxwell and his sister today. But they didn't tell them that years ago, something broke.

After the crash sounded, Aunt Tilda tucked her ten-year-old niece under the dining room table, the lace cloth Vera's only protection, and opened the basement door. She was gone for five minutes, exactly three hundred seconds. Vera counted. When Aunt Tilda returned, she said she'd recited the "prayers of protection." Everything was fine now. But when her parents got home, and Aunt Tilda informed them of the prayers she'd said, they realized she'd only completed two parts of a four-part ritual. That wasn't enough.

So they completed the rest themselves—seven days after the hurricane had wreaked its havoc.

Of course, they worried that something had been unleashed, but there were no reports of possession, no increased calls to the church. Seven years passed. They believed they'd contained it.

They could have been wrong. What if all the eerie co-incidences, all the accidents, all the deaths, even the *gas explosion*, traced back to that one horrible moment?

"The hurricane has nothing to do with it." Aunt Tilda stirred the contents of her pot, her wooden spoon sloshing.

"You can't know that," Vera countered.

"I do. I said the prayers. I was there when your parents said them. It worked."

"But what if it didn't?" Vera shook her head. "Aunt Tilda, the town changed after the gas explosion."

"Yes, because the explosion was horrific, but that had nothing to do with the hurricane."

"I'm not so sure. I think there's a connection." Vera stared at her hands twisting on the kitchen table. "I'm having dreams."

Her aunt stopped stirring. "What kind of dreams?" Her voice betrayed a touch of fear.

"About the past. I've dreamt about the hurricane," Vera admitted; the rush of that memory was so real she could practically feel the rain on her face. "And I've dreamt about things I couldn't possibly know. I dreamt about the man who caused the gas explosion. I dreamt about him going down to the basement of the community center and messing with the meter. Aunt Tilda, I could see the gas gauge—it looked like a little clock or a speedometer, with a needle that moves. I've never seen one in real life, but in my dream, it was so clear. I could draw it for you now. How is that possible?"

Her aunt slowly began to move her spoon again. "That day is still in the news constantly. Maybe you saw it on TV or online?"

She wasn't getting it.

"Maxwell and I were talking about the crash. The one earlier this year that killed my classmates?"

Her aunt nodded, not looking at her as she sprinkled various jars of dried seasoning into the pot. A warm basil mist swept through the room.

"That night I dreamt about the crash, like I was *in* it. I could see everything. The kids fighting, the driver laughing. In my dream, he let go of the wheel. On purpose." Vera stared at the back of her aunt's silver head. "And he had a statue of the Angel of Tears on the dashboard."

Her aunt dropped her spoon. "It's just a dream."

"They keep happening! I dreamt about this patient I saw at the hospital who almost drowned. I dreamt about Mr. Gonzalez and his wife. They feel like memories, *personal* memories, things I shouldn't know. And when I told Mom that I was sleepwalking, she acted like I was *inviting* in the demon. Like I'm weak or possessed, but I swear I'm not!"

Aunt Tilda sighed, her face growing worried with wrinkles. "You mom spends too much time with people who are *afflicted*. Sometimes her mind goes to the darkest place. But I'm here. I see you. You're one of the brightest souls I've ever known." She sat down next to Vera, reeking of steamed broth so strongly, Vera could taste garlic on her tongue. "Sometimes dreams are just dreams. Last night, I dreamt my podiatrist and I were in eighth-grade algebra and I was late for the final. That wasn't real."

"But that's a *normal* dream." Vera ran her hands through her hair. "When I dreamt about the gas explosion, I came *this close*"—she held her fingers close together—"to going down to the basement *in my sleep*."

"But you didn't." Her aunt patted her arm. "I know what you're thinking, but your mother's gifts, she's always had them, since birth. It didn't start like this—there were never dreams . . ."

"I'm not saying that—" Though Vera was thinking it, or more like hoping it. Because if she was gifted, that meant she had a bond with her parents, and she wasn't in the demon's power, she wasn't afflicted, and she wasn't turning into Maxwell's mother.

Aunt Tilda sighed, reading her panic. "You are being thrust into a situation you are too young to have to deal with. And you care about this boy, I can see it." Vera started to object, but her aunt waved her off. "I want to help him too, him and his sister—and we will—but for now I think your *fear* is manifesting itself in your dreams."

Vera tilted her head. Fear. Psychology. It was possible. But hearing it from her aunt made her second-guess all she thought she knew in the world. "You sound like a shrink."

"No, I sound reasonable. I don't want you scaring yourself any more than you already are. Everyone has dreams."

She stood, smoothed her apron, then returned to her pot. "I assure you, you're not becoming possessed, and you're not turning into your mother. You don't have *superpowers.*"

She mocked Maxwell's earlier choice of words, and Vera could see she was trying to lighten the mood. Maybe she thought she was comforting her niece, but for some reason, all Vera heard was, *You're not special, little girl. Wipe those silly thoughts from your head, because you'll never be one of us.*

In her dream, Maxwell's mother is a stunning beauty. She's wearing a yellow-and-white-striped sundress with spaghetti straps that cross at her upper back. It's the first really scorching summer day, and she's enjoying the sizzling rays on her skin. She strolls down Main Street to the local pharmacy with a shopping list that includes dish soap, mascara, and allergy medicine.

She drifts past a diner, smelling pancakes and gooey syrup so rich that Vera can taste the maple on her tongue. Max's mother's skirt catches a breeze, and she smooths it down. She saunters toward an art gallery, handmade jewelry displayed in the window. She lingers, trimmed nails tapping the glass in quick cascades as the smell of first kisses wanders in on a breeze—lilies.

It reminds her of him, the feel of his fuzzy beard against her cheek and a fresh bouquet clutched in his hand. Lilies are the gift of time travel, back to the days when they were young and happy and alive. Instinctively, she moves toward the florist's shop. His birthday is approaching—another year, another milestone. Without him. An ache stabs at her chest, a physical pain so sharp Vera grabs her abdomen in her sleep.

Then the woman's eyes move across the picture window, reading the name of the shop painted in hunter-green cursive letters. Durand Flowers. Durand? It must be his widow. Or maybe the son. She hadn't realized they bought the flower shop. Seth Durand died along with others—along with her person— and his family now sold flowers. They moved on.

The wound in her chest rips deeper. Why couldn't she?

Her eyes slip to the intimate staging in the window, two gold-trimmed chairs pushed into a round bistro table covered with bone linen. It's romantic, plucked from her happiest memories. There are two plates of fine china with delicate gold accents, real silver place settings, and between them an arrangement of bushy cream hydrangeas with powder-blue edges nestled in an antique brass watering can. Beside the bouquet, as if it were meant to be there, as if—of course—it would be part of the luscious table setting, is a statue of the Grim Reaper, sobbing. It's petite, only a couple inches high, with ivory wings reaching toward the heavens and an unlit torch resting on a yellow book. She's seen the hardback before, the cheery hats, the eclipsed suns. What was the name of the group again?

Her eyes strain to read the title and it's as if a burst of floral air crashes into her. She stumbles back, her vision cloudy, ears buzzing.

Whispers. She hears whispers.

Lilith. Lilith, I'm here. . . .

It's his voice. It's him. Where is he? Her head whips back and forth, searching, pleading, then her chest pulls toward the glass door, toward the scent of him. Her body knows where it wants to be. She tugs open a portal to the day their picnic blanket lay on the grass and he slid a flower into her hair, her first lily.

This family has the answers. They beat the odds. They'll help her find him.

"Vera! Vera, wake up!" a voice shouts.

Vera? Who's Vera? Where is her husband?

"Come on, Vera, wake up!"

I know that voice. He is mine. He belongs to me.

Then she feels a sting on her hand, like she's been slapped. All at once, she starts shaking.

Shaking, shaking, shaking.

"Wake! Up!"

CHAPTER TWENTY-FIVE

Max

Okay. I'm sleeping in Vera Martinez's house. And there's a bunch of demonic shit a few feet below me in the basement, and I'm supposed to act like that's totally normal. Max stretched his long limbs on the flowered sofa, all dusty pink and baby blue.

It wasn't comfortable. It wasn't even a pullout. But at least it was a sectional, so his feet sort of fit. Also, the room wasn't smoking, or located down the hall from a demon, so it had its perks.

God, my mom . . . that was my mom.

He rolled onto his side, his arm hanging off the edge of the cushions, skimming the shag area rug. He was lying on top of what he assumed were Vera's childhood sheets—pink polka dots—with a pink plush blanket. It was nearly July, and he sweated when he slept, so the fuzzy blanket was in a ball on the floor, but he appreciated the gesture. Aunt Tilda also bought Chloe a night-light and read her three books before bed. She was the first real parent Chloe had in a while.

I should get up. There's no way I'm sleeping. He popped

to his feet, shaggy beige fibers slipping between his toes. He should check on Chloe, or maybe sleep on her floor. If she woke up not knowing where she was, she'd be hysterical. He should call Alexis's mother tomorrow and see if Chloe could sleep there again. That was probably safer, away from all of this. He could tell Mrs. Tenn that he'd caught the same virus as his mom, drop the whole "it takes a village" line that parents love so much. That might work.

He trudged toward the kitchen, adjusting the hem of the Florida Keys T-shirt he was wearing. It was Vera's dad's. They ran out of his house so fast, he obviously never stopped to pack a bag, so Aunt Tilda put his and Chloe's clothes in the washer. Now he was creeptastically wearing the shirt of a man he'd never met, and Chloe was sleeping in Vera's night-gown. That wasn't awkward at all.

He padded to the fridge, not remotely hungry after Aunt Tilda's beef stew, but needing something to do. He couldn't lie on that couch anymore. He'd get a glass of water.

He opened the fridge, looking for a Brita, and let the cool gust of air wash over him. All of their fruits and veg-etables were organized in little Tupperware containers and the orange juice was in a glass pitcher. Everything looked so cared for. He dug his fingers into a cardboard box holding fizzy lime water and pulled out a can, the sound of the crack like a shotgun blast in the silent house. He hated the quiet; it made his brain think too loudly.

He wandered into the dining room, taking a sip. He counted six photos of Vera and her aunt, all of varying sizes.

Some were taken in the garden out back and others at the beach. Vera aged from a toddler in a floppy yellow sun hat to a teenager who towered over the gray-haired woman beside her. Her brown eyes glinted in the most recent picture, her smile wide and her legs long and toned in a short black skirt. She was photogenic.

Max took another gulp, turning toward the dining room table. He ran his fingers along the lace doily (he didn't realize people still bought things like this). Then he crossed the room, spying a photo of Vera and her parents. It was near the window on a big wooden desk, one of those old-fashioned kinds with a rolling door on top. He picked up the silver frame, which was surprisingly heavy. Vera looked like she was ten years old in the picture, and she was wearing a red graduation-style gown with a white shawl and a golden cross. Her confirmation, probably? Her mother wore a long-sleeved flowery dress and her hair was short and curly. Her dad had a mustache and bow tie. They looked a lot older than Max's parents.

So, one photo of them, six of the aunt. That was telling. Vera didn't spend much time with her parents. He wondered if that bothered her. Actually, he wondered if *all* of this bothered her. How old was she when she figured out what her parents did? That must have been a nightmare—being a kid and knowing, with absolute certainty, that demons, and devils, and evil, and Hell existed. And it was all *inside* her house. Max was scared, and he was nearly an adult. Yet Vera's voice never wavered.

Everything he thought he knew about her was wrong. Not just about what her parents did, but about who Vera was as a person. If it weren't for her, Max wouldn't be able to breathe through any of this.

He set down the photo and a creak sounded on the floorboards upstairs. His eyes shot toward the ceiling. Someone was awake. The hairs prickled on the back of his neck. It was probably Chloe. He should have slept in her room. He set down the can of water and moved toward the stairs.

A step groaned.

He paused, a wave of uneasiness coming over him.

Another creak.

"Chloe?" he stage-whispered, heartbeat accelerating.

A slender bare foot emerged, perfectly pointed, skin pale as milk and nails painted pink. That wasn't Chloe. The moon shone through stained glass, sending bits of ruby, gold, and sapphire swirling onto the exposed calf.

Vera.

Max grinned all the way to his eyes.

She descended leisurely, a graceful hand lightly brushing the polished banister.

"You can't sleep either?" he asked.

She didn't respond. She reached the landing halfway down the staircase and pivoted toward the living room.

That was when he saw her eyes—they were closed, lashes fluttering.

"Vera?"

Her mouth was slack, full lips slightly parted. He leaned closer, pulse picking up pace.

She was sleepwalking. She never mentioned this might happen.

Her foot hit the first floor, and Max reached out his arm, his hand lightly tapping her shoulder. "Vera, wake up," he said softly.

He pulled back. He wasn't sure if he was supposed wake her. He thought the same thing when his mom was sleepwalking.

Only, she was *never* sleepwalking.

His gut double knotted.

Vera made a sharp left turn, her body knowing where it wanted to go. Even in sleep.

"Vera," he whispered again.

Her black waves swung loosely, a tuft sticking up in the back from her pillow. She mumbled softly, the words unintelligible. He followed behind her perfect posture, shoulders back and neck long. Each step stretched lithely in front of her, moving with purpose. Where was she going?

They entered the kitchen. He'd heard stories of sleepwalkers pouring themselves drinks or fixing sandwiches, but the air was sizzling with tension, like this wasn't about to be a funny anecdote. His muscles tightened.

Then he saw where her body was steering.

No! His hand shot out.

Vera moved toward the basement.

The barnwood door seemed to pulse, the Xs bulging and swelling with warning: *Stay out. . . . Don't get any closer. . . .*

"Vera! Vera, wake up!" he insisted.

She couldn't hear him. Just like his mother.

"Vera, stop! Wake! Up!" he shouted.

She reached for the brass knob, fingers dripping delicately. Hell was behind that door, little pieces of Hell. She said to never open it, that they were safe as long as the door stayed shut.

He slapped her hand.

He didn't want to hurt her, but he was not letting her open that door. Not with his sister in the house. Vera paused.

She felt him. Good.

"Come on, Vera, wake up! You're sleepwalking."

Her hand rose once more, determined to turn the knob. This time he stepped in front of her, blocking her path. A rush of static electricity (that was the closest he could describe it) emanated from the door, pushing against his back and lifting the hairs from his legs to his head. He could have stuck a balloon to his skull.

He grabbed her shoulders. *I'm sorry. I don't want to hurt you, but . . .*

He shook her, fingers digging into her bare shoulders, her head rocking limply on her neck, soft waves fluttering.

"Vera, wake up! Wake! Up!" he shouted.

Finally, her eyes opened.

Her pupils were huge.

Max sat beside Vera on the couch. A rumpled pink polka-dot sheet was draped over their legs, and her warm body leaned against his shoulder. He liked the way her hair tickled his neck; she smelled of ginger.

"This is gonna sound weird," she said, breaking the silence.

"I'm not sure things can get any weirder than they already are," Max replied.

They hadn't said much since she'd woken up, blinking with pupils dilated to the size of quarters. Within moments, her gaze returned to normal, but still, Max couldn't help picturing his mother. She looked the same those first few nights.

Vera's head flicked around, taking it in, seeming shocked to find herself standing outside the basement. Then Max asked if she wanted to sit. She did.

"Does your mom own a yellow-and-white-striped sundress?" she asked.

What? Max's head wrenched back. That was unexpected. "Um, yeah. Why?"

"I dreamt of her, wearing that dress."

"Seriously?"

She turned to him, her hand resting on his shoulder. He liked that. "She was walking down Main Street, before all of this happened, and she looked *beautiful*."

Her words scooped the air right out from inside him. Max stared at the dormant TV, their reflections displayed in the black glass.

"What was she doing? In the dream?" he asked.

"She was on her way to buy allergy medicine, for you and your sister. I'm not sure how I know that, but I do. Then she smelled lilies in the air."

Max's chest slumped. *More lilies . . .*

"The smell, it made her upset. I could *feel* it." Vera twirled a lock of hair around a finger. "She saw the name of the shop, *Durand* Flowers, and she made the connection. You know, with the explosion?"

Max gritted his teeth. It was hard to forget the name of the family responsible for your father's death. They bought the florist shop a couple years ago, and since then, Max had avoided it at all costs. But his mother held no ill will against them. In fact, when she joined the son's self-help group, she told Max it was *because* it was connected to that family. She was inspired by their ability to keep going. She said Seth Durand's mistake may have destroyed the soul of this town, but now his son was trying to heal it. If there was anyone out there who understood her pain, she believed it was Anatole Durand.

Max disagreed. Or maybe he simply held grudges.

"She was about to walk away, but then she saw a tiny Angel of Tears statue. It was part of a window display, and it was sitting atop a yellow book. I don't know how the statue even caught her eye, it was so small, but your mom was *drawn* to it." Vera yanked her hair, her head jerked down a bit. Max reached for her hand and pulled her fingers free, lacing them with his own. He told himself he was showing her that she could say the hard things and he wouldn't get upset, but really he needed to touch her.

Max's fingers clenched hers. "What are you saying?"

"I'm saying I think the Sunshine Crew and the Angel of Tears are connected. Somehow. Maybe?" She pressed between her eyebrows, rubbing. "Or this is all bullshit, and my dreams are just dreams. I really don't know!" Her voice cracked, desperation leaking in. "My aunt thinks I'm over-reacting and my dreams are random Freudian textbook stuff. Meanwhile, my mom thinks I could be under the influence of the same demon that's inside your mother. She's acting like I'm *getting too close.*" She put air quotes around the words. "But neither of them feels right to me. And I just feel . . . messed up."

Tears spilled down her cheeks.

"You're okay. And you're making sense. We know my mom was in the Sunshine Crew. I don't know how people could go from *that* to devil worship, but both things are spreading through town. It's possible."

"It's also possible I'm freaking out and conflating two completely unrelated things just to make sense of my own fear," she croaked, a shiver rocking her shoulders.

Max leaned closer. "We'll figure this out."

"That's what I've been telling *you*."

He released her hand and reached for her, pausing. "Can I?"

She collapsed against his chest, and he hugged her tight, her legs pulled up and curled like a cat. He rested his chin on the top of her head.

When her breathing settled and he sensed she was falling asleep, her head sweaty against his chest, he didn't move her. He didn't want to.

CHAPTER TWENTY-SIX

Vera

Her parents called at eight in the morning. Finally. Vera was already awake, having opened her eyes at six a.m. with her head on Maxwell's chest, which was covered in her father's vacation T-shirt. The weirdness was too much for the early hour, so she snuck into her room before her aunt could find their bodies entwined. Vera never fell back asleep. Then the phone rang.

As soon as her mom said hello, Vera blurted everything.

"I think it's all connected," Vera insisted as she sat on the edge of her unmade bed.

She could hear Maxwell downstairs playing Jenga with Chloe. She told him that her mom was on the phone, and as much as she knew Maxwell wanted to speak to her parents, Vera wanted some time alone. She needed her mom. He understood.

"Mom, this shrine . . . it was in my patient's room, it's all over the hospital, and Maxwell's mom had it. There were, like, *worshippers* in her room. And I'm not just sleepwalking anymore. I've been having dreams, lots of them, ones

I didn't tell you about before. I dreamt of being in the car when my classmates died. I've dreamt of Maxwell's mom, hospital patients, the gas works employee. And I know what you said, but I don't think the dreams are coming from the demon. I think they're coming from inside *me*. I think I'm having them for a reason." There, she said it. She thought her mom was wrong, for maybe the first time. Ever.

Vera clamped the phone against her shoulder, waiting for a response, twisting a bedsheet over her wrists. She wrapped it round and round, forming a winter muff, holding her breath.

"Honey, there's something I need to tell you." Her mom's tone was unexpected, like she was bracing Vera for something. "I know this shrine. I've seen it before. In Chicago."

Vera dropped the sheet.

"Twelve years ago, we were called out by the local diocese," Mom continued. "There had been serial killings. Women were turning up mutilated. It was horrendous."

Vera slumped back on the bed, listening as the ceiling fan whirled above her, the beaded metal chain rocking with each rotation.

"The police thought the killings were human sacrifices, that it was tied to the occult. One of the victims survived. They found her half dead in the frozen Chicago River. She told the police that the four men who attacked her wore crimson cloaks. They placed her on an altar, beside a large ivory statue of what looked like the Angel of Death—a skeleton in a white robe, with soaring wings and black tears, holding a skull-engraved torch with its flame smothered."

"That's it," Vera sputtered.

That's exactly *it.*

"The church wanted me to interview the woman—they thought I could get a *sense* of what happened." Her mom drew a slow breath and exhaled with the control of a yogi. "What I saw wasn't just demonic, it was one of the darkest spirits I've ever felt. A cult leader managed to convince the four others that they were praying to a deity. He said the women were 'sinners,' and his followers believed him, without question. They left . . . parts of the victims . . . as offerings at the base of a shrine that they called the Angel of Tears."

"No, no, no." Vera wrapped an arm around her stomach, ready to heave. She rolled on her side, curling her legs. If her parents vanquished this demon twelve years ago, that meant there was only one plausible reason it was now festering *here*, in Roaring Creek.

"You didn't mention the shrine before!" Mom defended, as if seeing Vera's reaction.

"I forgot! There's so much going on, and the last time we spoke, it was only *one* patient. It wasn't connected to Maxwell's mom. But now it is. And it's in my dreams. It's all over the hospital." Vera looked toward the bedroom door, and for a moment she swore she felt the pulse of the basement reaching through the house and into her chest.

"I know, that's what we realized in Chicago. This demon

has the power to influence *many*. When we walked in, all four men were collapsed in front of the altar, lips smeared red, with their leader clutching a chalice of blood mixed with poison."

"A crystal chalice with gold trim." Vera didn't need to wait for an answer. That cup still haunted her nightmares. She knew exactly when it broke and where. "*We're* the reason Maxwell's mom is afflicted. The hurricane, the demon, it was in the chalice."

"No. Well, yes, but not exactly. We *trapped* it in the chalice, but demons don't want to possess *things*, they want to possess people. That's why we're able to contain it in an object, *if* the object belonged to the person doing the demon's bidding. The chalice was in the leader's dead hand, and I could still feel the evil attached to it. It called to me. So we performed the binding prayers right there at the altar. Then we brought it home to ensure its protection," Mom explained. "When Tilda told us that the chalice broke during the hurricane, and she performed the ritual, we thought we were okay. Even when we got home and realized she had missed some of the prayers, we still thought it was all right. The room and the object had been blessed as recently as a few days prior. But as a precaution we performed the ritual again, and we waited. Nothing happened."

"The community center exploded!" Vera sat upright.

"We thought it was a gas leak."

"You never considered the alternative? That it was intentional? Or demonic?"

"Of course we did, but the report said an employee made a *mistake*. It said he was grieving a dying child and was distracted. It made sense. Accidents happen."

"Mom, think of the timing!"

"*Months* had gone by before the explosion, and in our experience, demons don't patiently wait around for months. We thought if anything was let loose, we would feel the effects immediately. Not to mention, there's no reason this inhuman spirit would even stay *in* Roaring Creek. It could have gone halfway around the world, for all we knew. Contrary to what you may think, we do *not* know everything about how the demonic plane works."

Vera groaned, all her blood, all her sanity, plunging from her head. The room, the world, tilted.

"I can't believe this . . . ," she murmured, trying to form words. "This thing, it isn't just infecting Maxwell's mom. I think it's infecting the whole *town*. The shrine, all the deaths, the overdoses, the car accidents, Mom!" she yelped. "What if it's *all* because of us?"

"Honey, you're reaching. Calm down. . . ."

"You don't know that! You're not here! You're *never* here. Something is wrong in Roaring Creek. I can feel it, like this dread I can't shake. And now you're saying it started with a *cult*, which is exactly what Maxwell and I were saying last night. I think I know how it's spreading, and if I'm right, it's infecting *so many* people." Tears leaked without warning, cutting tracks down her cheeks. "How can all these people be possessed?"

"They're not. Not all of them. It's not that powerful. In Chicago, I think only the leader was truly overtaken by the inhuman spirit; the rest were just under the influence, so to speak, like they were drunk or hypnotized."

"Hypnotized by a demon!" Vera shot back, her breath hiccupping as tears fell. "Maxwell's mom—it's not mind control or hypnosis, it's *possession*. It's affecting her whole body, her face. She spoke in his father's voice; there was smoke coming out of her. I'm not sure how much longer her body can take it."

"Vera." Her mom's tone was suddenly stern. "We will be home as soon as we can. Two days, maximum. Do you hear me? I'm coming. In the meantime, you *must* stay away—"

"You've got to be kidding me! You expect me to ignore what's happening? I can help her." Vera *had* to help her.

"No! Absolutely not." Her words may as well have been aimed at a toddler reaching for the stove. "My gift, it's nothing like you're experiencing. I've always had it, as far back as my oldest memories."

"But some of my dreams are true—the hurricane, that was real. I know, I lived it."

"Which is what makes it a *normal* dream, but the other ones . . . Honey, what you're describing is completely different from me."

And different was wrong. Vera stared at the floor, her mother painting a white line through the room; Vera was on the other side. Her jaw tensed.

"You think I'm possessed too?" Vera spat.

"No, of course not. At least, not like *that*. I'm just saying you can't trust your dreams until we know where they're coming from."

Vera ground her teeth. Her mom just admitted to being wrong about the hurricane, about the danger of the object breaking. She could be wrong now. And even if Vera wasn't special, or magical, she had instincts. Everything inside her screamed she wasn't "under the influence" of anything demonic. Yet for some reason, it was easier for her mother to believe *that* than to believe Vera might have a power that rivals her own.

No. Vera's eyes squinted to slits, a million responses forming in her head, but none emerging from her lips.

Finally, her mom let out a heavy sigh, sensing Vera's ire. "I realize two days is a long time in a situation like this. I understand *that* more than you know. And I want to help this family. If you really feel time is imperative, then call Father Chuck. Tell him what's happening and explain it's an emergency. He'll have to go around the traditional channels, at least until we get there."

Vera curled in on herself, her chest tightening. She still said nothing.

"Vera, it's going to be okay." Her mom's voice was softer. "I know it seems dire right now, and you're scared, but it's going to be all right. I promise."

She couldn't promise that from Barcelona.

Vera felt insulted, scared, and clueless all at once. There was a boy in her living room expecting Vera to strap on a cape and save his mother. A cult was spreading through Roaring Creek. Shrines were multiplying everywhere she looked. Patients were praying to Death.

Vera paused, blinking away tears. Then she sat up straighter.

The hospital.

Samantha.

The Sunshine Crew.

No.

Vera popped to her feet, eyes searching for her purse, her car keys.

"Mom, I have to go."

———

Vera stomped through the hospital corridor, the fluorescent overhead lights adding to the queasiness in her stomach.

She'd sprinted out of the house, telling Maxwell she'd text him as soon as she could. She had to find Samantha. Only, before she did, Vera ran into the head of nursing outside of a ladies' room and held a ninety-second conversation on the dangers of the Angel statues. Vera insisted, rather desperately, that the shrines were tied to demonic worship, while trying not to explicitly state it was her mother who saw the figure on a satanic altar surrounded by body parts. It didn't matter.

"My hands are tied," the nurse said.

No, Vera wanted to correct her, *what's coming is so much worse than bound hands.*

Now Vera had to hope that at least her friends would believe her. She raced toward the cafeteria, peeking into patient rooms as she passed. On this floor alone, three doors were open. There was a shrine to the Angel of Tears in two of them.

An ache built behind her eyes, her fingers flexing with a desire to smash the statues into smithereens. *This is all my family's fault.* The din of the cafeteria rose, blending with the stench of burned meat. She stepped inside and scanned the crowd. Chelsea was in line for a rubbery personal pizza, while Samantha grabbed a mostly lettuce premade salad. Vera met them at the cashier line.

"I'm so glad you're back!" Samantha greeted. Her voice was cheery, but there were purple circles under her lashes, her gaze looked bleary, and somehow, her face was bonier. "Lou's been covering your shifts, and I swear if he tells me one more twenty-minute story about his pet hamster, I will bear no regrets for my actions."

"Seriously." Chelsea gagged as she paid for their food. "The other day he showed me an album of the hamster dressed up in costumes, like a tiny sailor suit. I almost committed murder by sporking."

"Glad you didn't." Vera faked a grin as she followed her friends to their table, wondering exactly how to segue the conversation. "Guys, there's something I gotta tell you—"

"Did I text you about my grandma? We had to put her in hospice," Chelsea cut in, her voice heavy, but her eyes looked at Vera like she was trying to communicate something else.

Vera's brow furrowed. "I'm so sorry. . . ."

"Why? Transitioning to the afterlife is the easiest journey she'll ever take." Samantha's voice was flat, lifeless. "She shouldn't fear it. No one should."

Vera's eyes shot toward Samantha, her gaze vacant. *She was direct-quoting* the Sunshine Crew? *How deep had she sunk?* Only, before she could ask, Chelsea cut in.

"My dad's having a really hard time. It sucks, but let's talk about something less depressing." Chelsea bit into her pizza, her expression begging, *Please. I know what you're going to say, but don't.*

Vera bit her lip. It was an impossible ask.

"How have you been?" Chelsea grumbled, mouth full. "Why weren't you at work?"

"Um . . ." Vera looked down at the table. Blurting *My friend's mom is possessed by a demon* or *You may be in a cult* didn't feel like the right opening line. "I've been busy. . . ."

"Whatever happened with that guy who came here?" Chelsea pressed, working hard to divert the conversation. "You still seeing him?"

"Yeah, actually," Vera admitted, lies of omission piling up on her shoulders. Maxwell was sleeping on her couch, though that wasn't what she'd come here to say.

"Ohhh!" Chelsea cheered, clapping her hands. "I need happy news right now! Give me details! What have you guys been doing? Where have you gone?"

Vera glanced out the window, unsure what to say. In the courtyard, patients were creeping along with walkers and gliding in wheelchairs. Fresh air and exercise were intended to lift their moods and promote healing. Meanwhile, Vera's world had become so dark lately, she'd half forgotten it was summer. Was it wrong to delay the evil details for a few moments, ease them into it?

"We've been hanging out at my place mostly," Vera said, sticking to what was true.

"Your parents are cool with that?" Chelsea raised her brows.

"They're in Barcelona."

"What?!" Both girls gasped in unison.

Vera bit her lip, basking in their reaction and knowing she was making this seem way cooler and way less satanic than it was. But the truth was, Vera liked Max. There, she admitted it. She liked him, and maybe she could have one conversation about the new boy in her life that didn't involve demonic possession. Was that so wrong?

"Tell. Us. Everything." Chelsea clapped her hands in time with the words.

"We've just been talking, mostly, but it's been . . . intense." Vera buried her eyes in her lap, hoping to conceal the realities she was holding back. "He lost his dad in the explosion, and his mom isn't doing well."

The girls nodded with understanding. "PTSD can last your whole life," said Chelsea.

"The Sunshine Crew says we need to embrace our pain and stop fearing our lives." Samantha's voice sounded distant, almost dreamy. She stared out the window, as if in a trance. "Besides, the pain doesn't really matter. It's only temporary. Soon we'll all be reborn. We should embrace it."

Every word was a needle piercing Vera's let's-be-normal bubble.

"What?" Vera asked, her jaw hanging. The last time she'd been at work, Samantha was skimming chat rooms and recommending herbal teas. What happened?

"How's he dealing?" Chelsea blurted, drawing Vera's attention and silently pleading with her to ignore the Sunshine Crew.

No way.

"His mom is in really bad shape." Vera's voice was measured, choosing the best way to describe this. "She was in TSC too—"

"Hey, did you hear Steam Punk is playing at the Vine this weekend? We should go!" Chelsea pulled out her phone, full-on blabbering now. "Lemme see how much tickets are. . . ."

"No," Vera snapped, her voice stern. "There's a lot you don't know about TSC—"

"Like *you* know anything about us," Samantha cut in, scratching her ear with nails chewed down to the little half-moons. *Us.* She said *us.* "If Maxwell's mom is a believer, then he must know the truth. Death is natural and beautiful. You just need to open your arms and let the warmth of the next life embrace you. If you're ready, and you sing from your heart, you'll transition to a higher plane. That's where my brother is now, and Maxwell's dad."

Vera was too late. She dropped her head into her hands, elbows on the table. That's what Mr. Gonzalez said the day he lost his mind, not long before he *died*.

"It looks like general admission is only twenty-two dollars," Chelsea jabbered, still feigning obliviousness as she booked their weekend plans.

What is going on?

"Sam." Vera slapped the table. Chelsea lowered her phone, wincing as if she knew the truth that was coming and really didn't want Vera to say it. Sorry, because this was long overdue. "I was going to phrase this more delicately, but I think I need to cut to the chase—you're in a cult." Vera paused, letting the words sink in. "TSC is not what you think. You've been brainwashed into worshipping death. . . ."

Samantha's blank eyes suddenly sparked with fire as they turned Vera's way. She aggressively shook her head, chapped lips pursed to the side. "If by *cult* you mean a bunch of happy people working to be our best selves and refusing to ignore the truth of our existence—then yes."

"Happy? You don't look happy!" Vera pointed at the lavender bags under Sam's eyes, and the protruding collarbones from what must have been significant and sudden weight loss. "This group isn't about truth, it's about death and darkness."

"It's about the great awakening!" Samantha tossed up her hands. "Your oppressive minds just refuse to let you see the wisdom of His teachings!"

Vera shot a look at Chelsea. "How long has she been this bad? What the hell?"

Vera knew her tone was accusatory, but by the looks of it, Samantha needed this intervention long ago.

"If I mention it, she just digs in deeper," Chelsea murmured, eyes downcast like she couldn't look at either of them.

"Don't talk about me like I'm not here! You're the ones refusing to see the true path, and you will pay the price in this life and beyond." Samantha stood up so fast, her chair tumbled to the ground behind her. She didn't pick it up. "You're both Oppressives."

She turned her back, marching through rows of tables toward the cafeteria doors. Vera grabbed Chelsea's wrist before she could storm after her girlfriend.

"This is worse than you think. The Sunshine Crew isn't just kooky; they're into some really dark shit. I can't get into how bad it is right now, but you have got to keep Samantha away from them." Vera's eyes locked on her friend's, hoping to convey her seriousness.

"How do you expect me to do that? She's a grown woman and her *mother* is into it." Chelsea yanked her hand away. "Every time I try to say something, she pulls further away from *me* and closer to *them*. And thanks to what you just did, I might have lost her forever. She's cutting everyone out of her life who isn't a part of that group."

"Chelsea, those Grim Reaper statues and the Sunshine Crew, they're connected." Vera's tone was heavy as she searched for whatever she could reveal without sounding like they needed garlic and silver bullets.

"How do you know that?" Chelsea's tone was disbelieving.

"Well, I don't have proof, but it's true. And it's a lot worse than you realize."

"Well, thanks for your conspiracy theories, but I can get that crap online." Chelsea jumped to her feet and collected her and Samantha's untouched lunch trays. "If you want to shut down TSC, you need *proof.* Bring me *that* and we can go to the cops together. In the meantime, leave Samantha alone. If she pushes me away too, then she'll be completely lost."

Vera sighed, rubbing her temples. That was why Chelsea was trying to shut her up. Vera had made it worse. Her fingers pressed harder. She didn't know how to deprogram a cult member. And she didn't know how to help Max.

Suddenly, her phone vibrated on the table, rattling against the Formica—a phone call, not a text.

She flipped it over: Father Chuck.

The screen might as well have read: *Last Resort.*

"Hello," Vera answered.

"I got your message. How soon can you get here?" the priest asked.

CHAPTER TWENTY-SEVEN

Max

The priest wore faded blue jeans. Max didn't know why that surprised him so much, but it did. He didn't know what to think when Vera texted him. On one hand, finally, a priest! He'd seen *The Exorcist*; he knew what priests could do. On the other hand, he'd seen *The Exorcist*. Green bile, spinning heads, last rites.

His mother was already spewing smoke.

Max fidgeted in the scratched leather chair, bouncing his knee and rocking the rickety coffee table full of brochures ranging from "Learning the Bible" to "The Gay and Lesbian Catholic Group." Vera said they were in the lounge of the rectory, which meant it was where Father Chuck lived. Max couldn't get used to calling him that. Shouldn't it be Father Whatever His Last Name Is? Though he didn't really have much experience with Catholic priests—or rabbis, or ministers, or monks. Religion was something that fueled other people—the reason wars were fought, genocides were waged, and people were treated as "other."

Even after the explosion, when Max was fed clichés about his dad being "in a better place" or "with the angels," he pretended to believe and smiled politely. Because where else was he supposed to picture his father? Of course the man was in Heaven, some ubiquitous utopia with white puffy clouds and magical harps. He never considered the opposite. Hell didn't cross his mind.

Now it did.

"I have soda, orange juice, water, or coffee," the priest offered as he dug through a humming beige refrigerator.

"I'm okay." Max's knee bopped harder.

"I'll have a water." Vera sat on a matching leather chair, not meeting Max's eyes.

She'd driven straight from the hospital to pick him up, and they hardly spoke the entire ride here. He didn't know if it was because things didn't go well with her friend, because she was sleepwalking last night, or because she spent the night wrapped around him on the couch. He really hoped it wasn't the latter, because honestly, holding her was the only good moment he'd had in a very long time. He needed that memory.

"Well, I need some caffeine." The priest cracked open a can of Coke as he strutted back in his cowboy boots.

He cleared a pile of newspapers and bulletins from the leather sofa, which was tufted with fat upholstered buttons, and sat down. His faded navy polo was untucked, and there was a stain that looked like coffee below his collar.

"You're eyeing me funny." The priest peered at Max.

Max shook his head, neck hot. "Sorry. I just, I mean, I don't think I've ever seen a priest out of uniform before."

"Oh." Father Chuck took a swig. "I used to wear the collar, but I find it turns people off." His graying mustache twitched. "Only bums approach me when I wear the collar. And I'm a real person—I ride the bus. I don't need that shit."

Max's eyes bugged, and he looked at Vera, who was suppressing a grin. She wasn't kidding when she texted the priest might be "just rogue enough" to help.

"Father Chuck is from Texas," she explained. "He moved up here to serve on Connecticut University's campus."

The school was fifteen minutes from Roaring Creek, and half their graduating class attended. They called it thirteenth grade.

"I was living every little boy's dream down there in Dallas. I was a cowboy on a ranch. Truth is, I wasn't ready to leave. But I was convinced it would be good for the kids up here, and I ain't sorry I did it. I met her folks." He nodded at Vera. "They called this morning, right after you did. Filled me in." His eyes flipped to Max. "Sorry about your mama."

Over the course of seven years, Max had grown accustomed to people giving him condolences. He'd lost someone "that day," and all of the victims of the tragedy were to be honored (#RememberTheCreek). But this was the first time anyone showed him pity for his mother, his currently *living* mother. He wasn't sure what to say, but he figured there probably weren't any "right" words for this situation.

"Give it to me straight—how bad is it?" The priest looked at Vera.

"I don't have the same frame of reference as you and my parents do, but"—Vera hedged—"something's inside her. It's taken over, and there's a shrine."

"I heard. Ain't the first time I heard about it, neither. I've seen the shrine, in cars, store windows—"

"The florist?" Vera asked, trying to be subtle.

Max was more straightforward. "Vera thinks it could be connected to the Durands and the Sunshine Crew."

"I reckon that's likely. I got thrown off when I saw it at the Mexican restaurant up there on Willow. Thought it was Santa Muerte."

Vera nodded. Max's eyes flicked between the two of them; their mutual understanding had him feeling like he'd missed the required Catholic reading. Father Chuck eyed his confusion.

"Santa Muerte's a folk religion down in Mexico. Church has hated it since the get-go, even blames it for the rise in demonic possession, but I think they just don't like it taking away the parishioners." He made grabby hands as he let out a chuckle. "Santa Muerte appeals to the poor folk, you see, the marginalized, the incarcerated. Folks who feel left behind by society, so they're lookin' elsewhere for a little help."

"But this isn't Santa Muerte," Vera confirmed.

"No, don't seem like it is." He pulled a smartphone from his back pocket and showed them an image—a feminine white skeleton was displayed holding a scythe and crystal globe. Around her neck and wrists were colorful strings of beads, and she wore a bright cherry robe embroidered with a rainbow of flowers pulled high over her skull. It looked like a female Grim Reaper dressed for a festive Mexican wedding.

"This what you saw?" Father Chuck's mustache pressed to the side.

Max shook his head no. So did Vera.

"Our idol's all white," Vera noted.

"With wings and a torch," Max added.

"And it's weeping black tears."

"Exactly. Santa Muerte ain't got wings. And the black tears . . ." The priest shivered. "I should have known better—the Bony Lady's big in Texas. Folks pray to her for healing, protection, and safe passage to the afterlife. They don't pray to her because they *want* to die, or because death is *better*. Whatever idol is ripping through our town is much . . . darker." The priest set his phone on the table. His lock screen was an image of horses grazing that was so serene, Max wished he could cross an electronic force field and step inside it.

"Did my mom tell you about Chicago?" Vera asked, her voice small. "About the shrine and the cult there?"

What? Max's eyes flung toward her. She'd been quiet the whole drive over, but he never considered it was because she was sitting on information that had to do with his mother. "What shrine in Chicago?"

"So . . ." Vera squirmed in her seat. "Remember the hurricane?"

"Obviously." He scoffed.

"Well . . ." She kept wiggling, the leather squeaking below her. "Something happened at our house that day."

Max's mind stilled as Vera relayed the story about the cult in Chicago, the human sacrifices, and the chalice of blood. That chalice was in her basement, a souvenir from devil worshippers. And it shattered.

"So let me get this straight." Max held up his hands, fingers stretched wide. "A hurricane hit your house and unleashed a demon? That's what's inside my *mother*, right now? But a few days ago, you said those objects were completely safe."

He slept in that house, so did his sister. They had an entire conversation about that basement, and at no point did anyone mention broken artifacts.

"When we talked, I didn't know. I hadn't spoken to my mom yet. She hadn't told me about the chalice. A lot has changed in a few hours. . . ."

"Would have been nice if you told me! So are these objects safe or not? My sister is there. What happens the next time a storm, a fire, or some clumsy cleaning person strikes? Will dozens more evil spirits be let loose on the world?"

"No. I mean, I don't know."

"Well, don't you kinda *have to* know? Otherwise, get rid of that stuff."

"The objects are safe," Father Chuck defended. "We bless them every week."

"Clearly, it's not working!" Max popped up, feeling like the room was shrinking.

It was one thing to think his mother had stumbled upon this demon on her own or was afflicted completely at random, but it was another to learn that it was *brought* here.

He cracked his knuckles, pacing on the olive-green carpet. "My mother is possessed by a demon that your parents encountered years ago and carpooled with to Roaring Creek. This means none of this would be happening if it weren't for—"

"Hey, if her parents didn't do the work they do, that demon *never* would've been bottled up, not for one minute. We all know the truth of that." Father Chuck stood, cutting off Max's pacing. "The evil would've gone hopping from those boys in Chicago to another and another, and folks would've kept dying, dozens, maybe hundreds. So I don't wanna hear you tossing blame. My eyes have seen what the Martinezes have rid from this world."

"How do you know that they've rid anything? Look at what's happening! Maybe your spells don't work."

"They're not spells, they're prayers, and they work," the priest insisted. "I've seen an evil spirit leave a body. I've felt it."

"Yeah, well, I've felt my mother turn into *whatever* was in that chalice!" Max snapped, eyes shooting toward Vera. He knew this wasn't her fault, logically, but he couldn't ignore that the evil coursing through his mom, his family, originated in *her* home. He dropped his head. "You're telling me *everything* my family's going through is because a cup broke in your basement?"

Suddenly Vera marched to Max with heavy steps. "I have spent my entire life dealing with the reality of what my parents do." Her voice was so steely that Max lifted his head. They faced one another, her finger pointed in warning. "I have been shunned, ridiculed, and so lonely you can't even fathom. I have resented my parents, I've avoided walking past a door in my own home, and I've learned to smile wide as person after person in this town—in my school, at *your* restaurant—treats me like a *ghoul.* But I can't anymore. You came to *me* for help, that's why we're here, but if you don't want it—fine. Because this isn't just about you anymore; this is about the entire town."

Max stumbled back, the word *ghoul* smacking him across the face. He couldn't lose her too. "I'm sorry. I shouldn't have taken this out on you."

"Good, that's settled." Father Chuck abruptly stepped between them. "Now, tell me about the Sunshine Crew."

Vera let out an exhale that puffed her cheeks, then she looked at the priest. "Half the town seems to be wearing yellow hats lately, carrying that stupid book. The group was started by Anatole Durand. Then, at the same time, shrines to the Angel of Tears start popping up in the hospital. I didn't realize the two were connected until I had a vision of Max's mom seeing the Angel and the book in the window of Durand Flowers." Vera pulled her fingers, marking the evidence. "If my dreams are real—and I think they are—then somehow the Sunshine Crew is brainwashing followers, and, I don't know, convincing them to worship a demon?"

Max dropped his head. For years, people in town joked about the yellow hats being a cult; it was said teasingly, sarcastically. He never considered it was true, not for one second. They had bake sales!

"I can't exactly go to the cops and claim my dreams are proof, but I *feel* like I'm right," Vera added. "You should have seen my friend at the hospital. Whatever this is, it works fast. She just started joining chat rooms a week ago, and now I don't even recognize her. I'm afraid if we don't stop this soon, what's happening to your mom could happen to everyone else in this town."

"Then we don't have time to waste." The priest stomped to a closet and began riffling through the clutter on the floor. "It sounds like this group is hiding its true face, drawing in folks with its self-help mumbo jumbo, and before they know it, they're leaving offerings for the devil."

"The men in Chicago didn't leave flowers, they left *body parts*," Max reminded him. How bad was this going to get?

"Well, sure, if you're aimin' to heal the sick, wine and crackers ain't gonna do it. Demon's gonna want something *big*."

"You're saying my mom's going to start leaving . . . ?" No. That wasn't possible. No matter what was inside his mother, Max had to believe that wasn't possible.

He pictured his mom curled on the rosy wingback chair in their living room, wearing her black-framed reading glasses that made her look like a teacher, that yellow book spread across her lap. He hadn't seen her smile that bright in a long time. She was focused—she got the restaurant out of debt and their finances in order. She never mentioned the part about the satanic altar.

"A body part is just one example of a supreme sacrifice for a demon." Father Chuck placed a heavy palm on Max's shoulder. "A soul is another."

Max swallowed hard.

"It's time for me to meet your mama."

CHAPTER TWENTY-EIGHT

Vera

They worried briefly that Max's mom might have finally left the confines of her bedroom sanctuary, but as soon as they turned the corner to his street, Vera felt a pulley system loop around her chest and wheel her close. His mom was still there.

Vera slowed the car, Father Chuck sitting in the passenger seat staring out the window while Maxwell bounced his knee behind them, rocking the sedan. In the light of day, his house looked like most others in Roaring Creek, completely forgettable. A petite white ranch house sulked in disrepair under an intolerably bright sky. The asphalt driveway, spread pitch-black when fresh, was now a dusty white, cracked and patched. An orange-breasted robin rested on the shingled roof pecking at gutters brimming with globs of rotten leaves. There was a garage, its door splattered with years of snow-shovel muck and hurricane slime.

The only remarkable aspect was the front door—the color of a perfect, plump tomato dangling on the vine. All the other homes on Stone Street had maple, ivory, black, or, at most, evergreen doors. But not the Olivers'; their door screamed to be noticed.

Only, no one noticed what was happening inside.

The neighbors abandoned this family. They left a boy to care for a newborn, then silently watched for seven years while his mother wilted with grief, seeking solutions everywhere, from a bottle to possessed strangers.

Vera reached for the handle of her car door, her heart kicking up a notch. Then she touched a foot on the pavement and instantly felt the rush of a ski's first slip down a black-diamond slope. The exhilaration returned, and with it a sense of absolute *rightness*.

She *needed* to be here.

And *it* wanted her here. Something had changed.

Father Chuck slipped out of the car, a black medical bag in his hand.

"Your parents asked me to keep you away." Father Chuck peered at Vera. "They don't think you should be here."

"My parents are on another continent." Vera stared him straight in the eye. "And you need all the help you can get."

The priest assessed her conviction, then nodded once. "Just follow my lead. It's not my first rodeo." Father Chuck made the sign of the cross, then kissed the crucifix hanging around his neck.

He'd been blessing their basement for as long as Vera was alive, sometimes even staying for Sunday dinner. Yet she never really thought much about him, other than the fact that he made her uncomfortable. Not because he did anything inappropriate, but because he was a priest. It was like seeing your high school principal in a bathing suit at the beach. Father Chuck was an adult in a position of authority, a vocation that was revered in her home, so of course, her natural instinct was to never look him in the eye and speak only when spoken to. Now, for the first time, they were walking side by side. Her mom would be livid.

They cut across the overgrown lawn dotted with the wispy wishes of dandelions. Max kept pace beside her, biting his thumbnail as they moved toward the door.

Vera pulled his hand from his mouth. "It's gonna be okay."

She had no idea if this were true, but Max slipped on an awkward grin.

The door was unlocked. Apparently, demons weren't concerned about armed robbery, or maybe they welcomed violent chaos. Father Chuck stepped a cowboy boot in the entry, and immediately a low growl reverberated down the hall, through the living room, and onto the stoop.

Maxwell tensed beside Vera, eyes flinching. That was the sound of his mother. This creature had taken her body and her face, his father's voice, his childhood memories, and his hugs and kisses. And it left that sound.

Vera grabbed his hand. "I got you," she whispered.

They stepped into the house together.

The chalky scent of smoke had grown in texture over the course of a single day—cigarette, marijuana, matchbook, and campfire, now tangled together and dried on their tongues. Max coughed into a fist, trying to force out the stench—or maybe their reality.

No electrical lights were on, and all the curtains and blinds were drawn. The only glow came from the wavering flames of every votive in a knickknack and every taper on a table.

They turned in to the hall, and Vera's chest seized. The layout, the actual physics of the home, looked warped.

Two candle wall sconces were lit, their flames starbursts, beams of gold too luminous and high, bouncing off the white ceiling in odd angles, making the space seem endless. The ivory moldings of the bathroom and bedrooms tilted left and right, zoomed in and out. Was it the smoke? Was it making her dizzy? The floor sloped downward, the gravitational pull adding to the force already reeling in Vera, but more than that, the pine boards seemed to breathe, bowing and heaving with her every step, threatening to give way.

A come-hither hiss slithered down the hall with a curled, bent finger, daring them to keep going. They did, her pulse accelerating and Max's breath in her ear. A gust of wind rushed by, gritty with dry heat, swishing back Vera's black shirt like a parachute. She smoothed it down. Then the front door slammed. Everyone jumped.

"You're back," greeted a baritone voice. "And you brought a priest. It's not even my birthday."

They all paused. This wasn't hypnosis, and this wasn't

some form of "influence." The demon speaking to them now was in complete control of this woman. It possessed her fully. Vera knew that for sure.

"I thought we should be introduced," called the priest, his voice calm, but the hand clutching his crucifix shook with betrayal. "Lilith, I'm Father Chuck."

"Don't waste my time. You're more boring than your sermons, Father. But not your frieeends. They're fun to play with," the voice singsonged, a chorus of guttural tones harmonized inside a human body.

Maxwell's grip grew clammy in Vera's fingers, and when the three of them finally reached the doorway of the master bedroom, Vera slammed to a halt. The space looked massive; his mother rested on the bed, but it seemed impossibly far away. And there was smog. Smoke no longer plumed out of her nose and mouth; instead it was everywhere, hovering in the room like a low-lying cloud. Vera could see his mother's face, but the legs of the bed were obscured. The fog stayed low, oily and swirling.

More black candles lit the room, covering the dresser, the nightstands, the hope chest, and the shrine in the closet. There were assorted bouquets of flowers, and crystal glasses full of dark burgundy wine. There was a dead goat rotting in the closet, flies zigzagging between it and a pile of charred chickens and pigeons, their bodies blackened. People had been here. A lot of people. A lot of offerings. She was holding court.

Vera clutched her stomach as the stench of decomposing flesh mixed with the smoke in the air.

"I would have cleaned up"—his mother gestured to the mess—"but I didn't know you were coming." She formed a Joker's grin.

"Mom?" Max's voice was unsteady, his head flitting around as if unsure where he was. "Can you hear me? Are you in there?"

"Ah, Maxie-boy, your mutha's not here. Wanna talk wit' me?"

Vera's eyes pulled wide, her mouth halfway to the floor. That had to be his father's voice. Max's skin turned dishwater gray, tears springing to his lower lashes.

"It's not real," she whispered.

"Oh, his dad's *real* dead." Its voice returned to a deep bass.

This was beyond cruel. Rage built in Vera's chest, which only added to the hellish joy in its expression.

Then its skin grew brittle. White foam oozed from the corner of its mouth, and its hair shriveled into crusty black cotton candy. But it was the eyes, brimming with fiery vengeance and intellect, that made Vera's chest burn like lava.

It wants you, Vera. Oh, how it wants you. . . .

She forced herself to stand taller.

"I know what happened, between you and my parents." Her voice was strong. Her parents had beaten it before. Or, at least, temporarily. And she was their daughter.

Serpentine sounds sissed with a flicking tongue. "They

failed. All these years, I was right here, and they didn't notice." It leaned forward, body swaying like a cobra. "Others have. Sooo many others."

"Because you prey on the weak," Father Chuck shot back. "Why not pick on someone your own size?"

"Careful, careful. Is that an invitation?" It took a deep inhale, the smog in the room heaving toward its flared crimson nostrils with such force, it lifted Vera onto her toes. "I . . . smell . . . fear. . . ."

Maxwell whimpered. It was involuntary, and Vera knew he was probably embarrassed, but she also understood that this was the person who kissed his boo-boos and tucked him in.

The beast laughed, a snarl of a hell dog barking with delight. "You like 'em weak, don't you? So malleable, aren't they? We have that in common." Its sinister eyes held Vera's. "Tell me—have any good dreams lately?"

Vera dropped Maxwell's hand.

Her dreams. It knew about them.

No, no, no . . . She'd hoped—no, she was convinced—that the sleepwalking and dreams were signs that she was growing into her gift, like her mother. She thought she was coming into her place in the family. She wasn't sure she wanted that, but she was positive she didn't want the alternative. Just the suggestion from her mother had been an insult.

Vera stumbled back a step, her shoulder hitting into the corner of the doorjamb.

"Death is just like falling asleep," it threatened. "Wanna try it?"

"In nómine Patris et Fílii et Spíritus Sancti," Father Chuck recited in Latin, making the sign of the cross.

"So predictable! Don't you see? You're . . . too . . . *weak!*" Its skull thrashed, arms rising. Then the sheet that covered its body fluttered up with its limbs, forming wings, bleached white and sprawling. All at once, the hefty curtains, made of long pearly blackout fabric, tore from the walls with the splintering crack of crumbling Sheetrock. The drapes tumbled to the hardwood floors, cheap metal rods clattering against the boards as the morning sun exploded into the room in perfect spotlight beams. Smoke rose in spiraling bits of grime, pirouetting in a blazing light so blinding, Vera squinched her eyes.

That was when she saw it. For just a moment, a vision crept up from deep inside:

Maxwell's mother is stunning in ivory linen pants and a springy floral blouse. There are balloons in the yard. No, there are three balloons. Maxwell and Chloe grip the milky globes tied with string, waiting for her. But she is here, inside this room, sitting on an unmade bed, her chest constricting so much Vera reaches for her own heart. It has been years, and the grief corroding her soul hasn't lessened. Not for a moment.

Until today.

Endless nights, she's prayed and prayed for a magical fix that will transform her very being back into who she was before, that will stop the constant agony found in moving through each day. But there are no answers. There is no respite.

Then she touched it.

Her fingers brushed against the cool surface of the Angel, and for a fluttering instant the perpetual ache that infiltrated her bones, muscles, organs, and breath lifted into the ether. It was only a flicker, but it was enough to convince her. It is enough to devote her. She wants more. She wants to feel that relief all the time.

Vera watches this woman, this mother, sit in her bedroom and lift the Angel of Tears from a crisp white shopping bag. She carries it to the shelf in her closet. "I can't keep going on like this. I miss you so much, and they deserve better," she whispers, laying fresh lilies on her newly formed shrine. "I just wish everything could go back to the way it was before. I want to feel like I did today, all the time. Make me forget what I lost. Help me move on without this pain. I'll do anything. Anything."

Then the flash was gone.

Vera was again standing in the bedroom, Maxwell at her side, while the priest recited prayers that Vera knew wouldn't work.

"You. Have. No. *Power!*" it screamed at Father Chuck. "I give life. I give death! I feed the mourning, the grieving, the damaged!" Its throaty intonation held dozens, maybe hundreds, of chanting voices inside. *"I bring the claws that slice the flesh of this Earth. They will all join me soon, and together we will fight as one. We will win. We will win! We will win over all!"*

"Hold her down! Help me!" Father Chuck rushed toward the bed. "Grab my bag!" Vera didn't think. She lifted the leather case and raced after him. Max was rooted behind.

Then the priest pointed toward the window, arm stiff, eyes wide. "Vera! No!"

She turned to look.

So did the demon.

The scream of a trumpet rang out from the depths of its throat, and when Vera turned back, a giant syringe was plunged into the beast's neck. The priest beat the devil with a made-you-look trick. Wow. This really wasn't his first rodeo.

"The straps! Now!" He pointed to his bag, and Vera dug into the satchel, navigating past a plastic bucket to find hunks of thick leather. She yanked them out, metal clasps clanging.

Maxwell's mom writhed on the bed. Its eyes rolled upward, neck so rigid Vera could strum the protruding veins.

Then the priest yanked a tan strap from Vera's hands and began securing it to the bed frame. He looped it around one wrist, unafraid to touch the demon, its body now sedated. Whatever was in that needle worked fast.

It let out a roar. Putrid wind gusted from its slobbering jowls, blowing the hair from Vera's cheeks.

Father Chuck darted to her side of the bed, not asking for assistance, and she was not sure she could give it. Whatever he injected weakened the body, but not the mind. Its infernal gaze still burned.

"You like him in your house, don't you?" It hissed. "You like him on your pretty floral sofa. Tell me, does your mother know your impure thoughts?"

Vera bit her lips, drawing blood, refusing to respond, to feed it.

Its bulging eyes blazed toward Max. "Maybe I should tell the girlfriend *your* thoughts? How relieved you are to have that little brat off your hands? How you resent the day your sister was born?"

"Shut up!" Max snapped, stepping forward with a clenched fish.

The corners of its mouth twisted in a sneer.

"Don't speak to it!" hollered the priest, struggling with the second set of restraints as it jerked and twitched. He reached for the plastic bedpan.

"Rather close, aren't you, Father?" It flicked its tongue, licking a glob of spittle from its mouth. "Tell me, am I hiding my true face now? Do you like my mumbo jumbo?"

A spiked ball lodged in Vera's throat. That was what Father Chuck had said an hour ago while discussing TSC. *It sounds like this group is hiding its true face, drawing in folks with its self-help mumbo jumbo, and before they know it, they're leaving offerings for the devil.*

It heard their conversation when they weren't in the room. It knew what her aunt's sofa looked like. It was aware of Vera's dreams.

It was everywhere.

Maybe it really was inside her.

The foul stench of skunked meat grew stronger than the smell of smoke, spinning Vera's already stunned brain. The beast broke out in a cackle.

Father Chuck made the sign of the cross. "Exorcizamus te—" But before he could finish the next word, the beast lifted its knee high and thrust its bare, curled foot so fast into Father Chuck's chest, Vera hardly saw the movement until the priest was reeling across the room.

His body soared as if electrocuted, his aging back cracking against the drywall, a web of fractured lines spreading across the wall's surface. He slumped in a heap by the closet, near the shrine.

Vera rushed toward him, medical procedures clicking through her brain. Then his spine contorted, chest heaving. He wailed, gripping at his rib cage. The muscles in his forearms strained beneath tufts of white hairs. Veins pulsed on his forehead. His eyes burst red with broken blood vessels. He groaned toward the heavens.

It's going to kill him.

Vera pulled at his nearly two-hundred-pound frame, not waiting for a stretcher, a neck brace, or any other protocols. If he didn't get out of this room soon, he was dead. Somehow, she hoisted him to his feet. He found his legs beneath him. She tossed his hairy arm around her shoulders and took his weight. Then she turned to the door, stumbling.

"You'll die! All of you! My gift of death will be unleashed on the world. Embrace me now. Know what others have seen before you. Join your mother! Your father!"

Its threats were a fuzzy buzz in Vera's ears. All of her senses focused on the rise and fall of Father Chuck's chest. His legs could move, and his back could shift. But before her, Maxwell had turned to granite. Smoke swirled at his feet, his eyes hypnotized. *No. Not you.* Vera didn't have time to gently return him to his senses, and she was not about to lose him. She barreled into him, crashing so hard, she practically threw Father Chuck's body like a battering ram. The shock was enough to push Maxwell out of the doorway and into the hall. He thudded against a wall, smacking his head and breaking his hypnotic gaze.

He rubbed his eyes; then, without a word, he grabbed Father Chuck's other arm and flung it over his shoulders.

Together they dragged the priest down the hall.

They heaved him out of the house.

They lugged him into the car.

Then, and only then, did Maxwell start to cry, his body shaking, tears silent.

Vera drove. And for the first time, she thought she finally understood what was happening.

CHAPTER TWENTY-NINE

Max

Max rolled down the rear window, the humid air smacking his face. They were rushing the priest to the hospital. Vera was afraid he was having a heart attack. Father Chuck disagreed. He wanted to return to the rectory. Or maybe to Vera's house? Max wasn't sure. Their words were traveling through a tin can, down a string, and into his brain, all garbled and jumbled by the time they got there.

He leaned into the wind, squinting. The whooshing air dried the sweat on his forehead and brought a din of static, but it didn't stop his hands from shaking or his body from shivering. The humidity was stifling, but his teeth were chattering. Why were his teeth chattering?

He wrapped his arms around his chest, curling in to stop the quivering. He thought he might vomit. A plop of liquid hit his forearm. He opened his eyes and stared at the little round droplet; it traced a path down the back of his hand toward the soft pocket between his thumb and forefinger. Another fell.

He touched his eyes. He was crying.

His house was smoking.

His hallway stretched like taffy and tried to gobble his feet.

His mother was a demon.

She spoke like his father.

She threatened to kill him.

Or did she threaten to kill everyone? Did it matter?

"Maxwell, Maxwell . . ." He could hear a voice calling to him. *"Stay with me, Maxwell. . . ."*

His mother was possessed, sputtering nonsense, and collecting carcasses.

"Max, breathe. We're almost there," said the voice.

It was Vera. That was who he clung to now. Vera Martinez. The entire future of his family—his mother, his little sister, *him*—all depended on a girl he never before said hi to in the hallways. They said hi now. They said a lot more than hi.

"Max, you're going into shock. Stay with me."

There was a fog *inside* his house, swirling and pulsing. And the master bedroom grew three sizes. Ha! Like the Grinch. *His mother's room grew three sizes that day!* But that wasn't his mother.

Her voice never emerged. But his father's did.

The car creaked to a halt. A hand tugged his arm. He didn't want to move. He was safe in the car. Safe was good.

"Max, I get it now," the voice said. No, *she* said. "I know how it lures people. I know why your mom bought the shrine, what she wanted."

His head turned toward her. He parted his lips to respond, but his mouth was too dry to speak.

She pulled his arm again, and he let her.

He rose from the car and he followed her into the hospital.

He was given an IV drip of fluids, but other than that, Max was fine. So was Father Chuck, bruised but nothing broken. The only things really damaged were Max's ego and his sanity. He almost wished he were having a medical emergency, because it would be a whole lot better than his current reality.

Vera took him home. Well, to her home. His house was currently under a dense fog advisory with an underlying demonic pressure system.

He sat on Vera's floral sofa, which the demon inside his mother had accurately described. (What else did it see?) A pink fuzzy blanket was wrapped around his shoulders as he sipped a mug of mint tea. He was getting used to the taste, and he wasn't sure if that was a good or bad thing.

"Feeling better?" Aunt Tilda asked as she tidied the room.

She'd already made a chicken casserole, given his sister a bath, read her three books, and put her to bed. Aunt Tilda was a better parent than he was, but the demon was wrong about how that made Max feel. He wasn't relieved to relinquish responsibility for Chloe, at least not in that way, and he didn't resent the day she was born (he resented the day his father *died*—same day, different event). In fact, Max was relieved Chloe was finally getting the parenting she deserved, the kind he'd had before the explosion. For the first time in a long time, he and Chloe were *both* being taken care of, and Max appreciated that.

That meant the demon could be wrong.

"I'm as good as I can be," Max responded, letting the blanket fall from his shoulders.

"That's all we can ask for," said Aunt Tilda.

Vera entered the room, her hair wet, forming black ringlets around her face. She was wearing purple plaid pajama pants and a white tank top, and she looked, well, really pretty. How had he not noticed this before? How did the whole school not notice?

Max was surprised the demon didn't reveal *those* thoughts, because he had them. All the time.

"You've got color in your cheeks," Vera said.

Yeah, I'm sure I do. Her skin smelled of vanilla, which reminded him of Delilah. She wore a similar lotion. When was the last time he replied to Delilah's texts? Or spoke to any of his friends? He imagined the essay he'd write at the start of school in September: "On my summer vacation, I helped to perform an exorcism."

Christ, I'm all over the place.

"Sorry I freaked back there," he muttered, staring at his hands.

"Don't apologize. I can't imagine. That's your . . ." She

didn't finish her sentence. Because it was too awful to say. *That's your* mom. *That person, saying those things, with* that *voice, is your mother.*

"How come I heard my dad today?" he asked.

"That's *not* your dad. It's just messing with your head."

"It's working."

Vera ran her fingers through her damp hair, her cheeks dewy from the shower. Then she exchanged a curious look with Aunt Tilda, who finished folding an afghan and placed it on the back of an easy chair. "I'll leave you two to talk."

Vera lowered herself beside him. "I had a vision at your house."

"A vision?" His eyes crinkled.

"I'm not really sure what it was, I've stopped trying to understand, but I *saw* something." Her voice was low and sounded as confused as he felt. "It's never happened to me before. It was different than the dreams, the sleepwalking. When your mom, when *it* lifted its arms, when it took the shape of those wings and the light flooded in, it was like I was hit inside my mind. A scene unfolded."

She peered at him, seeming worried about his reaction. Because *he* was the weakling; he was the one who went into shock and couldn't handle what was happening. He tugged at his knotted neck, glancing at the floor and realizing he cared a lot about what she thought of him.

"I saw you and your sister in your backyard, holding white balloons."

Max's head whipped toward her. How could she know that? How could she *possibly* know about that? He didn't even discuss this with his friends.

"Your mother was inside, in her bedroom, and she was . . . *sad*. Max, she was so sad I felt like my ribs were cracking and stabbing my heart." Vera grimaced. "She purchased the Angel of Tears the same day as the balloons. And it was like the moment she touched the statue, all the agony inside her went away—only for a second, though. I watched her set up the shrine in the closet, with some lilies. You and Chloe were outside waiting for her, and she mumbled that she couldn't 'go on like this.' She wanted everything to go back to the way it was before. She wanted that tiny pain-free moment to last, to forget, or feel numb, all the time. She said she'd do 'anything.'"

Max ground his teeth. *She* couldn't go on. *She*, the parent, was having a hard time.

He'd been going to school, working at the restaurant, taking Chloe to playdates, talking to the other moms, and trying to pretend like none of this was happening. His hands balled into fists. A lot of people lost someone the day of the explosion or in the days since (including him!), but they weren't worshipping demons, abandoning their children, or praying to forget their families. She did that, on *that day*.

"Are you okay?"

"No." He huffed like "okay" was a concept in science fiction. "I can't believe she bought a demonic statue on my dad's *birthday*. She wanted to forget him *on that day*. Every year we each write a note to him and tie it to the string of a white balloon, then we release it into the air. We never got a real chance to say goodbye, so this is sort of our way."

"That's really sweet."

"Yeah, for me and Chloe. Apparently not for her."

Vera reached for his hand and unfolded his fist, then she intertwined her fingers with his. "When's his birthday?"

"May eighth."

About a month before school ended. *She said she'd do anything.* Max repeated those words in his head.

"When I saw your mom in that vision, her grief was so profound it hurt to breathe." Vera released his hand, palm on her chest. "I think that's how the group goes from self-help to demon worship. Once the followers are good and brainwashed, swallowing all the crap the cult is shoveling, what's a little statue in the closet? The cult says that leaving gifts might solve their problems, then they give them one little taste of relief from their pain. That numbness, it's like a drug. Your mom would have done *anything* to feel that way again."

"Well, she definitely did *anything*." Max squeezed his eyes, pinching the bridge of his nose, his body flooded with shame. His mother had willingly done this. *Had she thought about him or Chloe at all?* "So now what?" His tone was exasperated. "How do we fix this? How do we stop this, if it feeds on grief and half the town is grieving something?"

"Exactly." Vera's voice perked up. He looked her way, and her big brown eyes sparked to life. "The explosion happened after the storm, and I think it was the first event, the first *big* event, caused by the demon. The explosion sent the town reeling into despair and shock, and that's how the demon started feeding, growing stronger. . . ."

Wait. Max jolted, eyes wide. "You're saying the demon didn't *arrive* with the explosion, but it *caused* the explosion. That means this thing is not only trying to take away my mother right *now*, but it already *took* away my father." He blinked, pegs falling into place. "It killed my dad. That's why it talks like him."

"I think so. Maybe."

Time froze. A gnat stopped its flight in midair.

Max should have realized. When she'd mentioned the hurricane and the chalice, he was so consumed with what was happening with his mom, he didn't fully deduce how it could tie into his dad.

All at once, something shifted inside him. All the desolation, all the confusion, all of the anguish he'd felt these past seven years, he now had a place to put it—in a sizzling pit of rage that burned with blue flames inside his chest.

This thing took his father—and seventeen other people from Roaring Creek. He thought of all the suicides, all the car wrecks, and all his dead classmates; they were brainwashed. It stole them. And now it was *inside* of his mother, gnawing on her and using her to infest the entire town.

"We have to stop it." His voice was firm.

"I spoke to my parents. They booked a flight that will get them home, not tomorrow, but the next day. They *will* stop it. Until then, Father Chuck's going to get some people to set up shop outside your house and make sure no one goes inside."

"How are they going to do that?" he scoffed. A handful of churchgoers against a cult and a demon sent from Hell?

"I don't know. They just will." She shrugged. "And I have to get those shrines out of the hospital. Maybe instead of the higher-ups, I'll go to the janitors, the orderlies, the food service staff. See if people will 'accidentally' dump the statues into the trash while patients are asleep. We *have* to stop this from spreading, at least until my parents get home. I feel so useless. . . ."

"How can you say that?" he spat, forehead wrinkled at the absurdity. Without her, who knows what would be happening to him and Chloe? To his mother?

"You heard the demon. It knew about my dreams—everything. All the sleepwalking, the visions, could be coming *from* the demon." Her voice broke, a touch of fear slipping through. Max noticed her hands were shaking. "I can't believe anything anymore."

Max placed a palm on hers. "That's not true. *I* believe you." His tone was certain. "The demon was wrong today. When it said I was relieved that your aunt took Chloe off my hands, that I wish she were never born, that *isn't* true. Yes, I'm glad your aunt's here and she's doing an amazing job, but that's not how I feel at all. And I'm not just saying that."

Vera peered at him, her head tilted like she was trying to translate his words from another language.

"If the demon could be wrong about *that*, then it could be wrong about a lot of things. It could be wrong about *you*," Max insisted.

Vera's gaze turned to the carpet and Max could see the endless questions swirling behind her chocolate eyes. Somehow Vera was so certain in the abilities of her parents, the priest, and a group of random strangers the church was assembling, yet she was unsure of herself. Since the day they started speaking, Vera repeated again and again that she wasn't special. Now she was having visions and dreams—that Max truly believed—while remaining remarkably calm in a house with the devil.

She had to realize how amazing she was. Max did.

But it seemed that after seventeen years of being treated like the outcast, Vera actually believed that she didn't deserve to be noticed, that she lacked any special gifts. In reality, it was always girls like her, the overlooked ones, the misjudged ones, who changed the world.

CHAPTER THIRTY

The Explosion

In a far-too-silent split-level home, a father watches his son. The child lies in bed, much too still. The time has come. The mother clutches his tiny hand, indigo veins popping beneath his nearly translucent skin. They are waiting on the edge of an hourglass, all the sand nearly slipped through. They pray. They beg.

He's only had twelve years on this Earth. That's not enough time. There's never enough time.

The mother's eyes are closed, hand clenched to her heaving chest, slick with tears.

The father's lips are pressed in a firm line. If he parts them, he'll scream. He'll howl. He might never stop.

His boy gets worse. The lights dim inside him; his soul flickers on a low wattage. This is wrong, all wrong. His breath grows shallow. Is his chest still moving? Yes, the father thinks. The machine still beeps. They need the machine. He hears it in his nightmares. He wakes sopped in sweat with the eerie tone of the dreaded flatline ringing in his ears.

The home-care nurse says they must prepare. It's weeks now. Maybe days.

They've done nothing wrong. This child has done nothing wrong. What kind of a God would do this?

Then he remembers: a friend from Chicago, years ago. He got a miracle. A dark, but oh-so-worth-it, miracle.

The father returns with a gift, telling tales of its power and beauty. He says it can heal.

They'll try anything.

He sets the statue of the angel by the boy's bed. Its wings point toward the heavens while the skeleton's hands clutch the skull carved atop a torch, its unlit flame pointing at his son's pale cheeks. Dark tears stain the angel's face, matching the mood in the room. The air is stagnant from sealed windows and growing despair, yet plaid sheets are pulled high to the boy's chin. The mother fears he'll catch cold. She bathes him daily. She brushes his hair. She cannot handle this.

No mother should have to handle this.

The father places a hand on the small marble statue and shuts his eyes. "Take me. Take me instead. Please spare my boy. Give him more time," he prays. But who is he praying to?

Nothing happens at first. So he does what he is told.

The next day he brings sweet red wine. Dessert wine. They can't afford it; they're buried under medical bills. What's one more debt?

Then he brings bread, so fresh that flour films the pads of his fingers as the room takes in the welcome new scent.

Next he offers salt, thick grains from the ocean, a natural force greater than all of them, as great as the universe.

He digs flowers straight from the garden, potting them in rich dark soil.

The sea and the earth. He is offering the world.

His boy keeps breathing, but he doesn't improve.

The man needs more, a grander sacrifice.

Words whisper inside, wheedling into his brain and implanting themselves deep in gray matter.

You know what to do, *they say.* You know, you know . . .

He does. The answer is tattooed on his mind. Buzz, buzz, buzz. Etch, etch, etch. He has been chosen to do this. It is his purpose. It is how he will save his son. He can't think of anything else. Anyone else.

This is his mission.

He wakes up for work. He eats crisp bacon and eggs scrambled with cheese, then swills a cup of coffee so hot it scorches his tongue. His last meal. It is bitter. He kisses his wife, his lips lingering longer than they have in years. The smell of her, sweet gardenia—somewhere in all of this grief, this torment, they'd forgotten each other. They'd forgotten to be people. He remembers her now in that red gingham dress the day they met, her long honey hair cascading over her shoulder. She smelled of gardenia then.

He says nothing, but somehow she senses. She knows him well, and she doesn't stop him.

He joins his crew, as he has for twenty years. His tan

coveralls are buckled on his broad shoulders. His work boots are laced. His white hard hat is firm on his head, though he needs no protection now.

They were hired to repair the one-hundred-year-old gas lines cutting below Roaring Creek and into the public buildings. The crews are massive, and no one notices when he slips away.

No one notices the fumes.

But he can smell them. Taste them. The power they give him, over life and death. His son's life. Nothing else matters. Not anyone else, and especially not himself.

He waits on a concrete step, hands folded in his lap, cracked and rough from a life's hard work. He doesn't cry, nor does he leave to save himself. He stays. He is the offering, the ultimate sacrifice. This is his choice, his deal with the Angel of Tears—his life in exchange for his son's. What parent wouldn't make that trade? The others are merely a bonus—dessert offerings, a little extra sprinkle to sweeten the deal.

It's an easy decision, but still his pulse pounds within him. He can feel it in his throat, his last pumps of life, and he savors them as he relinquishes control of this world. The Angel is everything. He will do anything for it, anything it says.

He hears it then, the tick, tick, tick of a stove's burner trying to catch upstairs. Instantly, flames erupt above him, a blast so colossal it might split the Earth. It takes only moments for the fireball to plume down the staircase. It's barreling toward him, toward everyone around. As the fiery mushroom *cloud approaches, he spreads his arms wide as wings. His last thoughts before the spiraling inferno engulfs him are* I've done it. I've done it for you.

He burns. Sheep shriek above him, sacrificial lambs roasting on an unseen altar.

It is over.

But only for them.

On the other side of town, as the flesh of the innocent are combusting to ash, a boy awakens. His mother is at his side, clutching his hand full of wires. She's always clutching his hand.

"What happened?" he asks. "Mom?"

Tears flow from her eyes in a steady stream as she kisses his head, that perfect blond head. He smells like a newborn babe wrapped in a receiving blanket, the fresh powder of a life starting anew. Spring petals sprout on his cheeks. His grip tightens. He feels strong.

"You're okay. It's okay," says the mother.

He's done it, she thinks. *He's really done it.*

She knows her husband is gone. She doesn't know how, not yet, but she knows. She can feel it as though someone whispered it in her ear. Or something.

She looks at the shrine by the son's bedside and places a hand on the Angel.

Thank you, *she prays.* You've answered our prayers. You've heard us. I will do anything for you. I will do anything now. . . .

She spreads its word.
She adds her offerings.
Her son gets better.
And the town grieves.

CHAPTER THIRTY-ONE

Vera

"Vera, wake up!"

Her aunt's fingers dug into her shoulders, and Vera felt her head rock limply with every shake. Her eyes opened to find she was standing on the precipice of the staircase.

"I heard your door open—caught you just in time," said Aunt Tilda, yanking her from the edge.

Vera stared down the steep steps to the stained-glass church windows below, knowing exactly where she was headed, where her dreams wanted to take her.

"I had another one." Vera was breathless, sweat gluing her hair to the back of her neck.

"A nightmare?"

"A vision." Vera corrected her.

They moved to Aunt Tilda's bedroom and sat on her mattress in the dim incandescent light of an antique glass lamp. Religious portraits hung from her aunt's walls, along with a crucifix and some spiritual carvings. Aunt Tilda encased herself with God to ward off the evil pulsating from the basement. It wasn't a bad plan.

Vera described her dream.

"He thought he was saving his son. That was why he did it. It felt so *real*." Vera plunged her hands into her hair. "Aunt Tilda, if these dreams are coming from the demon—like my mom thinks—then why would the demon want me to know *this*? Why would it show me the secrets of how it works? How it lures people? What it promises?"

"The devil plays tricks," her aunt stated simply.

"Do you feel the devil, right now? Do you *feel* any darkness within me?" Vera peered at her earnestly.

She may not be as gifted as her sister, but Aunt Tilda had an extra sense.

"No." Her aunt shook her head. "I don't."

"Neither do I. Maxwell said the demon was wrong today, about his feelings for Chloe. And I think it's wrong about my dreams. *That's* the trick. These dreams, these feelings, are *real*, and it wants me to believe otherwise." Vera's throat grew thick, tears collecting one on top of the other. "Aunt Tilda, Seth Durand wasn't a bad man. He wasn't evil, not before that day. He killed *all those people* as some sort of offering. How could he do that?"

Vera sniffled, unsure why she was crying. For him, because of him, for everyone who died? She reached for a Kleenex from the box on the nightstand. Seth Durand said he would do *anything*, just like Maxwell's mother did. Vera balled the tissue in her fist, squeezing out her fears, her throbbing head, her dark visions—she wanted it all out.

"He made a choice," her aunt replied. "People aren't born

evil. Lucifer wasn't always the devil. He was once the morning star, God's second-in-command. Then he *chose* pride and was sent to Hell."

"Clearly, he didn't stay there." Vera huffed.

Aunt Tilda nodded in agreement. "We've seen a lot of evil in this house, and we keep saying you have to invite it in, but maybe *invite* is the wrong word. The line that separates good and bad, it doesn't exist *out there* somewhere in need of an invitation." She twirled her veiny hand in the air. "It's inside you, but not like cancer, not like something you can't control. It's a *choice*. People know right from wrong. They know not to cross the street until the light says *Walk*, but sometimes they cross anyway; they think the rules don't apply to them, and they don't care who gets hurt. The man who caused the explosion, he made a choice; it was unthinkable, and we *all* got hurt."

"But he saved his son."

"And killed *seventeen* others, not to mention the permanently injured and the families he destroyed. All to do a demon's bidding. And now the son he saved is leading a cult."

"But the Sunshine people think the group is helping them, that they're learning empowerment and getting grief counseling." Vera considered Samantha and her mom. They were good people, smart people. How could they not see what was happening? If this group could get to them, it could get to anyone.

Aunt Tilda shook her head like it wasn't that simple.

"Yes, when they bought that book, they were seeking something to bring them peace of mind. But at some point, they let that man's words replace their own. They abandoned all logic and reason and agreed that he alone had all the answers. He told them *death* was better than living, and they agreed. Blindly." She handed Vera another tissue, the good kind with lotion. "He could probably stand in the town square and commit mass murder, and they'd somehow find it justified. Why? Because he said he could solve their problems, take away their pain, and that somehow gave them the right to inflict pain on others. The devil's in that."

Vera wiped her nose once more. "But Maxwell's mom, she didn't intend for *this* to happen. She didn't know what she was doing. She couldn't have. She was just hurting."

"You're probably right, which is why Satan, the Angel of Tears, cult leaders, seek out the most desperate and seduce them with magical solutions and impossible promises."

"And we're supposed to compete with that? There's all this evil in the world, and only Mom and Dad fighting it? That's ridiculously crappy odds." Vera slapped the mattress. Her aunt grabbed her hand, holding it flat between both of her own.

"There are a lot more than just your parents." Aunt Tilda's gray braid slid over her shoulder. "Sometimes people choose evil, but they can also choose to be heroes, like you, and Father Chuck, and Maxwell. That's how good prevails."

"You sound like that cheesy quote." Vera strained to remember her eighth-grade social studies teacher. She had a poster on the wall. *The only way for evil to triumph is for good people to do nothing.*

"Exactly." Aunt Tilda squeezed Vera's hand, her warmth spreading. "People sometimes face horrible choices, and it's not easy to choose the brave thing."

So exactly what was Vera's choice here? She wasn't an exorcist like her father, and she didn't have superpowers like her mother, but maybe she could get through to Samantha? If she could somehow show her, and everyone like her, that they were worshipping a demon, and not a guru, maybe Vera could halt the damage. She could prevent someone else from losing themself like Mrs. Oliver or becoming murderous like Seth Durand.

Vera was about to voice this idea to her aunt, when the slam of a storm door grabbed her attention. Her head whipped toward the window in time with her aunt's. It was nearly one in the morning, but she knew that sound, a metallic crash they heard five times a day, whenever Mr. Zanger let out his dog.

Vera rose from the four-poster bed and ambled to the curtains, swishing back the ivory lace. Her aunt pressed beside her in a fuzzy sea-green robe.

A motion sensor flicked on, casting a too-bright beam on Mr. Zanger and his tiny white puff. He rested the dog on the grass, and its twiggy legs immediately kicked backward.

"Seriously, he needs to get that thing a litter box," Vera muttered, and it was as if the dog heard her through the double-paned glass. Its head shot up, cocked to the side, white fluffy ear hanging down as its black eyes peered straight inside her. It started yapping. Not its normal bark, not even its I-want-to-eat-your-ankles bark. The pooch began spinning in circles, rapidly chasing its tail. Its high-pitched yaps bordered on squeals as it turned faster and faster.

"Snowball! Heel!" yelled Mr. Zanger. "Sit!"

The dog paused, then yipped and squealed once more, its round eyes pointed directly at Vera. It bounced on its tiny legs.

"What is wrong with that thing?" asked Vera.

Mr. Zanger's eyes sliced through the night. Maybe he felt them, or maybe he wanted to see what his dog was howling about—either way, the moment the man's eyes turned upward, the pet ran. Not toward his home, not even toward Vera's home, it ran *away*. The little puff streaked straight to the back fence, which consisted of two wooden horizontal beams designating the lines of the property. It offered no protection, no security.

"Where is it going?" Vera's body shifted toward the doorway.

She should go down and help. Mr. Zanger was too old to chase after an animal. It was dark.

Aunt Tilda grabbed her arm. "You won't be useful."

"The dog could get lost." Despite how the man treated her, Vera didn't want him to lose Snowball. That puff was all he had.

"Yes, but the animal hates us. If we go anywhere near it,

it will keep running. He'll have a better chance of calling it back if we're nowhere around."

Aunt Tilda had a point. But still, guilt sank to the depths of Vera's gut. Mr. Zanger's wife died years ago, he had no children, and no friends came to visit. He was about as pathetic as she was, only crotchety. He needed that pet.

"The dog will come back." Aunt Tilda patted her elbow. "Get some sleep."

Vera nodded. Her aunt was probably right. The dog correctly sensed the evil in their house, and so did Mr. Zanger. The Angel of Tears was released from these walls. Darkness lurked in their basement.

But Vera was not choosing to do nothing.

She marched to her bedroom and snatched her phone from its charging station. She didn't care how late it was.

To Chelsea: *Text me as soon as you get this. We need to talk about Sam.*

CHAPTER THIRTY-TWO

Max

It was his idea. Though Max had to convince Vera.

Her friend Chelsea, from the hospital, informed them that the Sunshine Crew was hosting a rally in the town square at noon. Actually, *rally* was probably the wrong word. It was more like a free summer camp. There was going to be an adult obstacle course with a rock-climbing wall, a dance party with a DJ for kids, and a stage hosting a smattering of speeches to encourage indoctrination. Chelsea agreed to approach their coworkers—janitors, orderlies, food service, anyone complaining about being creeped out—and convince them to "accidentally" remove as many Angel shrines as possible. She also promised to keep her girlfriend far away from Max's house, without even asking why. Vera said she just seemed happy to do *something*.

It was over the *something* that Max and Vera disagreed.

Vera wanted to break up the rally, bring a bullhorn and shout, *You're all worshipping a demon! You're in a cult and being brainwashed!* Like people would listen to *her*. Max couldn't say it to her face, but he knew she was aware of her family's reputation.

He gently encouraged a different approach.

Max slowed his truck outside the home of the *other* most notorious family in Roaring Creek. It was unassuming—an old split-level, half stone and half white siding. It had black shutters and a black door. There was a faux floral wreath. The sidewalk was cracked and the shrubs looked scrawny. It was a house fit for a mailman, a school secretary, or, apparently, a cult leader.

Max felt insulted for Vera. Legions of Sunshine Crew followers flocked to the home of the family that blew up the town, yet they thought *her* house was cursed. In seventh grade, on Mischief Night, the ultimate act of bravery was to run onto Vera's front porch and ring the doorbell. That was it. That's how scared their classmates were of her family. Given the fact that Max now knew there were actual demonic artifacts filling the Martinez basement, maybe his classmates had a point. But still, the Durand house had launched a demonic cult.

Max stepped out of his truck, Vera slamming her door shut in time with his own.

"If we get caught . . ." Her voice trailed off like she didn't want to finish the sentence.

"We won't," he insisted, with enough conviction he almost believed himself.

They started up the driveway, and a seagull shrieked

from the rooftop. The windows were dim, the inhabitants busy across town brainwashing new members. That was the basis for his plan. They had time. Maybe they could find evidence to tie the Sunshine Crew to the Angel of Tears, and the Angel of Tears to criminal activity, and then bring it to the cops. They could shut it all down legally. The odds of success were flimsy, but it was better than sitting on their hands waiting for a flight from Barcelona to arrive tomorrow.

Father Chuck called earlier. He said the "prayer circle" was still in effect outside of Max's house, near his mother's bedroom window. Max didn't know what the prayers were accomplishing, but he appreciated knowing his mother was still inside. She was safe—at least her body was. She wasn't in the town square morphing into a beast for all of Roaring Creek to see. She wasn't hurting anyone, aside from her children. As long as she was there, they had time to wait for Vera's parents to save her soul. And maybe they might find something inside of the Durands' house that could help them save her.

They reached the front door and Max peered through a long, slender side window. The living room could have been his own—plaid navy sofa, brick fireplace with a brass-trimmed screen, silk purple tulips on the mantel, and a remote on a Target coffee table. It was so normal.

Vera turned the knob and pushed. The door didn't budge. She squatted down to search beneath the gritty welcome mat. No key. He didn't think it would be that easy.

"Follow me." Max moved with purpose around the edge of the home, eyes flicking toward the neighbors. Not a curtain swished, not a shadow moved. He crept toward a rickety, handmade wooden deck in need of a new coat of stain that led to what was likely the kitchen. He moved carefully up the splintered steps, Vera close enough that he could hear her nervous breathing.

"Is this a good idea?" she whispered.

Probably not, but the house looked about as old as his own, with the exact same style of windows—screens on the outside of original wood-trimmed glass panes. Growing up, Max's parents were constantly at the restaurant, meaning he frequently returned from school to an empty house. More than once he forgot his keys and had to break in, achieving expert status years ago.

Max twisted his neck to peer at Vera, a rush of adrenaline coursing through him as he pressed an index finger to his lips. He then grabbed his keys and slid one into the seam alongside the grimy screen. It took surprisingly little effort to pop it loose. He gripped it with outstretched arms, placing the screen on the deck, resting it against the brick wall. Vera's face showed more fear than it did in his mother's bedroom. He restrained a smile. This was probably the most fun he'd had since he'd met her.

He reached for the mullions of the window, his fingers long and flat against the glass as he pushed up. It slid easily, unlocked. Now his smile stretched wide.

"After you." He swept his hand toward the now-open cavern—a dining room with birds on the wallpaper.

"What if they have a silent alarm?"

Max's brow furrowed. "This isn't Fort Knox. The guy didn't even lock his windows. I'm surprised the door's not open."

Vera didn't move.

"It's now or never." Max placed his hands on the windowsill, the rusty metal tracks cutting into his palms, then he hoisted his head and torso through.

No turning back now, Max thought as he wiggled his legs and landed on the hardwood floor.

He gazed through the opening at Vera, whose doe eyes were wide as the noonday sun backlit her hair, making the dark strands glow. For a girl surrounded by evil, it seemed she hadn't done much wrong in her life.

He extended his hand. "Let's see what the Big Bad Wolf is hiding."

For a moment, Vera's lips turned up and he caught a flash of excitement in her eyes. *That's the spirit.*

She followed him through.

———

They started with the bedrooms. No one hides criminal evidence in the kitchen pantry. (Actually, maybe they should.)

They tiptoed up the creaky stairs, Vera gripping the back of his black T-shirt as though they were in a haunted house on Halloween and a wicked clown might pop out at any moment.

"Which room do you think is his?" Max whispered as they reached the landing.

Three doors were closed before them, while another was open to a shared bathroom. The hall was small, so much so he could stretch his arms and almost touch every knob.

"That one." Vera pointed to the room adjacent to the bathroom.

Max didn't doubt her. He inched closer, a cloud of dust dancing in the light of the bathroom window. Moisture hung in the air from someone having showered recently without running the fan. Max wrinkled his nose, reaching his fingers for the scratched brass knob.

He was entering the room of the devil, or at least the room of the man who summoned the devil.

Max turned the knob and pushed it open, the wooden door scratching against the gray-blue carpet fibers.

The space was small. The walls were painted a cement gray and the full bed sat dead center, no headboard. There was a navy-and-green-plaid comforter rumpled at the foot, its hunter-green sheets twisted and unmade. Two maple nightstands sat on either side of it, mismatching. Atop the one closest to the window, with a bright ray of sun beaming down, was a small marble statue of the Angel. It sat on an ivory place mat that looked hand-embroidered, and it was surrounded by a pack of menthol cigarettes, a set of car keys, a small crystal bowl of what appeared to be sea salt, a conch shell, and a tiny bud vase holding a single bloom—a tangerine lily.

Max reached for his throat. He'd been in the room only seconds, not long enough for the pollen to cause a reaction, but he swore his throat was closing. Choking.

"The staff of the torch," Max croaked. "It's pointing right at his bed. How can he sleep like that?"

A skeleton dripping black tears gazed longingly at the pillow, waiting for its inhabitant. Watching. Ready. Max couldn't peel his eyes away, his pulse sprinting beneath his skin. That statue—all of the horror inflicted on his life was because of that twelve-inch trinket worthy of a novelty store. Max marched toward it, eyes reduced to slits. Someone blew up his father because of this. Something infected his mother because of this.

He lifted it from the makeshift shrine. It was so light and puny, a participation trophy from a Little League baseball team. His fingers tightened around it. It wasn't even marble. It felt like a cheap stone you could carve your name into with a steak knife. He made no conscious choice to bend his right elbow, to strain his shoulder as far back as it would reach and then slam the cursed hunk against the opposite wall with a satisfying crack.

He'd forgotten Vera was there until she yelped, black wavy hair swishing with surprise as cracked pieces of statue landed in chunks at her sandaled feet. Too close.

"Are you okay?" Max gasped, rushing over.

"I'm fine," she murmured, though her voice sounded strained. She didn't look him in the eyes.

Max stretched for the largest piece of remaining statue—the torso and two severed wings that now rested like an offering at her feet. The toothy edges felt sharp against his fingers as he held it out to her. "Want to take a turn? It's surprisingly satisfying."

Vera shifted toward the object, her gaze unfocused, head tilted as if unsure what he was presenting. Tentatively, she extended a delicate hand, cautiously inching as if the stone piece might be combustible.

Her nail brushed the surface of the wing, the slightest graze with the tip of her finger.

Then Vera hit the floor.

CHAPTER THIRTY-THREE

Vera

"Death is a superior state of consciousness. All confines of this plane do not exist once you cross over. You will be one spirit with the loved ones who have gone before you, and those you leave behind will reap the glory of your sacrifice. I know. I am living proof," insists the man, a healthy glow on his face, proving his righteousness. The spirit spared his life, and he has made it his mission to share his gift with the world.

Rows of tan metal folding chairs fill the cool cinder-block space, adding to the temporary feel of the group, of their existence. Around Vera, there are candles flickering high in glass jars perched on wall sconces, Walmart tabletops, and dirty garden pedestals. Sweaty bodies press together, too many for the seats. On the concrete floor sit children cross-legged, some only toddlers. Infants are cradled on laps.

Vera hovers above the worshippers in this basement that reeks of mold, cat urine, and Christmas potpourri. She watches their heads bow in reverence to the most average guy in the world. She is an ethereal observer. They can't see her in this room with no windows, no air.

"Join hands with your neighbors now, because you are not going alone. The sun that lights our days is also a star, just like those that light our nights. We are the same. Life and death are stages of the same existence, and soon we will embrace this next phase together."

Everyone nods, humming with a drugged cadence as his words burrow into them, digging so deep that all prior thoughts and beliefs collapse. Vera spies Samantha sitting in the front row, eyes glistening, mouth hanging open in adoration. A girl no older than five squirms on the ground in front of her, and Samantha's mother pats the child's curly red hair. Collectively the group leans forward. Toward him. It is all about him.

Lining the walls are boxes piled high like moving day, brown paper sides bulging. Vera floats toward them, gazing inside. Yellow hats with a stupid logo. Ceramic magnets. Piles of hardback books self-published with a Comic Sans font. Caches upon caches of shrines to the Angel of Tears.

"We are all sharing an insignificant, temporary experience on Earth. This life is merely a bus stop, a brief discomfort to be gotten through before journeying on to our true destination," the young man preaches, pacing before his worshippers. "The afterlife is endless harmony. Your loved ones yearn for you to join them. So I ask you, Why are we waiting? Why not ascend to that higher plane now? We are the chosen believers. Are you not ready?"

Eyes shoot up in unison, heads bobbing loosely, palms raised.

"Yes!"

"We're with you!"

"I'm ready!"

A baby wails, then there is a glint of starburst. Vera can't detect its source, but it draws her attention, pulling her near. Vera floats to the altar, fashioned from a cheap dining table and holding a supersized statue of the Angel of Tears. Beside it is another cardboard box.

Even here, even in a space outside of herself, Vera is chilled with icy particles of dread.

She hovers above the carton, peering inside.

Chalices.

Dozens upon dozens are stacked in bubble wrap, their gold trim gleaming through the rippling plastic.

They are waiting to be distributed.

They are waiting to be drunk from.

Together.

In unison.

One last drink.

Forever.

———

"No!" Vera shouted, eyes blinking rapidly as the bedroom came back into focus. She was on her back, goose bumps covering her arms, staring at a burnt-orange water stain on an unfamiliar ceiling. Had she fallen?

"Vera? Talk to me. You're freezing." Max's hands gripped

her shoulders, shaking her slightly as she returned to her senses.

God, this room. Her eyes danced around at the plaid bedspread, the dated furniture, the bland wall color. It was exactly as it had been when the boy lay there on the brink of death, his mother sobbing and clutching his hand while his father placed the statue by his side. The shrine wasn't just on that nightstand, it was the entire room, a devotion not just to the Angel of Tears but to his father, Seth Durand, to the man who blew up Roaring Creek. This was a time capsule to his sacrifice, his destruction.

"Are you okay?" Max's words were slow and deliberate, as though she might not understand.

"Yes. I mean, no." Vera sat up abruptly, the room spinning on a merry-go-round. She wobbled, and Max steadied her shoulders once more. "It's evil. *He's* evil."

"No kidding," Max quipped. "What happened? You passed out."

"A vision." She raised her hand to her pounding head, her fingers icicles. "It's mass suicide. That's what it wants. That's what they're planning—full Kool-Aid. I saw Anatole trying to convince them. There are *little kids.*" Her voice broke.

The rally, the carnival events. Anatole Durand was oozing through the town square right now recruiting more offerings to the Angel of Tears. That was the endgame—to consume Roaring Creek with enough grief that its weakened citizens would obey whispered commands to blow up buildings and down cups of poison. Once the monster overtook their small town, its empowered shadow would spread across the rest of the world, one mass tragedy at a time.

"Are you sure?" Max asked, sounding shocked.

Vera nodded. "The basement, it's full of chalices—boxes of them—just like the one that broke in my house during the hurricane. I'm not sure when, but he's going to fill them with poison and distribute them—"

"Not if he can't find them." Max popped to his feet. "Maybe we can't stop the devil ourselves, but we can slow it down a bit. Turns out I like breaking things." He nodded to the remnants of a statue littering the carpet around her.

It was a start, something they could do.

Max extended a palm and helped Vera to her unstable feet, her body swaying and her stomach sloshing. She took a slow breath.

"Can you walk?" He looked concerned.

"Just a head rush." She pressed her temples, hands still frozen. It was as if the chill of the room, the vision, stayed with her. This was new. Whatever was surging inside her was growing rapidly.

He clasped her hand. "I got you."

She followed Max out of the room and down the six steps to the cookie-cutter living room. Off the kitchen was another small set of stairs that would lead them to a finished basement, and below that, a few steps that descended to a damp cellar. Max nudged her toward their destination, but Vera halted, feeling a sharp tug—not physically, not externally—something inside, deep in her bones. She was being pulled in another direction. Vera's eyes shot toward the coat closet.

"Come on, let's go. We don't know how much time we have." Max pulled, her shoulder straining in its socket.

She was unmoving. Didn't he hear that? A buzzing. No, a whispering, a finger raised in a restaurant, gesturing *Check, please; look over here*. Vera turned toward the front door.

Something was in that closet.

"I'll meet you down there." Her voice was flat.

"What? I'm not leaving you. They could be back any second!" He yanked again, but she jerked her arm free, spinning his way.

"I have to do something. Give me a minute. Find the chalices. I'm right behind you!" She shoved his shoulders as confusion clouded his eyes.

"But—!"

"Do you trust me?" Her eyes were earnest.

"Of course."

"Then I'll meet you down there, sixty seconds."

"You've got one minute, then I'm coming after you."

"I'm counting on it."

He held her gaze, and for an odd moment, she felt the urge to hug him, even kiss him, reassure him. She resisted the sensation and turned on her heel. Then she marched to the closet, Max's feet barreling down the basement steps.

An instinct, that feeling you get when you know you've forgotten something but you're not sure what, took over.

She opened the closet door, a dormant part of her brain searching for what it needed to find. Then she dropped to her knees, and her jeans scraped against a raised nail in a floorboard, as her hands dug into the cluttered mess of rain boots and umbrellas. She stretched to the far back corner, and her fingertips brushed against the hard plastic she suddenly knew she was looking for. She grabbed the rim and pulled the object free.

A hard hat.

She clutched the molded cap, staring in wonderment. It was white, or it used to be. Now it was almost gray, a coating of soot baked into it. The brim was cracked, and the edge of one side was warped, maybe melted.

It was *his* hat. Vera saw it on the head of Seth Durand in her vision, the day he descended the steps into the basement of the community center, the day he lifted his wrench. It must have been given to his widow by the town after the case was closed. Only, the woman didn't memorialize it; she didn't place it with the shrine in her son's room. Instead, she hid it in a closet.

Why?

Though down deep, Vera felt she knew. She just needed to remember.

Vera rose to her feet, flinging open the front door and sprinting across the lawn toward Maxwell's truck. She tossed the hat inside, and it landed with a soft plop on the passenger seat. She wasn't sure why she needed it, or how she even found it, but somewhere inside, she knew she *had to* have it.

Her body slid out, and as she slammed the door shut, another chill overtook her, more severe than what she'd felt in the vision.

Something was coming. A sound revved, a motor.

Vera turned toward the end of the street as a van swung around the corner, midnight green with a business emblem adorned on one side featuring pink, delicate, cursive script: *Durand Flowers.*

They were here.

CHAPTER THIRTY-FOUR

Max

The chalices were easy to find. The concrete floor of the dank cellar was stacked high with boxes upon boxes overflowing with yellow hats, evil statues, and cursed crystal. Cheap, assembly-style folding chairs faced a makeshift shrine to the Angel of Tears assembled on a table worthy of beer pong. *This is the base of Operation Destroy the World? This is what drew my mother?*

Max reached into a carton and without a moment of hesitation, unfurled the bubble wrap from a delicate gold-trimmed chalice, and flung it against the butter-yellow cinder-block wall like he was a World Series relief pitcher. Glass sprayed out, the clatter sending a burst of exhilaration through him as glittering dust rained down. He grabbed another, smashing it at his feet, a stray shard ricocheting against his calf. Blood bubbled. He didn't care.

He lifted another, then another, then another. Each throw harder than the last, his grip so tight one shattered in his hand, slicing his palm. He kept going, his brow slick from exertion. Eventually, he picked up an entire box, warm slimy blood dripping from his palms, spilling down his fore-arms, as he upended the objects onto the floor and stomped with his sneakered feet. The shattering sang with the pitch of a piccolo. He grabbed another carton, hurling it at the wall, a pool of burgundy blood forming below him.

He kept slamming, box after box, glass after glass.

The racket was deafening. Until he heard the car.

Max inched open the front door and spied a man glaring at Vera. He was only slightly older than them, tall and built, with blond hair in a style not far off from a bowl cut. Beside him was an older woman in a frumpy dress, mustard yellow with bright tropical flowers that mimicked exotic parrots. A van that read *Durand Flowers* was parked in the driveway.

Shit.

"If you're interested in learning more about the Sun-shine Crew, I wish you would've come to our rally," said Anatole, stepping forward, his shadow cast on Vera. Max's fists balled, blood dripping. "We're expanding our reach in the hope that all souls, young and old, will learn to channel their inner wisdom and elevate their thinking to a higher state of authenticity."

What? Max's brow furrowed. *Are those even words?* He zeroed in on Vera, making sure she saw him. She did, but she didn't give away his position. The Durands had their backs to him.

"That's spectacular." Vera kept a straight face. "I'm really looking for a life hack that offers a holistic approach to ideation that would brand me an influencer on a hyperlocal scale."

Max blinked. Two points for the loner girl with her nose in a book.

"What?" Anatole asked, looking confused.

"Sorry, I was trying to see how many buzzwords I could fit into one sentence. That's what you do, right? Or are you more focused on the demon side of things? Tell me: what draws in more people, the Sunshine act or the Angel of Tears?" Vera's voice didn't waver.

Damn. Max grinned. Turned out her brand of badass wasn't limited to demonic possession.

"You really want to do this?" Anatole's words were clipped. Max stepped from the stoop, gently shutting the screen door without so much as a click.

"I'm not going to let you poison a bunch of people and their *kids*," Vera blurted.

Max held his breath, the air buzzing with the vibe that this was about to get bad.

"You need to end this." Vera's voice was strong. "Let Maxwell's mother go. Let them all go."

"Oh, gee, since you asked so nicely." Anatole puffed his chest, still oblivious to Max's presence. So was his mother. "I'm actually kinda glad you're here. Today's a blessed day. Wanna come in? Have a drink?"

"Kool-Aid in a crystal chalice? I'll pass," Vera spat. "We're going to stop you."

"Who's 'we'?" Anatole snorted, his face pressed toward her. Max edged closer. "From what I hear, your parents are out of town, and by the time they get back, it'll all be over. Oh, and tell your priest that the Bible thumpers he sent to watch the house are adorable. Maybe try sending bunnies next time?"

Max stopped. His mom. Where was his mom? If the church group left, then who was watching her? Fear slithered up his spine, hissing in his ear. He pictured all those people at the rally. The kids. She wouldn't hurt them. No, he had to believe she wouldn't hurt them.

"It's too late," interjected the mother. Mary was her name—at least, that was what Max thought he remembered from the news. She swished forward in her floral dress. "Lilith is evolving, *becoming.*"

At the mention of his mother's name, a fire lit in Max. His seething eyes searched the ground nearby, finding what he needed—a baseball-sized rock. He lifted it from beside a shrub.

"The Angel chose her," droned the woman, her graying hair blowing in a breeze too cold for the summer season. Max shivered. "We needed a vessel to bring Him to our state of consciousness, so He could guide us to the great beyond and show us the true path. Lilith was ready. It is her purpose. It is an honor."

"Shut the hell up," Max roared.

The Durands spun his way, shock spreading in wrinkles across their faces. Max extended his arm, dried blood coating his skin up to the elbow, a rock clutched in his still-bleeding hand. He must have looked unhinged, eyes wild, blood splattering his extremities. He pulled his arm back like a pitcher, displaying that he knew how to throw it. Anatole stepped away from Vera.

"We're honored you joined us." Anatole smirked.

"Well, I'd be honored to throw this rock at your head," Max bit out through clenched teeth. He cut down the lawn toward Vera, never taking his eyes off the demonic duo.

"We're so grateful for the gifts both your families have bestowed upon us." Anatole's gaze flicked toward Vera. "Your parents brought our great healer here, and for that you have my thanks."

"Your *healer* killed my father!" Max shouted, fingers tensing around the rock so aggressively a fresh stream of blood flowed down.

Anatole's eyes stretched, his pupils black and swollen. "The Angel of Tears saved my life. I am an *answered* prayer. I am living proof." He spat at the ground. "Soon, the world will know my father's sacrifice, and they'll tell stories of him. They'll sing songs."

"Not if they're dead," Vera rebutted.

"We all have a purpose." Mary's voice was melodic, her eyes raised to the cloudy skies. Hadn't it been sunny a moment ago? A seagull screeched above them, shooting off the roof toward a flock of four others. There was no perfect *V*, no graceful synchronization; the birds careened off one another, swarming and flapping in chaos above the house, cries overlapping, staccato trills echoing off the asphalt. "We all have our own winding paths. *We* were chosen to spread His word. And *you*. Oh, Vera, your moment is coming!"

"I . . . I have nothing to do with this," Vera stammered. And for the first time, Max heard fear in her voice. He stepped close enough that his shoulder butted hers. He might not be able to protect his demonically ravaged mother, but he could protect this human girl from human monsters.

"You don't understand, but you will. All these years, all our offerings. The spirit finally walks among us." The woman's ugly floral sleeves flapped like wings, her eyes empty as grommets as they turned to Max. "Your mother *chose* this. Don't you see? She was in so much pain, but now that's over. She is the supreme offering. And you, Vera!" Her thin lips pulled into a sinister grin. "Our great healer is coming for *you* next!" She pointed a wrinkled finger, her nail sharpened to a point as her face burst with hysterical excitement.

Vera slinked behind Max.

"It is time to join us!" Anatole called, spit splashing from his lips.

"Oh, Vera, I wish I could be there when it happens," the woman cried. "You're going to be so beautiful! It wants you! It wants you!"

"Let's go." Max grabbed Vera's quivering arm and tugged her to the truck. She stumbled behind, wordlessly.

"Yes, go! Go!" the woman cried. "The hour is near!"

Max guided her robotic figure into the passenger seat with a bloody hand, grateful she always wore black, and spied a random hard hat tumbling onto the floor. *Where is that from?*

Vera sat, unblinking, mouth hanging open as the Durands cackled on the street behind them. Max threw the stick into Drive, stomped on the gas, then blew through a stop sign.

"I smashed the chalices," he blurted, waiting for a response. She didn't twitch. "Not all of them, but most of them. Vera, can you hear me? What should we do? Go to your house? My house? The rally? Vera!"

She remained a statue, her skin ash-white.

She said nothing.

CHAPTER THIRTY-FIVE

Vera

Vera could see her hands shaking. She sat in Maxwell's truck as he drove, probably too fast, and watched as her fingers batted in time with hummingbird wings. *Wow, look at them go!*

"Vera, are you okay?" he asked.

Blood roared in her ears. He sounded underwater. *Veeeera, aaaarrrre yooooou ooookaaay?*

Silly. They weren't in water. They were on dry land. How did her ears do that? Or was it his mouth?

Her seat belt locked, digging into her collarbone as the truck jerked to a halt beneath a hulking tree on Elm Street. Huh, Elm Street. Perfect for nightmares.

Maxwell reached across her lap, tugging the latch on the glove compartment. He pulled out a dented white metal box with a scratched red cross on the top. He clicked it open and found a roll of sheer white gauze. He clutched an end with his thumb and palm, grimacing with teeth bared. Bloody prints blotted the gray leather steering wheel. There were drips on his lap.

"Are . . . are you okay?" she asked, her voice shaky.

"Thank God. Yes. Are you?" He sounded relieved to hear her speak. "I'm just scratched up, but I thought I was gonna have to take you to the hospital."

"Why?" Her face crinkled, still trying to process what happened.

"You looked like you were in shock. Seems to be going around." He turned his eyes back to his wounds, wincing as blood leaked from one hand while he pathetically swung the wrap around the other.

Without thinking, Vera unbuckled her seat belt and stretched toward him, kicking the hard hat. Why had she taken it?

She knew why.

Didn't she?

She couldn't think of that now. Maxwell was bleeding. This she could do. She grabbed the kit. "Let me do it."

He did.

She found a wet wipe and cleaned his skin. Then she tore open a small paper package and placed a square of sterile cotton on his palm. The cuts were plentiful, but shallow. Slowly, she wound the grainy fabric around his palm, his minty breath brushing her ear as she worked in the cramped space. With the engine off, and the air conditioner silenced, the July humidity filled the truck's cabin and soaked her shirt with sweat.

She secured the end of his bandage with medical tape,

then reached for his other hand. He shifted his body toward her to offer his left palm, and now they were face-to-face. His nose skimmed her hair as she worked, head down. She felt him breathing, a tickle against her skin. He didn't groan in pain or move an inch. In fact, his body was rigid, but his touch warm.

She taped his left hand, then peered up through her lashes. He was so near that the tips of their noses almost bumped. He didn't pull back.

"Are you okay?" she whispered.

A tingle spread through her body, that same sensation she'd felt in the house, the urge to hug him, kiss him. What was wrong with her? A murderous, cult-starting family was threatening to poison the entire town, yet somehow all she could feel was Maxwell's hot breath brushing her cheek. All she could see were his lips.

"I was going to ask you the same thing." His voice was low, different. She liked the way he sounded.

She glanced at their feet, unable to meet the heavy look in his eyes, and spied blood dripping from his ankle. "You're still bleeding."

She reached for the first-aid kit again, but he snatched her hand.

"I'm fine."

She glanced up, spying something else in his expression, something she'd never seen before. It was something she really, really liked.

He drew her closer, their eyes locked.

"What are we doing?" she mumbled, fighting the urge to pull away.

"Nothing wrong."

"Max . . ."

He kissed her, full lips hard on hers like he was done waiting, and the gasp that escaped her was almost embarrassing. She'd never been kissed before. She'd never been close enough to a guy to get anywhere near a kiss. Now Maxwell Oliver's lips were moving on hers in a way that stirred a feeling deep in her belly.

She wrapped her arms around his neck and pulled him closer. He groaned, and she loved the way that sounded. He smelled of humid summer boy sweat and, for some reason, that made her want to kiss him harder. Her lips parted, everything tangled, and, with his gauzed hands, he effortlessly lifted her body and shifted her onto his lap. The kiss was the anticipation of Christmas morning doused with a day in the blazing sun. But when his bandaged hands fluttered beneath the hemline of her T-shirt, she jerked away, her back hitting the steering wheel.

"Whoa." She blinked, mouth still open, still feeling his lips.

"Yeah, whoa." The look in his eyes said he didn't want to stop.

And maybe she didn't want to either. But they had to. This wasn't real. This was a stress reaction. This was adrenaline. This was a heightened emotional response to an extreme event. Wasn't that what she'd learned while working at the hospital?

"You're upset. We're both upset." She shook her head.

Max looked confused. "What? This is the first time I *haven't* been upset in weeks."

"No, I mean, you're upset about your mom and what's happening to her. Everything's mixing together."

"I am not mixed-up." He moved for her lips once more, yearning in his eyes, but she pulled away.

He sank back with a sigh.

"I'm trying to be considerate," she said.

"Of me? I don't need you to protect my innocence."

"I'm not. It's just . . ." She had to get off his lap. She couldn't think while sitting on him, while being so close. She moved back to the passenger seat, and he frowned. "Max, a few weeks ago, we'd never even spoken."

She stared at her lap.

"Is that what this is about? I know I was a jerk. But now—"

"Now you're in a life-and-death situation. Your family's on the line, and you don't know what you're feeling. This is an acute stress reaction. . . ."

"Stop talking like a doctor!" He smacked the seat, then winced from his injuries. She reached for him, instinctively, but he pulled away. "This isn't some medical thing; at least it isn't for me. I like you, Vera. I want to be with *you*."

It was as if his words spilled inside her and watered the bits of her soul dried and withered from seventeen years of loneliness. He didn't know how much she wanted to feel these feelings, but . . .

"You're overthinking this." He leaned toward her. "This isn't sudden. It's been growing, ever since we started hanging out. Don't you feel it?"

Right now, she felt like every nerve in her body was stripped raw, sizzling and exposed and reacting to too much stimuli; that's what she felt. But of course, she knew what he was saying. She was drawn to him too. But she was drawn to a lot of things lately—that was the problem. What was happening to her body—the visions, the impulses, the attraction—she wasn't sure she could trust it.

"Max, everything that's going on right now—"

"Is scary as shit," he finished for her. "But still . . . I feel *this*." His taped hand gestured between the two of them. "Do you?"

She chewed her cheek. "Of course I do."

Without warning, he plunged across the space between them and pressed his lips to hers. Her chest, her skin, her cheeks, felt flushed. It was the opposite sensation from inside that house. All the chill melted from her body.

"There's so much going on," she whispered against his lips.

"I know."

"I don't know what's happening to me. . . ."

"It's okay." He kept kissing, gently biting her lower lip, tugging. She closed her eyes. "Let's just be in this moment, right here."

He started to move on top of her, and she pulled him closer. She wanted to feel something else, something good. She wanted to let it all go.

Then her phone vibrated in her back pocket. Max froze, hearing it too.

It could be her parents, or Chelsea at the rally, or an issue with Chloe.

"My phone," she whispered.

Max sat back. His cheeks rosy, and his lips pink and moist. But his eyes—all the excitement, all the passion that had filled them a moment ago—were replaced by pools of dread.

Something was wrong. Vera felt it like a stab in the gut. So did he.

They both looked at her screen.

There was a text from Aunt Tilda:

Maxwell's mom is HERE. Come home. NOW.

CHAPTER THIRTY-SIX

Vera

Vera stared out the passenger window, hoping to hide the fear in her eyes. Aunt Tilda never texted, and she never sounded rattled. But CAPS lock?

"We should have gone the moment the Durands said the church people left." Max's eyes jerked about. "We knew my mom was in danger. The whole *town* is in danger. I can't believe I pulled over. This is all my fault."

No, Max, this is our *fault. We let our guard down.* Maybe that was what the demon wanted. Was everything puppet theater? Was anything real?

"If we kept driving, we would have gone to *your* house, and we would've missed your mom," Vera reasoned. "She would have already been on her way to *mine*."

"How did she even get there? What, did she carpool with the cult?"

Probably. Vera shrugged. "At least she's not at the rally."

"Text your friend. Make sure everything's okay."

"I already did. Chelsea hasn't gotten back." Vera stared at her phone.

Max slapped the wheel, then pounded on it with bandaged hands. "I should've sent Chloe to my grandparents. I should've driven her to New Hampshire! She is at your house, with Mom, right now because of me!" He was blaming himself, like whatever his mom did was his responsibility, because *he* didn't see it, and *he* didn't stop her.

"This isn't your fault," Vera insisted, but she knew he wouldn't hear her. Guilt and logic rarely met.

They pulled onto her block, a sudden fog tugging a thick gray blanket over his truck. It was sunny a moment ago.

"I can't see anything." Max slowed, flicking his headlights on as they rolled closer to Vera's house.

Hairs lifted on her arms and she felt the urge to hold her breath like a kid passing a graveyard, not wanting to let the spirits in. Slowly, the truck's beams closed on a figure hovering in the dewy grass dressed in white—a long flowing Victorianesque nightgown merely missing the chains it forged in life. And it was clutching something—no, *someone.*

"Chloe!" Max slammed on the brakes and Vera was flung forward, seat belt biting her collarbone.

His mother stood on the lawn with her black spiraling curls blowing in hurricane-force winds that hadn't existed a moment ago. She was gripping Max's sister, her own daughter, with bony hands clamped around the little girl's throat. Chloe's sobs melted Vera's heart.

"I'm coming!" Max shouted, his panic thicker than the air outside.

Where were her neighbors? And where was her aunt?

Vera jumped out of the truck, but Max was already tearing across the lawn.

———

Max

"Let her go!" Every ounce of training he'd had as a sprinter prepared him for this moment, because he dashed that hundred yards to his sister at Olympic pace.

"Back off!" it shouted in a hellish tone, knuckles whitening.

"That's your daughter! *Mom!*" Max shouted. She had to be in there. Somewhere, his mother had to be in there. If it was true, if she really was grieving so profoundly, then how could she bring more death to his family? She had to have some control. She had to.

"She is *nothing.*" It tightened its grasp around Chloe's neck.

"Mom, please!"

Vera darted in front of him, putting her body between him and his mother, or what used to be his mother. He nudged forward but she held out her arm, straight and low, a mom stopping her kid from darting into traffic. He didn't need her protection. This was *his* family.

"You don't want her. You want me," Vera said.

"No!" came a voice charging from the front porch. "Vera, don't!"

"Do not get any closer to *it*," yelled a man.

Max flung his head and saw Aunt Tilda and Father Chuck bounding down the porch steps, each clutching a black leather-bound Bible.

"In nómine Patris et Fílii et Spíritus Sancti." The priest made the sign of the cross in time with her aunt.

Then they chanted in some language (Latin?) while reading from a book, reciting lines Max had never heard before. His mother laughed. No, *it* laughed, that same throaty, cursed sound.

"You are all fools!" It lifted Chloe by her slender throat, her bare feet kicking frantically at the dewy grass. She was wearing her long cotton twirl dress. She had begged their mother to buy it for her last birthday. It was her favorite, with blocks of fabric in varying shades of blue, and she only wore it when she was happy. That meant she had been happy today—until her mother began to choke her.

Max leaned toward his sister, heart hammering in his ears.

"No!" Aunt Tilda shrieked, halting her prayers. "Don't touch them!"

"It's killing her!" Max yelled, and Vera grabbed his arm, staring at her aunt with the same look of terror.

They couldn't just stand there.

Aunt Tilda and the priest chanted again, their tones monotonous. The priest tossed water. Max looked at his mother's reaction. Nothing. Chloe kept kicking, eyes bulging, curls wildly whirling in a wind that spiraled around the house. No, it spiraled *at* Vera's house. A sudden cyclone formed, Vera's home at the center, the fog whipping colorful petals, cut grass, and stray leaves around the wooden structure but never touching it.

An awareness came over him. His mouth fell open, gritty bits of earth hitting his tongue.

"It wants *in* your house," Max said.

"I know." Vera gripped him tighter. "It can't get in."

"Why?"

"I don't know."

The priest kept praying, going through all these motions, Aunt Tilda following along. "The blessings on the basement, the artifacts, I think they're keeping it out," her aunt shouted, overhearing their conversation. "I think it wants to release what's inside—all the demons, all the darkness. We can't let it, Vera. Come! Help us. We have to stop it."

Vera looked at her aunt, then at Max's mother, then back at Aunt Tilda, then at Max. He could see the rattled confusion in her eyes as if he were looking in a mirror. She didn't know what to do. No one did.

Then Chloe yelped, strangled pain in her voice, a child struggling to breathe. "Max!" she squeaked out.

He shook off Vera's hold. He couldn't wait any longer. These prayers weren't working. A splash of water wasn't working. He wasn't going to stand here and let this *thing* kill his sister while he watched. He wasn't going to let his *mother* do that to her own child.

The beast turned toward Vera.

"Ready yet?" it asked.

CHAPTER THIRTY-SEVEN

Vera

It wants in the house. Max and her aunt were right.

Vera stood on the lawn, the chaos of Hell consuming them, and felt in the deepest part of her soul how much the monster wanted inside her house. Why? Aunt Tilda guessed it was to shatter all the objects the house contained and release those demons on Earth. It was possible—the result would be catastrophic, apocalyptic. But it didn't feel right.

For some reason Vera couldn't quite explain, the rationale was wrong.

Beside her, Max bounced on his toes, ready to attack, while her aunt and the priest chanted exorcism prayers that felt . . . off. It was the *binding* prayers on the objects that were working; they were keeping the demon outside the home. That was clearly why it hadn't come after Vera's family before. In these seven years, it stayed away because it *had to* stay away. It couldn't break in. Now the cult had made it stronger.

It wants you. It wants you.

They'd been saying it all along, all of the afflicted—

Mr. Gonzalez, Anatole and his mother, Max's mom. They'd been telling Vera directly, plainly, what the demon wanted.

"*Oh, Vera, I wish I could be there when it happens. You're going to be so beautiful!*"

It. Wanted. *Her.*

"*The line that separates good and bad, it doesn't exist* out there *somewhere in need of an invitation. It's inside you . . . It's a choice.*"

It wanted Vera to choose—Chloe's life, or her own. The lives of every brainwashed cult member, or her own. The lives of innocent children, an entire town, the entire planet, or her own. Would Vera let the monster take her?

As though hearing her thoughts, the demon turned her way. The depths of Hell she saw in its pitted eyes could have sucked a person's sanity.

"*Ready yet?*" it hissed, then tightened the stranglehold on Chloe's neck.

The girl yelped. Vera bit her cheek, warring with herself, the coppery tang of blood filling her mouth. *Why* did it want her? Because she was her parents' daughter, because they had fought *this exact demon* before and won. The cult leader knew her parents were out of town. The demon wanted her to submit while they were gone, ensuring their devastation when they returned. It was striking first before her parents could strike at it. Before her parents could bind it. Again.

There was a click, an audible flip to the machine working her brain.

It didn't want to release the other demons in the basement. Demons don't hang out with the other *cool* demons and get each other's backs. It wanted inside her basement to destroy all remnants of the chalice, to destroy the shards of the object that bound it. Her parents had the power to do it, and it thought Vera could do the same.

Demons don't want to possess things, *they want to possess people. That's why we're able to contain it in an object*, if *the object belonged to the person doing the demon's bidding.*

It didn't want to be vanquished.

The sleepwalking. The strolls to the basement. Her body was trying to open that door in her most unconscious state. Her mother was wrong; her dreams weren't demonic. Something was awakening in Vera that she'd repressed for years, maybe her whole life.

Instinct was leading her to that door.

Because that was where the solution was.

Her aunt's words returned: *Sometimes people choose evil, but they can also choose to be heroes.*

Vera sprinted to the truck, letting the whispers of intuition guide her. Her scientific mind couldn't process what was in front of her, couldn't rationalize a plan, but something else inside her could. She tore open the passenger-side door, grabbed the hard hat, and sprinted across the lawn with lungs gulping misty air, blood thundering in her ears.

Her aunt yelled. Father Chuck bellowed for Vera to stop. And the beast followed her every move with its obsidian eyes.

Vera bounded up her porch steps in two giant leaps and dove through her front door. The hat was clutched in her clammy hand as she shook the old wooden house with her thwacking sprint to the basement door. Her sandals skidded to a halt in the kitchen as the brass knob came into view.

Never open it. Never touch it.

Her entire life she'd been afraid to brush that surface with so much as a pinkie finger, her covers pulled high to block the nightmares swirling behind it.

Not anymore.

Her breath shuddered in time with her hands as she wiped her sweaty hair from her forehead.

A voice rose up inside her. *Don't think. Just do.*

She took two large strides and placed her hand on the chilled metal knob.

With one final gasp of air, she turned it.

The creak of the door's hinges ripped open the forbidden portal.

Then Vera broke the plane of the doorjamb and placed her foot inside.

The room smelled musty, the old water stench reminding her of the flood damage years ago. She flicked the switch that illuminated a bare bulb and descended the steps into a chill much like the one she felt at the Durands'. She knew where she had to go. Somehow, despite never so much as glancing into the room, she knew.

She walked across the floor, her sandals slapping the painted spinach-green concrete, her eyes on the third shelf of a bookcase. A black velvet satchel rested, its drawstring pulled tight.

Vera's hand trembled as she lifted the sack, a clattering of broken glass rumbling inside.

All of this over broken glass.

She loosened the strings and peered into the black mouth. Fangs of shattered crystal loomed, untouched for seven years.

Vera poured the razor remnants into the scorched gas worker's hat. This was why she'd taken it. Some piece of her knew this moment was coming.

Filtered light from a tiny basement window reflected on the fragments—so small, so delicate, so destructive.

Vera shifted back toward the basement door, feeling that familiar pull, understanding the ramifications of the rule she'd broken.

Something was waiting for her at the top of the stairs.

CHAPTER THIRTY-EIGHT

Max

When Max watched Vera tear off into the house (was she carrying the hard hat?), he spun toward his mother, refusing to let his girlfriend, or friend, or whoever she was, risk her life for his family while he stood outside flat-footed.

"Put my sister *down*!"

Only, his mom wasn't looking at him, or his sister. Her eyes were locked on the house, as if tracking Vera's movements inside. It was distracted. This was his moment. He had to act.

He shifted his weight to his toes, and as he did, his eyes caught on a sudden flickering shadow. The fog parted and a tiny white apparition emerged, its barks high and yappy. Max squinted, struggling to discern the shape of the beady black eyes sprinting closer, yipping like a record skipping. In his mother's bedroom, she'd mimicked the sound. It was the neighbor's dog.

His brow furrowed as the fluffy animal raced toward his sister.

Then Chloe started choking, hacking, flailing.

His mother's knuckles protruded as they tightened around her daughter's neck, lifting her higher from the ground. Guttural bursts erupted from Chloe, her feet desperately kicking for purchase. Max had to charge. Yaps reached a crescendo and Max watched as a tiny barking puff flew through the air and latched itself onto his mother's calf.

For an instant—he barely saw it—his mother snarled, charcoal eyes flashing with fury in the animal's direction. And Max reacted like a starter pistol fired in his brain.

Three things happened in quick succession: his mother flicked her leg, sending the little dog soaring; Max barreled into her hips, shoulders low, head down; Mom's fingers lost their grip on Chloe's neck. His sister collapsed onto the wet earth with the lifeless limbs of a doll. Her legs bore no weight as she tumbled onto her side, her head smacking the grass and bouncing once.

Momentum carried Max a few paces beyond the collision, and he stumbled to keep his balance. He spun around, ready to assault again, and caught his mother gliding to the house, leaving the scene behind her, wind swishing her hair.

Max scrambled to Chloe, his bloody ankle brushing a tuft of fur. He peered down and spied the white pooch, not more than a couple pounds soaking wet. There were streaks of crimson on its white mustache, his mother's blood. A door slammed in the distance.

"Snowball! Snowball!" yelled the voice of the elderly neighbor charging out of his house on rickety, arthritic legs.

Hope you're okay, little guy.

Max dove toward his sister. She wasn't moving. Her hands weren't on her throat. There was no coughing. Her eyes were closed.

No.

No!

"Chloe!" he yelped, tears forming a solid mass in his throat. He gently lifted his sister's head, placing it on his lap and smoothing her black spirals from her face. "Can you hear me? Breathe. Breathe, okay?"

She was so still.

Please, God. Please! . . . I'll do anything. Please . . .

"Move aside." A hand clamped his shoulder.

Max looked up into the face of Father Chuck.

The priest dropped on all fours in his faded blue jeans. "Priests are teachers, and teachers know first aid."

The man carefully lifted Chloe's head from Max's lap, bracing it between his palms to keep it as straight and still as possible. He set her skull on the ground and placed his ear to her chest. Then he began pressing on her heart with his hands laced together. CPR.

"Is she okay? Should I breathe into her mouth? What should I do?" Max didn't know any lifesaving procedures, but he'd seen enough movies to think it counted.

The priest slammed on her frail chest, mumbling words (prayers?), his hands thumping, counting, pulsing.

Finally, Chloe coughed.

Holy shit, she coughed.

She rolled onto her side, hacking, eyes fluttering.

"Chloe, can you hear me? I'm *here*!" Max hugged her face, her curls sticking to his leaking eyes.

"Where's Mom? She tried . . . Why . . ." Then Chloe sobbed, thick bursts erupting from her chest, and Max hugged her tight, cradled her close, buried himself in his sister's hair as a wave of anguish pulled her under.

That was when he heard the voices.

Max looked up, slowly realizing they were no longer alone.

A crowd had gathered.

And they were chanting.

———

Vera

When Vera emerged out of the basement, the beast was waiting for her. Inside her house. She had what it wanted. She'd pried open the door and broken the prayers of protection.

Finally, it was in.

Vera worked to hide her unsteady hands as she clasped the hard hat filled with shards of a crystal chalice that once poisoned its followers in Chicago, all in service to a demon. The biting chemical scent of a gas leak rose from the hat, melding the sins of Roaring Creek with the sins of the past.

An endless inferno of black gleamed in the beast's eyes as it snarled at the objects, lips peeled back from its pointed teeth.

"It's time," it rasped, tongue unfurling against the rotted skin of its chin, eyes wild with hate.

Then she heard the crowd of voices soaring outside the windows, encasing the house. Gauzy lace curtains blew in the dining room, exposing a mob of wide-eyed strangers bedecked in yellow hats droning as one. The rally had moved. The cult was here.

Aunt Tilda rushed inside, Bible clutched like a shield, but its protection useless. The beast's entry gave it power. Vera could feel it consuming their energy, drawing from the demonic evil trapped inside the basement, trying to absorb it, obliterate it. Obliterate them.

Father Chuck rushed beside them, a cross in his hand. The beast laughed.

"Let us be done with this endless agony. Life will never bring you peace," the monster growled, arms wide as its mangled toes lifted from the floorboards.

It was floating! Dear God, it was levitating. Max's mother's body rose from the ground, her feet, its feet, hovering inches from the gritty hardwood. Its arms lifted with the grace of a swan, white nightgown fluttering in a breeze that now blew inside the house. Its pocked face oozed and pointed toward the heavens. No, the skies. Heaven wasn't here right now.

"*You're all dying. You have been since you were spat onto this Earth. Why continue to suffer? Rush to me. Now! Now! Now! My children, the time is now!*" it bellowed.

Crimson blots blistered before Vera's eyes as its rhythmic words rang in her head.

The cries from the crowd outside gathered in force.

"*The human constructs of this inhumane world brought about your pain. It is time to shed the limitations of the flesh.*"

A baby screeched, an ear-piercing shriek, and the beast broke into a feral grin.

Acid burned up Vera's throat.

"*Step over with me, my children. Find our new beginning! Now! We must go now!*"

Its words sank in as she floated up.

A wind blasted through the kitchen, a warm wind, a summer wind.

Wings. Were those wings? Vera swore she could feel the tickles of feathers on her skin as white light filled the room. She stared at this figure, this beast, in a ruffled ivory nightgown, transfixed, wondering if Max's mother wore it often. Was it her favorite? The gown clung so perfectly to her hips, her chest. Vera never slept in anything so dainty, so feminine.

And now she had wings!

"*Rip your souls free! Do not delay. Go, go, go!*" it called.

It called to *her*. She could end this. It wanted her. Wasn't that what everyone said? It wanted to inhabit her. It wanted to *be* her. How simple would it be to give it what it wanted? It would all be over. It wouldn't hurt. Numbness. No one else would suffer. How simple, how simple . . .

"Vera!" A voice shouted. "Vera! No! Step back!"

Was she moving? She wasn't moving. She was standing still. She was watching. But its face was getting closer. Those eyes, those fathomless eyes, what secrets lay inside that abyss? She could know. If she let herself, she could know everything. Just a simple invitation.

"Vera! Listen to me! Stop! Wake up!" a voice continued to shout. Where was she? Why did everything feel so far away? Was she floating?

A hand clutched her shoulder. The grip was firm, pulling, yanking. "Vera, hear my voice. Come back. Stop. Please. Come back to *us*."

Us.

What us?

Was there an us?

"Vera, please, for me. Do this for *me. Don't leave me.* I can't lose you too. We need you. All of us."

She blinked.

Max. It was Maxwell Oliver.

He was beside her. He was holding her. He was holding her *back*.

Her gaze flicked about.

She was still in her house. She was still in her kitchen. Her eyes were awake.

She was no longer sleeping.

She peered down at the cursed hat in her hand, full of glittering glass. Her breath gusted in heavy bursts. Wind smacked her face, shoving her back. She was tired. So tired. It was draining her life, her will, her . . . everything.

Vera scrunched her eyes, gripping the brim of the hat with all her might, and with a clarity of mind she didn't know she possessed, she began reciting all four stages of the binding service she'd heard echo from the basement over the course of her seventeen years. She breezed through the first two stages quickly, as far as her aunt had gotten after the hurricane. This was why the words only protected *them*, their family, and their house, when the demon was unleashed. The town—the world—remained at the mercy of the monster, because by the time they said the final two phases, it was already gone.

Fingers brushed against hers, gripping the hat, but Vera kept her eyes closed. She couldn't look. She couldn't risk that hypnotic stare pulling her in again.

Somewhere in the distance, a gurgle rose up, bloody and liquified, booming and powerful.

Vera kept chanting. She moved on to stage three. "I exercise my power to expel all evil spirits. I command them to leave. I renounce all forces and bind them to these objects. . . ."

Her aunt's voice surged in time with hers. Then Father Chuck's. They recited the words with the force of their beings, drowning out the humming chants outside, their fingers cramping, their breath unified.

A power lifted Vera's chest, rolling her onto her toes. It was their power. Her power.

A ragged roar of agony shook the room. Gales blasted Vera's face, whipping her hair, pushing against her. She didn't let go of the objects. Instead, she squinted tighter, her blood boiling hotter. Sweat saturated her shirt, her hair.

Her lips never stopped moving.

The fourth stage, the final stage: "I attack this evil. Bind its powers, end its darkness, confine its wrath. . . . I command this demon to leave, transfer to these objects forever. I command it to leave this body. I command it never to come *back.*"

The shrill wail that ricocheted off the surfaces of their house was inhuman, not of animal, not of man. It was a sound not of this world.

Vera finished the last line of the final blessing and opened her eyes.

The rotting, tortured being crashed back to earth, muscles convulsing, tendons popping. Blood poured from its nose in a congealed burgundy gush. Its head heaved back, brittle curls lifting, then abruptly its chest flung forward and it gagged, blood vessels bursting in its eyes as it retched, still fighting their prayers.

Then black greasy liquid spewed from split lips with a bubbling gurgle, and Vera thrust the objects beneath it. The hard hat, black with the ash of the dead and full of shattered, poisonous glass, caught the inky secretion that spilled from the monster. On impact, the liquid absorbed into the shards of the crystal chalice, dissolving, disappearing, erasing. The beast hurled, chest cast forward and seizing, until the body was wrung clean.

Then it stopped.

Everything.

The room was silent.

The winds stilled.

The cries ceased.

The chanting halted.

Not a finger twitched.

Not a hair blew.

Then the body before them rested a hand on its knees and pushed itself upright.

"Maxwell?" she said.

CHAPTER THIRTY·NINE

Max

"Mom?"

Max rushed toward her, throwing his arms around his mother for the first time in . . . what? Weeks? Months?

She curled into his chest. "What happened? Oh, Maxwell. I'm so *sorry*."

She sobbed with a force he hadn't heard since *that* day, since they stood outside the community center.

"Mom, you're okay. I got you." He stroked her hair. It felt soft, almost silky.

He pulled back and looked at her face. Her tan skin was red and blotchy as tears stained her cheeks, but her lips were no longer cracked. Her nose was no longer bleeding. No oozing sores covered her skin. Her eyes were a dark, rich maple, not burning hunks of coal. How could this be?

He turned to Vera.

Her lips were parted, eyes blinking like she couldn't believe the scene was real. Or maybe she couldn't believe that she had done this.

Yes, *she* did this. She saved his mom.

"Thank you," he mouthed, feeling language lacked words big enough to describe how he felt.

His mother flung herself at him again, gripping him like a life raft.

"I'm so sorry," she pleaded.

"I know. I know." He patted her hair.

"Where's Chloe?" Aunt Tilda asked.

"*Chloe!*" his mom howled, collapsing.

"In my truck. I locked her in. I think she's okay," Max said.

Aunt Tilda nodded as if accepting her mission and started walking toward the door.

Then Vera reached out. "Aunt Tilda!" she called. Her aunt spun around. "Thank you."

Seriously? Max thought, feeling as though the thanks in this situation should only be pointing in one direction.

The aunt smiled, smoothing her gray hair behind her shoulder, still wild from the wind. "No. Thank *you*. I'm so proud of you."

The aunt's eyes looked the same way Max felt, as if she knew her words weren't enough to convey what she really felt.

Vera was a superhero.

Vera

Vera watched as Max hugged his mother, and for the first time in a long time, the tug she felt on her chest held no fear, no psychic pull, no demonic energy. Max smoothed his mother's curls from her face and comfort food poured into Vera's soul.

"She's okay," Vera croaked.

"I think so," said Father Chuck, stepping beside her. "How did you know what to do? Your aunt, she thought the chalice, the basement, was *giving* it power. She thought it was feeding it with demonic energy. But you . . ."

"I don't know." Vera shrugged. "I really don't. You know how sometimes you drive someplace and don't remember how you got there? Your body just does it?"

The priest nodded.

"That's the best I can explain it."

"It takes no bravery to drive a car, but what you did—"

"It's what my parents do." In fact, they had done exactly this yesterday and were going to do exactly this tomorrow when they got home. It was nothing special.

Father Chuck placed a heavy palm on her shoulder. "You saved a woman's life." His voice was heartfelt. "I have a feelin' you'll spend a lot of time reflecting on what happened here. I imagine we all will."

Vera's face flushed as she shook her head no. He was making too much of it. Her actions, she didn't consciously make them. She just did them. She wasn't a hero. Anyone would have done the same.

"The folks outside, the yellow-hatters, I think I oughta take a look at how they're faring." Father Chuck turned toward the windows, strangers milling in her front yard, aimlessly pacing with blinking, vacant eyes.

He left the house and Vera shifted back to Max, still hugging his mother—not *it*, but Mrs. Lilith Oliver. Lilith gazed up at Vera through thick, healthy lashes and smiled, her teeth as white and straight as a toothpaste ad. Her eyes leaked uncontrollable tears.

"Mom," Max said. "This is Vera. She saved your life."

"No. I didn't. I just—" Vera shook her head.

"She's amazing," Max added.

The way he looked at her in that moment, the way his honey-brown eyes gleamed, was a picture Vera hoped she'd hold in her mind and her heart forever. Whenever the world got too cold, and her life got too dark, she prayed to every force she'd just summoned that she would always be able to picture his face gazing at her in exactly this way.

EPILOGUE

"You didn't order the scampi. You ordered the crab cakes," Max insisted as he set a plate in front of Aunt Tilda. "But I can get you the scampi if you want it."

"No. No. You're right. I couldn't decide. The crab cakes look lovely. I'll have the shrimp next time," said Aunt Tilda as she nestled beside Vera, sipping a glass of iced tea with a wedge of lemon.

Vera glanced around the crowded restaurant. It was a Saturday night in early August, and it seemed the tourists were finally venturing back. The darkness had lifted from Roaring Creek, not just from Max's mother, but from everyone.

"Who ordered no tomatoes with balsamic?" asked Mrs. Oliver as she approached their picnic table with a tray of side salads.

His mother was stunning. Sometimes Vera found herself staring at her, wondering how this could be the same person. She looked so much like Chloe, with those bouncing black curls. Her skin glowed.

But her eyes sometimes fell with the weight of remorse.

Vera insisted Mrs. Oliver go to the hospital after everything settled. A full workup was imperative, but it was an uncomfortable consultation. You couldn't exactly put "possessed by a demon" on a patient intake form, but after Vera called in a few favors, the doctors ran as many tests as her insurance allowed. She was given a clean bill of health, aside from some malnutrition and dehydration from not eating properly for several weeks. But it was her mind Vera worried about, the aftereffects.

She spent two weeks at an inpatient facility to recover from "exhaustion," and she finally admitted it would take time, and regular therapy, to deal with her grief. She was willing to do the hard work. Max, however, blamed himself, insisting he missed the signs that her self-help fixes had shifted to something more sinister. It took some talking—*a lot* of talking—to convince him that it wasn't his job to regulate her every move. He was her son; she was the adult. She needed to handle this herself.

Max's grandparents moved into the house, taking care of him and Chloe while Lilith was away. Father Chuck arranged for a priest with a doctorate in psychology to treat the entire family. His mother's memory was spotty—chunks of the experience were missing—but Chloe suffered from nightmares. It was hard to explain what happened to her, and to convince her that she couldn't talk about it with anyone outside of their circle. Vera knew that horrific experience, Chloe's brush with death at the hands of a monster that wore her mother's face, would change the person Chloe would turn out to be. And that reality stabbed at Vera's heart.

But in the end, the experience changed all of them.

"All right, Grandma, Pops—we got a fried Captain's Combo and broiled crabmeat." Max set two steaming plates in front of his grandparents—his father's parents.

They didn't know what happened to his mom. They just knew she was still grieving their son, and she was sober. She needed time. Aunt Tilda had convinced them to move to Roaring Creek, to be a part of this family instead of breaking it up. Max's mother needed her children, but she needed help as well. They listened. Max's grandma even taught Aunt Tilda how to make jerk chicken and stew peas. Pops played the harmonica on the porch every evening and told stories about Max's dad. He also befriended Mr. Zanger. Turned out they had a lot in common—they were both veterans who grew up in Brooklyn. Sometimes he even walked Snowball.

"All right, scooch over," Max said as he set a plate of shrimp stuffed with crabmeat in front of Vera. His hip pressed against hers. "Look how packed it is."

His gaze flitted about the open-air restaurant, a grin on his face.

"It's like the fog has lifted." Vera squeezed his forearm, finding any excuse to touch him.

"Ain't that the truth." Max pumped his brow. "We got another call from a reporter."

"Ugh." Vera groaned.

After his mother came back from some unseen Hell dimension, they were smacked with real-world problems. Max and Vera had broken into the Durands' home, and they confessed this to the police. They swore that Anatole and TSC were behind the Grim Reaper statues. The cops suspected this already—the figurines had been showing up at crime scenes and car accidents connected to Sunshine followers—but they couldn't prove any criminal activity. Max and Vera insisted they go to the basement of the Durand home. Eventually they got a warrant and discovered the makeshift altar, boxes of statues, Sunshine merchandise, shattered chalices, and containers full of cyanide. The Durands had already skipped town by that point, but they were easy to find. A follower had posted a picture of them on Instagram.

It was ultimately the cult members who offered the most damning evidence. Once the trance was broken and they were no longer under the influence of the demon, they could finally think clearly. They realized how close they'd come to dying, and they submitted statements to the police, detailing stories of being coerced to worship a demon and distribute poison. The cult was deemed a criminal organization and the media devoured the story.

Max and his entire family refused interviews. So did Vera's coworker Samantha, who said she remembered everything she did as if she were drunk, her brain not in control of her actions. It was probably better that way. Chelsea was helping her through the aftermath.

"Did you hear the mayor is talking about another memorial sculpture?" Max asked, biting into corn on the cob dripping with butter.

"It's a nice gesture." Vera smiled.

Max rolled his eyes.

The families who lost someone the day of the explosion had filed a class-action suit against the Durands. It would take years to wind itself through the legal system, but it gave them somewhere to place their blame. It gave them an answer to the darkest question: why did this happen? It gave the town a way to finally close its bleakest chapter. The Durand trial was scheduled to be broadcast live. And a documentary was already filming.

"Your parents get back tomorrow?" Max asked, his mouth full.

"Yeah, false alarm." Vera's parents were working another case.

Their plane touched down from Barcelona the day after the demon was vanquished. It might have been the first time in Vera's life she knew, with utter certainty, that her parents were proud of her. It was like that day finally solidified her as a member of her family. And Vera wasn't sure how she felt about that. She didn't want to have to earn her parents' love, and she didn't want her parents' lives. She hated the idea of spending weeks or months traveling, away from the people who loved her, and she wouldn't mind going her whole life never again seeing a nightmare-inducing hell beast. Dipping her toe into the demonic was enough.

But Vera couldn't unsee what she saw. She knew what existed, and now she was more committed than ever to becoming a psychiatrist. She wanted to know that someday, if a poor afflicted soul was ever admitted into a hospital, there would be someone there to consider *all* options.

That was her purpose in life. She knew that now more than ever.

"My mom wants to have dinner with you," Vera said as she ripped a tail off a stuffed shrimp.

"They want to come here?" Max gestured around.

"You eat here all the time. She wants you to come over to *our* house. Don't worry, Aunt Tilda will cook." Vera nudged him.

"Well, how can I say no to that?" He pecked her lips, and as he did a loud pack of teenagers stumbled through the door.

Vera turned to see their classmates, Max's friends, though he hadn't seen them much lately. He said that wasn't Vera's fault, and she shouldn't feel guilty, but she did. She didn't want to take him away from who he was or those who were important to him.

"Max!" Leo yelled, his hand raised high to show an August sweat stain on his blue T-shirt. Jackson tumbled behind him, tripping in his flip-flops.

Delilah stood at their sides.

"When are you off work?" Jackson asked, his hand on Delilah's shoulder. She clasped her palm with his, aiming a smile directly at Max. It was an intentional gesture. They were together, and she wanted Max to know it.

"Um, guys." Max stood. "I'm hanging out with Vera tonight. Family dinner." He nodded to the crowded picnic table that included Vera's aunt, a priest, Max's grandparents, his little sister, and his mom.

Delilah's mouth set in a hard line. "Oh, that's . . . great."

"Yeah, maybe tomorrow." Max placed a palm on Vera's shoulder and squeezed.

They were together too. There was no point in pretending anymore.

The darkness was behind them now. The steely clouds had lifted from their small coastal town, and all it had taken was a lonely girl dressed in black beating a monster.

THE TRUTH

Santa Muerte

The shrine at the center of this novel, the Angel of Tears, is fictional. Its basis draws inspiration from the folk religion of Santa Muerte (literally translated as "Saint Death"), which is most commonly practiced in Mexico, along with the United States. Death figures have existed in Catholicism since at least medieval times, rising in popularity and number during the Black Plague. Some scholars tie Santa Muerte to Spanish colonizers who brought images of La Parca, the Grim Reaper, into the lands they invaded. Others say the religion is born from Mictlantecuhtli, the Aztec god of the dead. Worshippers pray to a female skeleton wrapped in a colorful robe or wedding gown, often wearing jewelry, decorated with flowers, and holding a scythe or a crystal globe. Devotees create altars and leave offerings. These rituals are derived from indigenous practices, Spiritualism, Santería, Catholicism, and New Age philosophies. While some devotees remain active in the Catholic church, in 2013, the Vatican declared Santa Muerte a "degeneration of religion."

Notably, the practice is popular in areas with high rates of poverty and violence, among those who are most marginalized by society and feel death is imminent. They seek healing, protection, and safe passage to the afterlife. The saint is sometimes invoked for vengeance and illegal activity, including murder. The religion, however, is *not* a cult. Unlike the Angel of Tears, which was created for this book, Santa Muerte is *not* a Satanic mass. Santa Muerte worshippers are *not* praying to the devil or demons. There are an estimated ten to twelve million followers of Santa Muerte worldwide. It should be noted that Santa Muerte is separate from the Day of the Dead.

Jonestown and NXIVM

The cult-speak used in this book is original, but it draws inspiration from the recordings of real-life cult leaders. In November 1978, in Jonestown, Guyana, Jim Jones convinced more than nine hundred of his Peoples Temple cult followers to drink poisoned Kool-Aid, including more than three hundred children. Prior to 9/11, it was the largest single incident of intentional death of American civilians. Jones didn't drink the Kool-Aid, but he fatally shot himself immediately following the death of his followers.

Keith Raniere is the creator of NXIVM, an expensive faux self-help group based in Albany, New York, that spread worldwide for two decades. Promising success and spiritual enlightenment, the group included a cult that branded, exploited, and abused women and children. Raniere was convicted for his crimes in June 2019, and in October 2020 was sentenced to 120 years in prison.

The Chicago Ripper Crew

In the 1980s, a satanic cult composed of four men committed a string of horrific homicides in Chicago. Known as the Ripper Crew, the men were responsible for brutally killing at least eighteen people at a makeshift demonic altar in their ringleader's home. An eighteen-year-old woman who survived her attack provided the police with details that led to the men's arrest. One of the murderers was released from prison in March 2019 at the age of fifty-eight.

The Warrens

The author's imagination was sparked by Ed and Lorraine Warren, the renowned demonologists who are the basis of *The Conjuring* films. For over fifty years, the devoutly Catholic husband and wife team were routinely called on to investigate diabolical phenomena throughout the country, including demonic possession. They are best known for their work at the haunting in Amityville and the possession of the doll Annabelle. For decades, objects connected to their work, including Annabelle, were housed in the basement of their home, which later was turned into the Warren Occult Museum. Both now deceased, they are survived by their daughter; her husband is the director of the occult museum.

THE TRUTH SOURCES

"An apocalyptic cult, 900 dead," *The Guardian*, November 17, 2018 (theguardian.com/world/2018/nov/17/an-apocalyptic-cult-900-dead-remembering-the-jonestown-massacre-40-years-on).

"NXIVM founder sentenced to the remainder of life in prison," CNN, October 27, 2020 (cnn.com/2020/10/27/us/nxivm-keith-raniere-sentencing-supporters/index.html).

"The Ripper Crew abducted and murdered women in the '80s," *The Chicago Tribune*, March 29, 2019 (chicagotribune.com/news/ct-met-ripper-crew-thomas-kokoraleis-release-20190327-story.html).

"Santa Muerte: The rise of Mexico's death 'saint,'" BBC News, November 1, 2017 (bbc.com/news/world-latin-america-41804243).

"Santa Muerte: The miraculous pagan divinity who doesn't snub anyone," Al Dia, November 1, 2019 (aldianews.com/articles/culture/social/santa-muerte-miraculous-pagan-divinity-who-doesnt-snub-anyone/56733).

"Who Is Santa Muerte?" JStor, October 5, 2020 (daily.jstor.org/who-is-santa-muerte).

Biography of the Warrens pulled from the family's website, warrens.net.

ACKNOWLEDGMENTS

It's odd to begin an acknowledgments page by thanking people I've never met, but if it weren't for real-life demonologists Ed and Lorraine Warren, this book wouldn't exist. When I watched *The Conjuring* film for the first time, I was struck with that mystical writerly inspiration, "Ooo, what if . . . a hurricane hit their basement full of occult artifacts?" Then I began to wonder what it was like to grow up in a home where monsters are real and the proof is right downstairs. So thank you to the Warren family for sharing your stories, so the Martinez family could emerge with their own.

My publishing journey has been a long and winding road, and I am so grateful it led me to my agent, Lane Heymont at Tobias Literary. We sold this book in a pandemic! Your creative and dogged approach to the submission process got this book on the shelf. Thank you for your consistent enthusiasm, because it inspired me to believe in myself at a time when I really needed it.

Thank you to my film agent, Emily Dayton at the Gotham Group, for representing this project before it even found a publisher. Your excitement, and the interest you generated, made all the difference.

Thank you to Wendy Loggia for acquiring this project

for Underlined and for bringing me under the Delacorte umbrella. I think every aspiring author dreams of being published by Random House, and you helped make my dream a reality.

To my amazing editor, Alison Romig! It has been such a joy to work with you. Your thoughtful suggestions took the ending to a new level and added a layer of depth throughout the novel. Thank you for championing the project in all stages of the publishing process.

To Nicholas Moegly, the artist who designed my gorgeous cover, I love it more than you know! It perfectly captures the book, and I still don't know how you create such realistic illustrations. And thanks to everyone at Underlined, especially designer Casey Moses, and copyeditor Marla Garfield.

Lane and I met via Tweet during #PitMad, so thank you to Brenda Drake for creating the online pitch fests that have propelled so many careers. I had several beta readers for this project who helped hone my craft as a first-time horror writer. Special thanks to Gaby Triana, whose notes on sensory details elevated my creepiest scenes. Thank you to Megan Kelley Hall for being an early reader multiple times in my career. Thanks to Jennifer M. Eaton, whose notes on the opening pages inspired me to move "The Storm" later in the book. To my friend from the fourteenth floor of Warren Towers at BU, Amazon editor Grace Doyle, thanks for reading this book and offering much-needed career advice. And thank you to Lucina Stone, author of the novel *Santa Muerte*, for answering my questions.

I am grateful for my high school friend, producer and director Marguerite Henry, and her business partner, Vanessa Shapiro, for developing my last YA series, Proof of Lies. Optioning that project (during a pandemic!) helped push *Small Town Monsters* to the top of editors' desks. I am also grateful to all the authors who offered advice before I signed Hollywood contracts, especially Frank Morelli, Gretchen McNeil, and Alisa Valdes.

Thank you to Chris Klock, and his amazing wife, Sheri—this is our fourth author photo together! To the friends who have stood by me for decades—the Ridley Girls, my BU roommates, my Spain friends, and everyone who comes to my book signings—thanks for keeping me laughing during the year 2020.

I'm an alum of an amazingly supportive university; thank you to everyone at the College of Communication at Boston University for publicizing my books and inviting me to speak. Alumni relations director Jacqueline R. A. Dragani—you were the last person I had lunch with before the world shut down, and I'll never forget that!

I am lucky that my in-laws are not only incredibly kind but are also incredibly good copyeditors! Thank you to Paula and Larry Wallach for catching countless typos over the years. And thank you to all the Wallachs for your support, especially Matt and Cristina, whose former home has given me my first real office.

To my Rodriguez family—who will undoubtedly be the most scared of anyone I know when they read this book—if

I didn't grow up in such a Catholic home, I wouldn't have been able to write this novel. I promise I'm okay, this is all fiction, and I'm not summoning demons into my life. To my brother, Lou, who will definitely think I'm in danger of being possessed, thank you for that long talk at Tierra Colombiana about mystical coincidences and the nature of good and evil. It worked its way into these pages. To my sister, Natalie, thanks for having a walking doll when we were little that scared the bejeezus out of us. To my parents, who are always the first people I call when something good happens with my books, thank you for believing everything I write deserves to be read and seen by the world. I promise I won't put an Angel statue in any of your bedrooms while you're sleeping.

To my husband, Jordan, the greatest compliment I have gotten on this book so far came the morning after you finished reading it. You turned to me and said, "You wrote this? Who did I marry? This is some dark shit!" That meant more than you know. Thank you for watching the kids when I was forced to have quarantined staycation writing retreats locked in our guest room. Without your support, my books wouldn't be here; so, readers, you should thank him too.

To Juliet and Lincoln, you are not remotely old enough to read this yet, but I look forward to the day you are and I really get to creep you out.

A killer after-party
you won't want to miss . . .

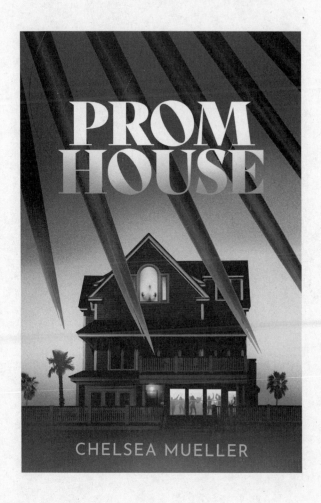

PROM
HOUSE

CHELSEA MUELLER

one

I WAS *not* prepared for a house this swanky. As I stood out-side on the wide, wraparound porch, I couldn't help but gape at the glamorous dark paneling and white trim. Rentals—*especially* party rentals—usually came with shabby carpet and dripping refrigerators. Judging by the exterior, this Jersey Shore mansion was none of that. It was movie-level luxe, and I was staying here with my friends for an epic prom weekend.

"Yes!" I whispered.

My best friend, Aubrey, who had been standing shoulder to shoulder with me, opened the door without knocking. I stepped forward to catch the door before it closed behind her, the porch planks creaking in my wake. Crisp, cold landscaping lights shot up from behind the green bushes, illuminating the command-ing white columns at the front of the three-story house.

"Kylie, you coming?" Aubrey had both hands wrapped around the crossbody strap of her overnight bag, like her clothes were about to make a break for the beach.

I shrugged my considerably lighter bag higher on my shoul-der and walked inside. "This place is ridiculous."

"Right?" Even in the low light of the huge foyer, I could see that Aubrey was beaming. Her auburn hair was pulled tight into a perfect ballerina bun, but she sauntered toward the living room with the grace of a newborn giraffe.

"Watch the—"

The tip of her shoe snagged on the rug, and she pitched forward. The sofa caught her before I could.

"Rug?" Her laugh was clear and high. Nothing was going to ruin this weekend for her.

I needed to get in the same mindset, even if this plush furniture and the wildly ornate candlesticks sitting on the mantel above an oversized fireplace made me feel even more out of place. My house had a standard stoop, not this wraparound porch fanciness.

"Who rents out a party house and leaves so much breakable stuff?" *Overly trusting adults,* I guessed.

Aubrey shrugged. "People who have money to burn."

"People ready to make a quick ten grand off seniors." Aubrey's boyfriend, Cam, sauntered into the house behind me. He let out a low whistle at the interior.

"You mean like ten *thousand* dollars?" Even saying that number aloud made my throat squeeze.

"Wait, so Kylie didn't front the cash?" Cam didn't bother disguising his sneer. He'd buzzed his hair a couple weeks ago, and it somehow made him look meaner.

Aubrey planted a fist on her hip. "Don't be a dick."

"What? I'm kidding." He rolled his head from side to side, like he was preparing for a fight. "Kylie, the house is covered. Don't freak."

"That's not an apology," Aubrey muttered.

This was supposed to be our first weekend of freedom. But within seconds of stepping inside this incredible party house, Cam and Aubrey were already sniping at each other.

"Babe."

"Don't *babe* me."

He shuffled closer to her. His shoes screeched against the hardwood floor. "Let it go, Aub. You wanted to do this."

He cradled her face in the palm of his hand, and I had to look away. This is what they did. A fire-and-ice routine that left her crying every other weekend. Jabbing at each other until he made promises he wouldn't keep. I started toward the stairs. Aubrey's pouty "I wanted to have the prom you promised me" followed me, but I didn't look back to see if she was caving to his dimples.

This rental was the most secluded house I'd ever seen on the Jersey Shore. We were out on the end of a long road and right up next to the beach. Which was great, knowing how loud we could get when we partied, but I wasn't supposed to be alone here with just Cam and Aubrey for company. Especially not when they were already going at it.

"Liam? Holli? Rory?" I started shouting my other friends' names to see who might call back. A precursor to the round of Marco Polo we'd most likely play in the pool after we got back from the dance.

"Noah told me he's already here. He's probably staked out primo digs upstairs." Cam's voice was raspy behind me. I turned and found him and Aubrey standing at the bottom of the stairs; Aubrey's cheeks were heated. *That resolved itself quickly.* She pulled her phone from the front pocket of her oversized week-ender. A swipe and a trio of taps later, she announced, "Dani and Hudson are already here somewhere, too. Rory is stuck in traffic, and everyone else is in her car."

"Everyone?" The tightness in my chest tried to strangle the word. Seven of our friends were joining us for the weekend: Noah, Dani, Hudson, Rory, Holli, Vic, and . . .

Aubrey got a dimple in her cheek when she smiled. "Even Liam."

"Oh, good." Though I could tell my cheeks were burning, Aubrey didn't call me out. Liam was my boyfriend, but we hadn't been dating long, and I knew clingy wasn't a good look. "He thought he'd be here first."

Aubrey darted past me. "Did anyone call dibs on rooms beforehand?"

"This is a finders, keepers situation, Aub." And the sooner I found a room to claim, the sooner I could distract myself with prom prep. I was banking on Aubrey pinning my deep brown hair into a prom-worthy updo. She'd brought the flat iron for some 1920s-style finger waves but promised she wasn't going to burn my ear again. Third time's the charm, right?

And speaking of prom-worthy, I couldn't believe I'd landed my dream date. Liam and I had had classes together for years, but we'd only started dating a month ago. I almost hadn't recognized him after winter break; he'd grown what seemed like six inches. When he leaned forward with that messy black hair flopping over his green eyes, I went gooey. All languid limbs, bands of tension snapping up from my hips to my chest, and rushes of effervescent bubbles to my brain. Every. Single. Time.

I wasn't sure I was prepared for how he was going to look in a tuxedo. Or how I was going to handle being with him in this house. Aubrey had made me pack the skimpiest swimsuit

I owned, and I was already cringing at the thought of poolside wardrobe malfunctions. Not to mention the more pervasive mental image of me purposefully pulling the string on the back of my bikini because I wanted to show Liam more. *Did I?*

The first room we passed had two twin beds pushed up against opposite walls. A desk with a stack of leather-bound books was wedged beneath a windowsill.

Aubrey didn't even pause. "Pass."

Cam grumbled behind me. "It's just a place to crash for a couple nights."

The hallway pivoted right. For a tall, square house, the interior was oddly serpentine. The next door we passed was closed. I gripped the brass knob, but before I could twist it, a high-pitched squeak slipped out. I flinched, then realized the sound was coming from inside the room. There was another squeak, and another. *Bedsprings.* I peeled my fingers away from the knob before I alerted the couple on the other side.

Aubrey's eyes widened.

I mouthed, "Found Hudson and Dani."

Cam simply smirked. "A bed's a bed, ladies."

Aubrey and I had to scurry down the hall with our hands clasped over our mouths to keep the laughter from spilling out.

Safely up on the third floor, we found bedrooms across the hall from one another, and a bathroom between them that was big enough for prom prep.

"We each get a room?" I still couldn't believe it.

"I know how you are. Told everyone we needed megaspace for maximum cuteness," Aubrey said.

The four-poster bed in my room was enormous. Five people could sleep in this bed. I mean, they wouldn't, but the *space.* As

I was reveling in its sheer size, Aubrey slipped into the room. She'd ditched her shoes, and her toenails were painted a posy pink. I toed off my own canvas sneakers. She nodded at my riotous lime-green polish. "Niiiiice."

"Cam settling in?" He hadn't followed her.

"Said he needed to 'set up' for the party." She rolled her eyes, which meant he had to be toting in coolers of beer.

I dove onto the bed, landing starfish style at the center. The mattress threatened to swallow me in downy softness.

"I still can't believe my mom went for this," I said to the textured ceiling, refusing to let Cam and Aubrey's relationship drama ruin prom prep.

Aubrey flopped down next to me on the bed. "She knew I'd be a good influence."

I rolled my eyes at her. "She said it was about proving I was a responsible young adult." I tried to mimic my mom's serious voice, all stoic and concerned.

"I just told mine I was rooming with you." Aubrey tapped her heels against the footboard.

Even when I stretched, my toes barely made it to the wood at the end of the bed. Would Liam fit? His feet had dangled off the edge of my bed at home, but he hadn't slept over, so it didn't matter.

No, I chided myself, I wasn't going to think about what might happen in this bed tonight. I was going to focus on getting ready for prom. My ears burned anyway. Stupid brain.

"It probably helped that Liam and I are such a new thing. I mean, he's thoughtful and my mom likes him." When I said our names together, the words had this umami tang, like I was testing a new flavor. Maybe Mom thought I wouldn't rush into anything serious with Liam, the same way I refused to choose a mom-approved dress for graduation. The difference was I *liked* the way Liam felt against me, unlike all of those scratchy dresses.

"Yeah. Wouldn't have worked with my mom."

"It's not like you and Cam are new," I countered.

"Well, he does sneak out of my house at least once a week." Pink splotches dappled the sides of her neck. New or not, grumpy or not, Cam was it for Aubrey. "And calling it sneaking is generous. He's so bulky. I love it, but he's even less coordinated than me."

A door slammed somewhere downstairs, followed by a flurry of muffled voices that shook me from my thoughts. This weekend wasn't about sneaking. I wouldn't have to hide my beer, I wouldn't have to hold back with Liam if I didn't want to, and I wouldn't have to worry about steering clear of drama. It was prom weekend, and we had super-fancy digs. Tonight was going to be one hell of a rager.